Praise for THE CLOTHES ON THEIR BACKS

by Linda Grant

"Gripping and written with keen understatement, it manages to be a domestic coming-of-age story even as it takes in the tumultuous sweep of the twentieth century. . . . It is, in other words, that rare thing, a novel of big ideas that never forgets to tell a story. Any frocks and bolero jackets you happen to come upon along the way are just the icing on the cake."

—*The Evening Standard*

"There is nothing lightweight about its themes and yet it is so artfully constructed that you barely feel you're reading it at all, so fluid and addictive is the plot. But like all the best books, the serious ideas it raises stay with you for a long time afterwards. . . . This is a wonderful, tightly written novel that charts one woman's emotional life while weaving in politics, history and morality. . . . This novel is above all a quiet masterclass in the perils of hypocrisy. No man is all good or all bad. And a decent suit can make you overlook a lot."

—*The Observer*

"This vivid, enjoyable and consistently unexpected novel is like Anita Brookner with sex. Sándor's mix of the endearing and the repellent takes on a life beyond that of an absorbing and unexpectedly ambitious story."

—*The Telegraph*

"We are what we wear because clothes reveal our personalities, but as Grant makes clear as she guides us through a dizzying ethical maze, they also conceal them. . . . In this meticulously textured and complex novel, beneath Grant's surface dressing, what she is talking about is more than skin deep."

—*The Times*

"Such is the richness of Grant's plotting that the story encapsulates many untold narratives . . . while the significance of other narrative threads can sometimes seem strangely opaque. But that is really the central theme of the novel—that life itself is opaque. You try to analyse it as best you can, but sometimes it is impossible to see past the surface of things."

—*The Sunday Times*

"This is a terrific novel, bursting with life and vivid characters."

—*The Mail on Sunday*

"Richly imagined . . . her novel is at once a beautifully detailed character study, a poignant family history and a richly evocative portrait. . . . It is a joy to welcome such a vibrant and thought-provoking book."

—*The Independent*

"Like money, clothes have real, symbolic and psychological value. Linda Grant understands these dimensions implicitly. Stitched beautifully into the fabric of her latest novel is an acute understanding of the role clothes play in reflecting identity and self-worth. . . . Grant's own particular beam reveals the way we acquire our sense of self from what gets reflected back to us, either in the mirror or in our relationships with others. She is as at home writing about the thrilling ripple of a skirt as she is charting social tensions."

—*The Sunday Telegraph*

Also by Linda Grant

FICTION

The Cast Iron Shore

When I Lived in Modern Times

Still Here

NONFICTION

Sexing the Millennium: A Political History of the Sexual Revolution

Remind Me Who I Am, Again

The People on the Street: A Writer's View of Israel

THE CLOTHES ON THEIR BACKS

A NOVEL

LINDA GRANT

SCRIBNER
New York London Toronto Sydney

SCRIBNER
A Division of Simon & Schuster, Inc.
1230 Avenue of the Americas
New York, NY 10020

Originally published in Great Britain in 2008 by Virago

First Scribner edition November 2008

For information about special discounts for bulk purchases, please contact Simon & Schuster Special Sales:
1-800-456-6798 or business@simonandschuster.com

Text set in Goudy

Manufactured in the United States of America

1 3 5 7 9 10 8 6 4 2

ISBN-13: 978-1-4391-4319-3
ISBN-10: 1-4391-4319-6
ISBN-13: 978-1-4391-4236-3 (pbk)
ISBN-10: 1-4391-4236-X (pbk)

To George Szirtes and Clarissa Upchurch

But this is the soul
Prepared for you, these garments that glow
In the dark and burn as fierce as coal.

George Szirtes, from 'Dressing'

This morning, for the first time in many years, I passed the shop on Seymour Street. I saw the melancholy sign in the window which announced that it was closing down and through the glass the rails on which the clothes hung, half abandoned, as if the dresses and coats, blouses and sweaters had fled in the night, vanished down the street, flapping their empty arms.

There was Eunice, behind the counter, patting her blue-black lacquered hair with silver nails. How old she looked, and how forlorn, her chin sinking for a moment on her chest.

Then I saw her rouse, and raise herself up, lifting her chin with a cupped hand. She mouthed a couple of words to herself. *Be brave*!

An impulse took me through the door, a strong pang of sympathy. I stepped inside and her perfume filled the room, inimitably Eunice – Revlon's Aquamarine, the scent of eau de nil and gold.

'You!' she said. 'Vivien, is it really you, after all this time?'

'Yes, it's me.'

'I thought so. How come I never saw you before?'

'London is very vast,' I said.

'A woman gets lost easy, but not me, I've been here all along. You knew where to find me.'

'But I wasn't looking for you, Eunice. I'm sorry.'

You never went to see how Eunice was? my uncle's voice cried out, in my head. *You left her all alone like a dog, my Eunice! You couldn't even pop in to buy a pair of gloves?*

'Well,' she replied. 'That's true. You and me had nothing to say,' and she gave me a haughty stare, raising her nose high and pulling back her shoulders. 'How is your family doing?'

The shoulders filled out her jacket, she smoothed the box pleats of the skirt. Three gilt buttons engraved with fleur-de-lis flashed on her jacket sleeve above the swollen bone of her wrist, lightly freckled. I recognised her gold watch. My uncle gave it to her. It was an Omega, his favourite brand, still revolving on quietly, tick-tock.

'My father died last week.' How strange it was to refer to him in the past tense, to think that I would never see again that cantankerous old man. Whatever was unresolved between us would stay unresolved unless we met again in the *yane velt* – that life, that other life.

'I only saw him the two times, neither was a nice occasion, you'll agree – your mother, though, she was very different from him. Is she still alive?'

'No, she died sixteen years ago.'

'That's a shame, now she was a true lady. I'm sorry she went before her time. And what happened to the boy? Don't look at me so innocent, you know who I mean.'

Yes. I remember. A sudden laugh, sharp little teeth, a lascivious mouth, his hands rolling his cigarettes, his red canvas boots, his spiky dark hair. His T-shirt. His guard's cap. His fish tank. But particularly I recall his smell and what was in it: and the whole arousing disturbing sense of him flooded my veins, a hot red flush of shameful erotic longing.

The red tide subsided. 'I don't know what became of him, he must be in his late forties now.' A residue of sadness, imagining the sultry, sexy boy as a middle-aged man for he had had nothing much going for him apart from youth and all its carnal excitements.

'You are a careless person, Vivien. You always was, you've not changed.'

'Oh, Eunice, you don't know anything about me. It's been nearly thirty years. You can accuse me of anything you like, but careless! No, not at all.'

'OK, OK, I take that back. So tell me, where have you been living all this time?'

'Abroad for a few years, but I'm back in London.'

'In that flat round the corner?'

'No, of course not. I have a place near Regent's Park.'

She looked me up and down and I knew what she was thinking – that I didn't dress like a woman from Regent's Park. Where were the pearl necklaces, the Chanel handbag, the diamond earrings, the fur coat? Eunice had an exact understanding of the clothes that rich people put on when they got up in the mornings; she read all the magazines, but I was more or less in rags. Those jeans!

And she had not spent most of her life in the retail trade without knowing how to seize an opportunity. A rich woman badly dressed is in need of a clever saleswoman. 'Well, well,' she said, 'you want to buy an outfit? I've got something that would fit you. We're low on stock because we're closing but I could find you a nice bargain.'

I smiled. *Me* of all people, being offered a dress. For I no longer bothered to look at my reflection in shop windows as I passed, let alone cringe in front of a full-length dressing room mirror with strong overhead lights, and if I did I would not recognise what I saw. Who was that dreary woman walking up the steps of the tube with lines around her eyes, jeans, boots, leather jacket, chapped hands, a ruined neck? That middle-aged person you see hesitating at the traffic lights, trying to cross at Oxford Circus, with her dyed hair and untended roots?

For some time – several months, but perhaps it was longer – I had let myself go, just drifted away from even thinking about how I looked, had let go the self which once stared in the mirror, a hand confidently holding a mascara wand, a person who cared about how she appeared to others.

There are mitigating circumstances. This is not my true personality. A year ago my husband died, thirteen and a half months, to be exact, and then my father. Too much death gets in your hair, in the crevices of your nose, your clothes, it's a metallic taste in the back of your mouth. My daddy was ancient, a toothless old man in a dressing gown and stained trousers; my husband had muscled forearms with reddish gold hairs and a thick neck which he had trouble finding collars to fit. He was so full of life and energy and humour, had a go at things whether he was any good at them or not, then cracking jokes about his own failures; only Vic could get lost on a golf course.

Twice this has happened to me. In the middle of my life here I was, as it was in the beginning. The same pearl grey horizon with no distinguishing features has reappeared.

And today of all days, on my way to my father's flat to get it ready for the house clearance people, a woman I had not laid eyes on for nearly thirty years was looking me up and down, remembering me as a young girl in her early twenties when I *was* careless, as charged. And curious, full of yearning, longing, passion, hope, indignation, judgement, disdain. Full of conviction, of course, about what not to wear. Yet now I stood with a line of white at the roots of my hair, in my jeans and plucked at the green silk scarf round my ruined neck, for no one looked at me any more the way Vic had looked. And despite my sturdy legs, the roll of fat around my waist, I felt like a ghost, only half here.

But Eunice was renowned for always wanting a woman to make the most of herself, whatever her drawbacks, whether imposed by nature or self-inflicted. 'I don't say you are the skinny girl you was when I saw you last, you filled out quite a bit,' she said, 'but look, this is for you. I can give you a good price.'

The dress she handed me was red, the colour of dark wine held up to the light in a glass bottle. I held it tentatively, rubbing the fabric between my fingers then holding it up against me. I didn't really get it. I couldn't see how it was supposed to fit.

'It looks nothing on the hanger,' she said, 'but you try it, you'll see. It's just right for your colouring, your black hair, and when you fasten it round your waist it pushes up your bosom. It's a *wrap* dress. You never seen one of those before? They're all the rage. And the fabric is silk jersey so it's going to do wonders for your bottom, you wait. Try it on!'

I get dressed quickly in the mornings and rarely bother with make-up apart from a balm to keep my lips from cracking. My daughters bring me round miracle skin creams that they read about in magazines, and saved up to buy me a weekend break at a spa, for which I have not yet got round to making the booking. Sweet girls, they turned out; more confident, straightforward and loving than I was at their age, for which they have their father to thank – and being the products of a successful (though hardly perfect) marriage. His light colouring came out in both of them, the reddish hair, the rosy cheeks and dimpled smiles.

'You're closing down,' I said, looking round trying to remember the place in its heyday, when I last came here in the seventies, and it did not seem so different. Perhaps the colour of the walls had been altered, and the carpet, but let's face it, I was more changed than the shop.

'Yes, after all these years, the owner Mrs Post, she died and her daughter Carolyn took over but she is not a saleswoman, she doesn't know how, and then the ladies that used to step in here to buy, my loyal customers – Mrs Cohen, Mrs Frame, Lady Parker with the false breast from after the operation – I remember them all but they don't come any more, they stay inside their flats. No excuse, I say. Look at me, I'm that age and still I'm on my feet. Go and try that dress, right now.'

'But I don't want a new dress, I have all the clothes I need.'

'*Silly* girl.' She looked at me, with dark, inquisitive eyes. 'What's your age now?' she said. I told her. 'Not such a bad one. Shame you got that skin that falls into wrinkles, though a good cream wouldn't do no harm, either.'

'Well, you look marvellous, Eunice.' I said this in deference to that iron determination of hers: never to surrender to what she could conquer with her own will – her weapons an eyeliner pencil, a lipstick, and a pair of stockings with no runs in them. But then her son was no good, and she had nothing to live for, in that direction, unlike me.

'I work at it, Vivien,' she said. 'All my life I made sure I never had a torn fingernail or my shoes needed heeling. Many times I had no dinner when I got home at night so I could take my business suit out of the dry cleaner's. You going to try that dress on or not?'

'I'm too fat. Look at me, I'm as big as a house.' It was an exaggeration, I had put on a couple of stone since she last saw me but then I marvel at how thin I was in those days. I put my hands across the bodice of the dresses I once wore – I had no chest to speak of. Children round you out. I'm not so much overweight as neglected for there is self-abuse and then there is self-desertion.

'Don't be ridiculous, a woman is never too big for a nice dress. This is going to take pounds off you, you'll see.'

And Eunice stood there with the dress in her hands, this old woman facing the emptiness of her enforced retirement. She was holding a dress and urging me to try it, she was reminding me of what I had once intimately understood and had forgotten, that surge of excitement, that fizz, that deep pleasure – for a new dress changes *everything*.

'Go *in* there, try it on, that lovely dress.'

Alone in the little room with its velvet-covered stool, its hooks to hang my clothes, its flattering mirror and its clever lights, unzipping my jeans, pulling them past legs covered in a fine dark down that I went for months without remembering to shave or wax, I could not even recall the last time I bought something new. But the sight of the red dress was enough to intimidate me. How were you supposed to put it on?

I called out to Eunice. 'See?' she said. You inserted your arms in the sleeves and threaded a long belt through a slit at the side, wrapped with clumsy fingers the other belt around your waist and tied it in a bow. When I had managed to complete that awkward manoeuvre the dress acquired a life of its own, taking charge of my body, rearranging it to assume a completely different shape. Breasts *up*, waist *in*. I looked at least ten pounds slimmer.

The dress felt dangerously silky, it felt as if it might cling to me for good. And in the mirror a startling visitation from one at first I barely recognised or remembered, the one whom I had let go, that slim, exciting girl, that former me, silvery in the glass, smiling back at a fifty-three-year-old woman with white roots in her hair. Vivien Kovaks!

The red dress was glowing like rubies against my skin. I stood on tiptoe to mimic the effect of high heels. I thrust my right leg forward and put my hands on the place where I last remembered seeing my hip bones. Without the camouflage of my silk scarves, the wrinkled neck was exposed but the skin on my breastbone was unlined. Oh, the tricks your body plays, the fun it has with you, you have to laugh. Well no, not really.

'What do you think?' I said.

She looked me up and down with her appraising shop assistant's stare, darted forwards and rearranged the neckline in a couple of quick movements with her hands. 'See that? *Now* your bosom is uplifted. You need a good bra, by the way, Selfridge, they've got a nice selection. And make sure you get measured before you buy anything, you're wearing the wrong size.'

The dress dissolved and mingled with my flesh. Who knew where my skin began and the silk jersey started? I was falling ridiculously in love with a piece of cloth.

'I'll take it.'

'Now don't go buying it as a favour. I've got a nice pension from Mrs Post. I don't want for anything.'

I noticed there was a beige mark at the neckline. Another customer had left the trace of her make-up and Eunice hadn't seen it. It would come out with dry-cleaning yet I felt a wrench of sorrow that after a lifetime of close examination of herself, she had lost her own keen eyesight. Her irises had a milky opacity. I didn't say anything about the mark but she seemed to feel some small dissatisfaction in me, a criticism, perhaps of her. The balance adjusted itself again, and not in my favour.

'Why did you come in here, today?' she said, in the old sharp tone I remembered, like being battered by icy needles. 'You saw the closing down sale and thought you could get a bargain one last time?'

'I was just passing,' I said. 'That's all. Just passing.'

'You never passed before?'

'To be honest, Eunice,' I said, 'I always took another street, or I crossed to the other side of the road. I didn't *want* to see you.'

'So. You couldn't even look me in the eye.'

'Oh, come on. You tell me what I did wrong. I didn't—'

'You! You were a nasty, deceitful little girl. You broke that man's heart. And after everything he went through.'

'Yes, he had a hard life but that doesn't—'

'Doesn't what? Doesn't give him the right to make himself

comfortable, for the old age he never had *by the way*, thanks to your meddling?'

She slammed the dress down on the counter and threw it into a bag, unfolded, without tissue paper.

'A hundred and twenty pound. Cash or charge?'

I took out my credit card.

'Oh! *Platinum*. You've done well for yourself, money always comes to money, I always say. A rich husband, I suppose.'

And here we were again, back to where we started, Eunice and me. There would be no parole, no probation. I was still the nosy niece of her tormented lover, my uncle – and all the sorrow I inadvertently brought him, the girl she blamed for his premature death. Because he was the love of her life. That incongruous pair: the black manageress of a Marble Arch dress shop and the refugee slum landlord from Budapest.

She pointed a brown-lined finger at me, the silver nails chipped, a slight tremor at the fingertips. She began to speak and then for no reason her eyes welled up and she started to cry. I had never seen this, not even at my uncle's funeral when her face was hidden by a hat with a small black veil splashed with black net roses. But now all the past had overwhelmed her, the love she bore him, set in stone, turned molten in her chest.

'You don't know how it was that a man should look at me the way he did, after . . . that other thing,' she said.

'What other . . .?' I began, but just as soon as they had started, the tears stopped. She slipped a smooth brown veil over her features; an old sadness was set in them, like stains you cannot remove.

'I'll wrap up the dress for you properly,' she said. 'I'm sorry I snapped at you, Vivien.'

'It's all right,' I said. 'I understand.' For it was nearly thirty years since he died and still she suffered. Was this what I had to look forward to – thirty years of hard grief ahead of me?

Tentatively I reached out to touch her arm; her bones were fragile under her jacket and I was afraid that if I held her she would break. We had never touched before, apart from that first handshake on the street outside my uncle's house, her blue-gloved hand in mine.

She allowed me to rest my hand on her jacket. The silk of the sleeve surrendered slightly. She raised her face to mine, vivid and radiant.

'I have so many feelings for that man, every day I think about him. You ever visit his grave? I do. Once a year. I take stones to weigh him down so he doesn't rise up again and wander the earth in torment and in my flat I put a vase out with fresh flowers and a card on the mantelpiece, in memory. Did you see, I still got that watch he gave me, and the gold heart and chain with the little diamond in it. I only ever take that necklace off for a wash, and the lighter, I've still got that too, though I don't smoke no more. I could have got a lot of money for those things but I never sell them. Never. They're all I've got left of him, that *wonderful* man.'

I walked up Marylebone High Street, the strings of the carrier bag swinging, containing the dress, my ruby-red silk jersey dress.

This morning I had been forced along a different route by a police cordon set up because of a terrorist scare: a man was on a balcony with a towel wrapped round his waist, police marksmen had their guns aimed at him. There was supposed to be a bomb-making factory in the flat behind him. Last year there were blasts, deep in the tunnels, just as Claude predicted nearly thirty years ago, the stench of burning flesh, then rotting bodies deep down in the Piccadilly line.

Diverted by terrorism, which led me to Eunice, and this red dress.

I turned off at the familiar corner. My territory. I grew up here, these are my streets. I am a Londoner. I accept this city with all its uncontrollable chaos and dirty deficiencies. It leaves you alone to do what you like, and of where else can you say that with such conviction?

This is Benson Court, where I was born. No programme of modernisation and refurbishment was ever agreed on by the squabbling residents of the flats. The same dusty brass lamps suspended from the ceilings, and the same Canaletto reproductions in tarnished gilt frames hanging on the walls. The lift's cage, its clanking metal gates opening and closing, the groaning cables, the wood-panelled cabin with its pull-down leather seat, all unchanged. A tenant died in there last year. My father pressed the button to go downstairs and a corpse ascended, sitting upright with her shopping – the retired ballerina, dead with her head becomingly to one side. That old girl always knew how to strike a pose.

I let myself in. Silence. Dust. Smells. Memory. I went into the kitchen, which was the worst room, to make a cup of tea. Things were in the fridge that didn't belong there, books and pens my father used to write his bizarre letters to the newspapers, advertisements cut out of discarded magazines left by the bins – a disembodied hand displaying a diamond watch.

I sat down at the table and drank my tea. The stove on which my mother had heated countless tins of soup stood as if it did not know that in a few days, when the house clearance men arrived, it would be broken up for scrap. No one wanted that charred and grease-blackened engine, gas wheezing through its pipes. Not even a museum would take it. Vic, my husband, tried to make an omelette on it, once. There was something badly wrong with the heat distribution of the burners, he said; they flickered like guttering candles. I'd die for one of his omelettes, flecked with chives or plump cubes of pink ham. I'll have one again, some day, in that place, that other place.

By Friday, everything would be gone. All traces of my parents and their nearly sixty-year residence of these four rooms would vanish under coats of new paint, the old lino torn up, the place fumigated. The flat was encrusted with our lives. I had left long ago, my mother was sixteen years gone, my father wheezing out his last breath in his TV armchair, a copy of the *Radio Times* still in his fingers when I found him the following day. Sixty years of their interminable tenancy. How strange it was that people could acquire such apparent permanence, that nothing, not a bomb, could shift them (and bombs had fallen, not on this flat, but nearby during the blitz, my parents below ground in the air-raid shelter in the garden and back up in the lift the next morning to the kitchen in time for breakfast). At the end of the week nothing would remain. In a month, strangers. And for the rest of my life I would walk past Benson Court without the key to unlock the front door, without authorisation to ascend in the lift. No doubt they would throw away the old hessian doormat. A new welcome would take its place.

A sigh of wind against the window. Opposite, a drawn blind. The lift was silent; it had not moved from the same floor. The whole mansion block was still, and I was alone in there, with nothing for company but a new dress. '*Clothe me*,' I thought, '*I am cold.*'

A bell chimed in the hall. My uncle's voice echoed through the flat. I heard him suddenly, like a hallucination.

The uncle who was the love of the life of Eunice, the manageress of the Marble Arch dress shop, the uncle who could be killed by many methods, dead but unwilling to lie down, was speaking, *shouting*.

I have not forgotten our summer together, when I learned the only truth that matters: that suffering does not ennoble and that survivors survive because of their strength or cunning or luck, not their goodness, and certainly not their innocence.

And then I laughed, for he *was* there. For almost thirty years my uncle had been in hiding in a cardboard box. I had brought it back to the flat myself a few months after he died and placed it in my mother's wardrobe, pushed to the back.

I went into the bedroom and I parted her clothes to reach it, past her brown felt waistcoats, her wooden stick which my father refused to throw away. Not since she died had I seen that stick and I reached out to touch it, at first gingerly, then tenderly, rubbing my fingers against the grain. I felt the wearing down of the wood that her hands had gripped for so long, the satisfying curve in the neck – the cells of her body were all over that thing.

Here he was: my uncle had come to rest in his sister-in-law's wardrobe, next to that stick, which was the object that first drew her to his attention, and as a result of this she married my father and they left Budapest and came to London, and I was born, and my daughters born, and everything follows.

Not literally in the wardrobe. He was still under his marble stone in the cemetery, but his voice was alive, in the series of tape recordings and sheets of paper on which I had painstakingly typed the transcripts, and of course his own account, which he had tried to write himself.

Tapes, stick. These objects, this ordinary rubbish belonging to people who were dead, had survived them all. And the girl I had let go was also there, somewhere, just waiting for me to put on a red silk jersey dress to make her presence known. I was looking for her. She was somewhere in this flat – not a ghost for I am still alive, very much in the world, I don't pass through lightly or silently. I am my uncle's flesh and blood, after all, and nothing *he* ever did was without an impression.

This is the place where I was born, this mansion block off Marylebone High Street, my mother going into labour in the lift while my father was out at work; writhing and screaming, riding up and down. The metal doors unfolded like an accordion and a surgeon from the Middlesex Hospital saw her, in a pool of her own broken waters. He pushed her into his flat and delivered me on the sofa. I came into the world staring at a pre-war Bakelite light fitting and an oil painting of Highland cattle above the fireplace. High summer, 19 July 1953, and I was named Vivien, after the surgeon's wife.

At 2.30 in the afternoon the surgeon telephoned my father at work to convey the news, but he did not leave until 5 p.m., his usual time, despite his boss, Mr Axelrod, telling him he could go home at once. I understand his insistence on not having his routine disrupted. My father was terrified of change. When change was in the air anything could happen, and he already suffered from an anxiety: that any small disturbance in his circumstances would bring everything down – the flat, the wife, the job, the new daughter, London itself, then England, and he would slide down the map of the world, back to Hungary, clinging on uselessly, ridiculously, with his fingers clutching the smooth, rolling surface of the globe.

Benson Court. Built around the turn of the century, in overdecorated red brick. At the back a garden with a lawn, low-maintenance bushes, and a couple of flowerbeds which our flat did not overlook. We had a side view from our kitchen of the mansion block next door; the other rooms looked out on to the street, a quiet cut-through for pedestrians, with a one-way sign at the end which got rid of most of the traffic. You could not drive from our front door to anywhere useful like Marylebone High Street or Euston Road. But so what? Neither of my parents could drive, let alone own a car.

I am the child of old parents, a pair of cranky, odd Europeans with weird opinions. Oppressive ideas formed in the stale gloom. My father became very crazy in his last years without my mother's restraining influence. Without her, he filled himself up with the gas of his own thoughts and floated off into another dimension. At the end he became a fervent admirer of the American president, George W. Bush: 'Not a smart man, but that's what you want – the last thing we need is for the intellectuals to gain power; I tell you, some ideas are so ridiculous only a professor could swallow them.' From the time he retired, he took to writing smudged inky letters to the newspapers which he gave me to post and I never did. What was the point? They were illegible, he could barely see the paper himself.

Our flat was rented, for a pittance. The bowler-hatted ladies of the Women's Royal Voluntary Service found it for my parents when they arrived in England in 1938 as young refugees from Budapest. There is a photograph of them turning the key in the front door, their smiles like wooden postboxes. Safely on the other side, they bolted it, and tried to come out as little as possible. They had brought with them a single piece of furnishing: an ivory Chinaman with an ebony fishing rod which was a wedding present from my mother's aunt. For the Coronation of the Queen they bought a television which they coddled with their constant anxious attention, worrying that if they left it off too long it would refuse to turn back on, for sets in those days needed 'warming up', and suppose it got too cold? Would it die altogether, out of spite for their neglect?

The landlord was a philanthropist who had property all over London. Every week he sent a man in a Harris tweed overcoat and a trilby hat to collect the rent, which my parents had ready in an envelope. They were never late with a payment. The philanthropist would try raising it, to get them to move on, but my parents paid up without a murmur. No work was done on the interior; the fixtures and fittings grew more old-fashioned, my parents didn't care. It never occurred to them that a flat off Marylebone High Street, a short walk from Oxford Circus, the railway stations and the BBC, might be worth a lot of money. They genuinely believed that the philanthropist (and when he died in 1962, his heirs) would rent the flat to another set of arriving refugees once they were gone. They had *no idea*.

The reason for this cluelessness was that my father spent all day with his eye focused on a small point, a few inches away from his nose. He was a master craftsman in the back room of a jeweller's in Hatton Garden, the street in Farringdon where you go and buy gold and diamonds weighed out on tiny scales. The gold and the diamonds are brought in from Antwerp by men with black coats, black beards, black hats, black briefcases handcuffed to their wrists, talking on their mobile phones in a variety of languages, and minds that are very quick with numbers, but my father had absolutely nothing to do with them. He was always in his dusty workshop, crowded with boxes and paperwork, under an intensely bright lamp, restoring broken necklaces and putting old stones in new settings. That was his work from the age of sixteen until his eyesight finally failed at eighty-one, when a black cloud came down, as if God had sent one of his plagues upon him.

Many people passed through Benson Court over the years. The surgeon and his wife moved out to Finchley when I was five, and although a card would arrive on my birthday, eventually they went to Canada and we lost touch. In the kitchen window across the passage between the two mansion blocks, new curtains, new blinds and new people appeared; we never met any of them. I saw a woman once, standing there crying, alone, in the middle of the night, her mascara running and the fluorescent light overhead tingeing her blonde hair green. In 1968 a small child dressed in red clown shorts climbed on to the ledge, balanced, for a moment, toppling sideways, until a large arm hooked itself around him and brought him in to safety. A politician lived there for a bit, I saw him once, on the news on the living room TV, and then a minute later, when I went into the kitchen to make a cup of coffee, there he was again, boiling a kettle in his shirtsleeves.

Years go by, people come and go. The radio announcer with the exquisite voice and the war-hero boyfriend with the special medal moved in; the ageing ballerina, and her husband, the Persian carpet dealer, and dealer in much else, I suppose, since she habitually referred to him not as my husband but as 'the plutocrat'; Gilbert, the newspaper cartoonist who drew pictures of politicians with long spiteful noses, whether they had them or not. You saw them running up the stairs, you heard the noise of parties, saw famous faces. And many others who hid themselves behind their doors and drank, or wept, or ran companies whose business was obscure. Sometimes you heard foreign tongues in the lift. An attaché at the Indian embassy kept his blonde mistress in a flat.

But in all that time I was always the only child in our building, I don't know why. Maybe there was something in the lead pipes that frustrated fertility, though my mother and father had managed it to make me. Or perhaps it was just that Benson Court was the kind of place that people came to because they were lonely and needed the stimulation of the city. Or they were in transit. Or maybe there was a child-free policy that had been overruled for my parents the refugees. I know there were no large pets, or if they were, they hid themselves carefully.

A solitary upbringing. I lived mainly in my small bedroom overlooking the street, with a single narrow child's bed and a white candlewick bedspread. On the opposite wall was a framed picture, a scene from *Swan Lake*, the *corps de ballet* as cygnets, snow, rosy dappled water, and on the chest of drawers, my books, held in place by a pair of chipped plaster horse bookends and an ornament, a glossy china dog; a spaniel, I think. My only friend was the ivory Chinaman in the living room, which my parents had brought from Hungary. I called him Simon and he often spoke to me. I did not tell my parents this.

The clothes in the wardrobe were strange. Most of them were hand-me-downs from the WRVS: tweed skirts and ivory-coloured rayon blouses with Peter Pan collars, all done up to the neck in pearl buttons, and rimed with discoloured lace like dirty snow. There are no pictures of me wearing them. My father never owned a camera or knew how to operate one. As far as I knew, no evidence existed that I was ever a child.

What I remember, when I think back, is not a childhood, but Benson Court itself, and me in the corridors and the communal garden, or in my room with my dictionary which my parents had handed over in embossed wrapping paper, as if it was the keys to the kingdom (which for them, whose native tongue was not English, it was), and so the liking for words was born in me, an immigrant trait. I was trying to puzzle out the many mysteries of my simple existence, just lying there thinking. Not about homework, but playing with thoughts, as another, more athletic child might continuously bounce a ball with a tennis racket against a wall or throw it into a hoop. I thought about the distance between us and the sun, and then the moon, then Australia and so on, until I put my finger to the tip of my nose and practised how close I could get to it without the two surfaces quite meeting, and whether there was a measurement for that. Everything felt too near, yet eerily distant at the same time. The outside world looked as if it was seen through the thick glass window of a speeding train, or at least how such an experience had been described in a book, for I had never been on a train. I did not get outside the perimeters of London until I was eighteen.

I floated through time and space. I had complicated dreams, occasional nightmares. I thought I saw ghosts in the lift. I was neurotic, shy, prone to colds, flu, tonsillitis. I preferred the stillness of bed – the counterpane, the eiderdown quilt in winter – the enclosed space of my room, and smaller and smaller environments.

Full of unfulfilled yearnings for what I couldn't describe or understand, I bit down on things in frustration. I bit my nails and for a period of several weeks when I was eleven, drinking glasses, which bloodied my mouth. 'Where does she get the strength in the jaw?' my father asked, baffled.

There was a short time during puberty when I had what is now called an eating disorder. I would only eat white or yellow foods, but since this left bread, butter, potatoes, chicken and cake, I got fat, not thin. Then suddenly I craved red: beef, tomatoes, apples, baked beans. My parents would talk about me when I had gone to bed, and I would pass them in the hall on the way to the bathroom for a night-time wee. They disagreed about whether or not I should see a doctor. My mother was for it, my father against. 'Don't worry,' he said, 'she'll grow out of all this.' 'You don't have to pay, you know,' said my mother, 'if that's what you're worried about.' 'It's nothing to do with paying, she's fine, all girls are hysterics anyway. Not you, of course, Berta.'

In time I calmed down and began to look at life more philosophically and started to appreciate that the pain of being alive was normal and to be taken for granted.

In adolescence I acquired self-consciousness and began to look at myself in the windows of shops when I was coming home from school. I started to observe others, in crowds and as individuals, and acquired the trick of being part of the rest of the human race. I made tentative overtures to other girls at school, the quiet outcasts, and became part of a studious group which went to the cinema at weekends, to the Academy on Oxford Street where we watched films in the foreign languages we were learning. Afterwards we went to Soho for a frothy coffee. Then I'd go home to Benson Court where my parents were watching light entertainment, quiz shows, soap operas and comedy half-hours on the television with a tray of supper on their lap. Ideas were categorically not their thing.

My mother was born with one leg shorter than the other. I never knew her without her brown stick and the brown felt waistcoats she made for herself 'to keep my back warm'. Coming home from school one day, I saw her trying to cross Marylebone High Street, by the pub, when the traffic was heavy. She didn't see me. As she waited, nervously, for the cars and vans to slow, pushing the stick down the step of the pavement, readying herself for the little descent, a bird, a sparrow, alighted on her head. She must have felt the claws dig into her scalp, but she didn't scream; she put her hand up and felt its cold dry wing with her fingers, and it did not fly off in a fright, or try to peck her eyes out. It hovered for a moment, an inch or two away from her nut-brown hair, before flying away, leaving a small white deposit on her head.

Ashamed to be walking home, arm in arm, with a woman with bird shit on her hair; a woman not only with bird shit, but also with a thick wooden stick with a rubber tip; a woman who took her daughter's arm and crooked it in hers, automatically, because she thought this was how a mother and daughter should promenade through the streets, to demonstrate their affection – not wanting to be seen with my own mother, I doubled back along Moxon Street and took a series of right turns to get me back to the same spot, and arrived home a few minutes later.

I found her in the bathroom, washing her hair, smiling and singing a little tune from the radio. 'You know,' she said, 'I had a visit from a little bird just now, and though it's not very nice at first, when this happens, I hear it brings good luck. Yes, I will be lucky tomorrow.'

And she was. A letter came in the morning's post: we had won £10 on the premium bonds. 'It was the bird,' she said. 'Thank you, bird!'

So that was her.

Until I was ten I was completely unaware that I had a relative. Then one day the doorbell rang. My father opened it in the same way he would open the door to anyone, with the chain on, peering through the crack.

'Who is it?' he said in his piping, immigrant's voice with its mangled vowels. 'I know who it isn't, because it isn't rent day so don't pretend you have come for your money.'

A couple of thick fingers felt their way through the gap and grasped my father's sharp knuckles. 'Ervin, let me in, it's me, your brother.'

The moment my father heard that voice he slammed the door shut with such a bang that it shook the flat and my mother and I came running out into the hall to see what was going on.

'We're no relation!' my father cried, breaking out into a sweat on his nose. 'Go away or I call the police.'

'Ervin, I bought a beautiful bar of chocolate. Wait till you see the size of it! Let me in and we'll sit down and talk.'

'*Khasene hobn solst du mit dem malekh hamovesis tokhter*!' my father screamed.

'Ha ha! He wants I should marry the daughter of the Angel of Death,' my uncle said to the girl he had brought with him and gave her a kiss on the cheek with his wobbly lips.

'*Fransn zol esn dein layb!*' yelled my father, and opened the door so that his brother could appreciate the full force of his voice which he knew was quite little and needed uninterrupted air to amplify, with projectile spitting.

I was standing with my hands on the door frame staring at the visitor with saucer eyes. I had never in my life seen anyone dressed like him, let alone the girl. A man in an electric-blue mohair suit, black hand-stitched suede shoes, his wrist flashing with a fancy watch attached to a diamond bracelet. And the black girl on his arm, in a nylon leopardskin coat with matching pillbox hat, carrying a plastic crocodile handbag with a gilt clasp.

An uncle!

The man looked at me. I was all black eyes in a sallow face. A dark little child, taking after my mother; he and my father were fair in the complexion with reddish hair. This volcanic eruption had sent me into a state of catatonic shock, I couldn't speak, I couldn't move. We *never* had any visitors, apart from the rent man. I saw no one except the refined residents of Benson Court, some of whom spoke to me and gave me sweets, after being carefully vetted by my parents so I just stood there, rigid with surprise, as if the moon, the silvery ball, had lowered itself down from heaven on ropes and pulleys and the Man in the Moon had opened a trap door and climbed out in our hall.

'What did he say?' asked the girl, in a hoarse voice.

'He's wishing venereal disease on me,' my uncle translated for her, rolling his eyes. She giggled and coughed.

'In front of the child!' my father screamed. 'Vivien, go into your room.' But I didn't budge. I didn't know what venereal disease was. I let the word roll over my tongue, and committed them to memory, for later, when I would consult my birthday dictionary

'Oy, Vivien, come here to Uncle Sandy, I got chocolate for you.' He opened the gilt clasp of the girl's crocodile bag and pulled out a bar of Toblerone the size and weight of a hammer. 'I bet you never saw one of these outside a shop before. It's from Switzerland, you know, they make the bar of chocolate like the shape of the mountains!'

'*Migigul zolst in henglayhter, by tog zolst du hengen, un bay nacht zolst du brenen.*'

'Now he wants for me to be a chandelier, to hang by day and burn by night. My own brother.' My uncle grabbed the mohair crotch of his trousers and gave his penis a yank. The girl started laughing: she opened her mouth and let out a series of high-pitched yelps, gulping for air with each one. I saw inside her pink mouth, and her big pink tongue and the metal fillings in her teeth.

'You are no brother, you wolf!' My father was going mad, I had never known him so enraged. His eyelashes were magnified and pushing up against the panes of his dusty, black-rimmed glasses. I pressed back further against the door but had no inclination for flight. I had never been to the theatre. This is what I thought it would be like – shouting and large gestures. People transformed.

'What are you talking about?' my uncle said, laughing, his bulbous lower lip shaking up and down. 'The same mammy bore us, blood of our blood!'

'May she rest in peace. Don't you desecrate her name with your filthy mouth.'

'*Ervin, let me in.*'

'You'll never set foot in this house. Not while there's a breath left in my body.' And my father slammed the door, went into the living room and turned on the TV to its loudest volume, a higher notch than he had ever dared before.

On the other side of the front door my uncle let out a theatrical sigh, shrugged, turned away, walked down the stairs in his hand-stitched suede shoes, and I could hear the girl ask him what he was going to do with the chocolate. 'You can have it,' he told her. I ran to the window and looked down at them in the street, the West Indian girl standing on the pavement, chocolate round her face and my uncle with his fabulous car, the silver Jaguar, opening the driver's side and calling to her to get in, not opening the passenger door like a gentleman, because he was no gentleman and she was just a teenage whore. But this sight remains with me to this day, that sunlit Saturday morning at the door of Benson Court in 1963.

Eight months later, he was in prison. *Agony* for my parents, night after night for five weeks, to be forced against their will to watch the reports of the case on television, unable to switch off the set because then the living room would turn into a tomb of unbreakable silence. And to try, and fail, to shield their daughter from the man in the dock with nearly the same last name, who came from the same place, who talked English with the same accent as my mother and father, whom I had seen with my own eyes at the front door of our flat, arguing with my daddy and calling him brother.

A brother is, to a person's daughter, an uncle. There was no way round it. I had a relative.

'But what has that man *done*, Daddy?' I asked, at once.

'Don't ask questions. No one ever had a quiet life by asking questions, and a life that isn't peaceful is no life at all.'

But my parents' life was not so much peaceful, to me, as inert. A quarter of a century hibernation.

For the rest of my childhood, my parents and I rolled slowly and quietly like three torpid marbles across the lino floor, while below, under the plaster ceiling rose and the ornamental cornices, the longest-serving resident of the flats moved silently about in perpetual semi-darkness, her lamps fitted with low-watt bulbs and shrouded in fringed shawls to dim them down to hazy areolae of amber light, like car headlamps on a foggy morning. Occasionally, she played an unrecognisable gramophone record. Every night, around 8 p.m., she dressed up in a fox-fur coat and down-at-heel suede shoes with torn grey satin bows, to tramp the night streets of London; a vagabond coming home just after dawn, when you were woken from vertiginous dreams by the elevator's clank and the slamming of the front door and the rattle of the stained glass panel in its wooden frame.

Who knew why she kept these odd nocturnal hours, or why she made herself up with shaky hands – the eyes of her lined face rimmed with smudged kohl, her doll-like dots of rouge, her Cupid's bow lips painted blood red, as if she had bitten into someone's flesh and sucked out its goodness? Maybe she had a werewolf in her. We all have these inner drives, like dogs biting our intestines. I know I do.

Until mid-afternoon she slept, unless she was lying, eyes wide open, memorising what she had witnessed on her voyages across the city. She had been seen as far away as Kilburn, climbing the streets, heading further and further north, before dropping down with exhaustion as the light rose. Why did she walk, to what purpose? What was she searching for or what was she escaping? I have no idea, even now forty years later.

One evening when I was seventeen, I was coming home late after the final rehearsals for the school play, which was the story of the Romanov princess Anastasia (or rather that girl who claimed to be her, the Polish peasant Franziska Schanzkowska). I wasn't acting in it, I was the prompt, an unseen voice. It was the fifth of November. Fireworks had begun to explode in back gardens. A roaring bonfire was being lit on Primrose Hill. Mrs Prescott was standing on the steps of Benson Court fastening the buttons of her coat when an almighty explosion rocked the street from behind the mansion block opposite. She stood, mute, trembling.

'Are you all right?' I said.

'I don't like the bangs,' she said, in a papery voice.

'I expect it reminds you of the war,' I replied, sympathetically, because this is what my mother always said, every year ('the horrible bombs!')

She shook her head. 'I never liked bangs.'

'Perhaps you shouldn't go out tonight,' I said. 'It will be bangs all the way.'

'I like the coloured lights. I just wish they were silent. I like to look, not hear.'

Silver rain showered above the chimneypots. A rocket whistled. She shuddered. Her vulnerability affected me, it reminded me of my lonely years in the bedroom. She smelt of roses and face powder and sadness. These scents caught and held me, there on the step. I am only five feet four inches, but still, I towered over her.

'I think you're right, I won't go until it's all over,' she said.

She turned back. I noticed how her Cupid's bow bled into the lines above her mouth. I had never seen this phenomenon close up before, because my mother, who also had lines, never wore make-up. I thought she must spend hours in front of the mirror painting her lipstick into the cracks with a tiny brush. You would need good eyesight and a steady hand, neither of which she seemed to possess, for she continued to tremble and her eyes peered at me as if I was someone she once knew.

'You live in the flat below us,' I said. 'We hear your records, sometimes.'

'I don't play any records.'

'But you do.'

'That's not me, it's a visitor.'

I had never seen a visitor, but then not everyone had seen Uncle Sándor.

We ascended in the lift.

'Is your father the one with the accent?' she said.

'Yes.'

The doors of the lift clanked open at the second floor.

'Perhaps you would like to join me for a glass of sherry,' she said, turning to me, as she stepped out.

I followed her into the flat, entering twilight. She poured the sherry into a glass and a dead spider floated up on the surface; I fished it out with my fingers and dropped on the floor next to my chair. I licked the inner surfaces of the glass, cautiously, to try the taste of alcohol, which was sweet and heady. After she had looked at me in silence for several minutes, which did not bother me at all because that was what my father did, she practised opening her mouth a few times, began to form a word, halted, paused, started again, then finally said: 'Why do you dress like that?'

'It's my school uniform.'

'I mean when you are not at school.'

'I don't know. I just wear what's in the wardrobe.'

'You know what I would like? To wash your hair.'

'Why? My hair is clean.'

'I'd like to style it. Come on.'

She put her hand delicately on my arm. Her eyes were gentle, not crazy, a faded watery blue, the Miss Havisham of the windy, chaotic, dangerous streets. If you grow up in Benson Court, you take it for granted that people are different, not all the same. She was weird, but so were my parents. And she was both frail and strong at the same time, frail in the body but tough to survive the night.

I got up and followed her into the bathroom. She ran the taps and lightly pressed my head down over the sink. The water coursed over my head, and I felt the cold trickle of shampoo on my scalp. Her fingers, suddenly strong, began to massage the liquid into a foam. My body was suffused with delightful tingling sensations.

For several minutes she rubbed my scalp with a towel then began to wind my hair around large rollers. Her fingers knew exactly what they were doing. I looked in the mirror. My head had expanded into a series of large metal curls clamped with pins.

'Now sit by the fire,' she said, 'while it dries completely.'

A long time passed. Outside the explosions were getting much worse and cats were shrieking in terror and dogs barked like they'd lost their minds. She put her hands over her ears and shrivelled up behind her cushions. Flashes and sparks and a hail of light penetrated the curtains.

'It's going on for ages,' I said.

'Every year it's more loud.'

At length, she removed the rollers and began to brush my hair.

'Look,' she said and pointed to the mirror.

I had entered the flat with a black bush of tangled, frizzy curls, flattened and held down by brown kirby grips and two tortoise-shell slides. Now I had a smooth dark helmet of waves. I found myself in two halves, the interior and exterior of my own head. It was such a profound alienation at first, such a mental crisis that I began rocking back and forth on the rubber soles of my school shoes.

'You see, when we started you were quite an ugly sallow girl, but now you look like Elizabeth Taylor. I'll show you a picture.'

'Is this really me?'

'Yes, of course. It's who you really are.'

'Thank you.'

'My pleasure.'

The explosions were dying away. Only an occasional bang interrupted the night.

She put on her coat.

'I can go out now,' she said. And we left the flat together. She went down in the lift and I walked up the remaining flight of stairs. I heard her come in much later than usual, around 7.30 in the morning for she had had that delayed start.

My mother screamed when she saw me and my father went white. 'What have you done?' she cried. 'And who did this to you?'

'What, are you a tramp, now?' said my father. 'Do you go with men?'

'A girl from school did it,' I said, 'and don't tell me to wash it out because I'm not going to. I'm seventeen and I'll do what I like.'

My parents were flabbergasted. They had not brought up a

daughter to talk back to her parents. They saw me descending into the world, which seemed to them to be the dark forest of fairy tales, prowled by wolves, bad elves, and other creatures of the Middle European night. A short walk away in Hyde Park, the year before, the Rolling Stones had played a concert and the noise of the guitars and drums had echoed as far away as Marylebone, even through the windows of Benson Court where my parents sat, holding hands, as if the music were the sound of marching bands, ahead of an army come to shoot them.

The next day, after school, I went to Boots the chemist and bought a red lipstick in a gold case and painted my mouth with it in the evenings to wear while I did my homework. A few days later I ventured into the territory of mascara, after a lesson in its application from the sales lady. I never wore any of this stuff outside the flat, but I began to stop at dress shops and look inside. I tried to do my hair as Mrs Prescott had styled it but without much success and eventually I asked the hairdresser who cut it every three months for advice. She sold me a lotion I was to put on after shampooing and she told me where I could get a second-hand hairdryer cheap. From this time on, I spent a lot of time straightening my hair.

Like Louis Jourdan in the film *Gigi*, it was Gilbert, the cartoonist, who first noticed that a little girl had grown up, and invited me into 4G for a drink and then rolled a joint. I floated away down Marylebone High Street and an hour or so later I lost my virginity to him – an afternoon of intense rain which flooded the gutters, and lightning flashes that hit a pigeon in the communal gardens. Afterwards he made me toast with Gentleman's Relish, and drew me, for his private collection of sketches. I only did it because I had read a lot about love in books. It wasn't satisfactory, it was wet and uncomfortable but it drew my attention to the next set of possibilities. I was precocious in that department, what they call *an enthusiast*.

They say you get a glow about you once you have had sex. I must have done, because all the old goats in the building were after me now. The retired ballerina used to go out twice a week for lunch at the Fountain Room at Fortnum & Mason to meet her old chums and reminisce about days long gone when they were Odette and Giselle. The potentate prowled the halls looking for me. 'I want to show you my first editions,' he said. He was a tubby chap with a pink cravat and owned one of the earliest telephone answering machines, which his wife didn't know how to operate. It allowed him to organise his complicated love life.

I was planning to apply to study philosophy at university because of all that lonely thinking in my bedroom, but then I started to try on characters in novels for a day or two, to see how they fitted. I'd dress like them, think like them, walk around being Emma Bovary, with no understanding at all of either provincial life or farming, but boredom I knew *very* well.

The last time I saw Mrs Prescott, she was hovering on the step looking worn out. Only because of the time of night could I know if she was coming or going.

'I did the trick,' she said, in a voice as flimsy as tissue. 'Much improved.'

'Thank you.'

'I think you should eat some red meat, you need iron and protein. You are going to be a very strong girl. It's your frame, your bones. You come from peasant stock.'

'I don't think so.'

'Oh, yes. That's quite certain.'

'Can I come with you?'

'Where?'

'Wherever you're going.'

'No, my dear. I wouldn't want that.'

And she walked off lightly along the street, faster than I had expected. I followed her for a little way, as far as Edgware Road, before turning back. I saw her waiting at the lights at Hyde Park Corner, her own hair sparkling under the light rain.

Everything was lit up with an amber radiance: the traffic lights seemed held forever on amber. I was filled with sudden exultation, like a person aroused from a coma. It was a joy to be alive, a pleasure.

'Mrs Prescott,' I cried, 'tell me—' but she ran across the road and however fast I followed, I never caught her, that night or another.

She was a missionary, an expeditionary. She was an explorer, she was a huntress, and glory be to her and the glory she left me. She expired like a railway ticket, on the Edgware Road ten days later, at the corner of Frampton Street, with no explanation.

Everything was taken away by a man in a stained leather jerkin and studded boots. As he was hefting a trunk its rotten bottom fell out, showering the hall with silks, satins, velvets, broiderie anglaise, lace and feathers, in peach, apricot, grape and plum-coloured shades: a dazzling momentary rain of richness, that my mother ran to gather in her arms and then she raced up the stairs, slamming the door of our flat, panting.

'A thief she has made me,' she whispered, 'a pilferer of dead woman's clothes. But look at this, Vivien, look at the beauty of it, I never saw things like this except on the Hollywood stars, come on help me, what do we have here? Gold buttons – no, gilt, it comes off if you scratch it.' A smell arose of lily of the valley scent, old pre-war flowers overwhelming a mouldy odour that permeated the trunk.

She held up a dress against her, but her form broadly overlapped its seams. 'It's too small, I knew it. Well these are much too good to go to waste, but they will not fit me, I'm afraid. Vivien, you must try. For parties.'

After I had exhausted all the possibilities of Mrs Prescott's clothes and began to acquire a taste for the tailored, the bias cut, the calf-length skirt, the bolero jacket, the wide high-waisted Katharine Hepburn pants, and the Dietrich shoulder pad, I started to frequent second-hand clothes shops, where in those days you could still quite easily find outfits from much earlier eras. The inhabitants of the many mansion blocks of London died and their wardrobes – flappers' fringed dresses, cloche hats, the occasional Fortuny silk pleated robe – were emptied out by grieving relatives and carted off by the same house clearance people who had tried to take away Mrs Prescott's outfits, before my mother had nabbed them.

Amongst us aficionados of what is now called 'vintage', who refused to wear the ghastly styles of the period, the wide lapels and lurid tank tops, the huge collars, all the brown and orange, certain addresses were passed around, quietly, as if they were the hideouts of drug dealers. The most sought after were the places where you rang a bell in a side door and were buzzed up to a dingy room above a shop where racks and racks of treasure stood slovenly together, the moth-eaten furs with the Schiaparelli jacket. The owners knew exactly what they had. They were old-clothes men. Rag dealers. They did not understand why a procession of young girls traipsed up their stairs and handed over folded pound notes for worthless rubbish, when brand new clothes were freely available in the shops; we must be a bit touched in the head or terribly poor. But they, the dealers, were bright enough to understand that certain labels sold for a good price and it didn't matter whether the label was attached to a little blouse or a sensible winter coat. The label was the point.

There was rarely anything like a dressing room. A bit of curtain was slung across the corner of the shop and after a while one calculated that the angle of the mirror on the ceiling was in line with a second mirror outside, and worked out that, if you were adept at it, you were going to need to change from one set of clothes into another without actually stripping down to your bra and pants.

The shop I went to most often was on Endell Street in Covent Garden, above a butcher's, and the whiff of pork, lamb, beef, livers and kidneys hung around the clothes so you had to wash them a few times or have them dry-cleaned before you could wear them. An old Pole ran it, bearded, and swaddled in boots and sheepskins during most months of the year except the really high summer, when he wore a tweed jacket and a cap. If you came in regularly, he would offer you a filthy drink from a bottle of Cyprus sherry and smile in gratitude when you refused. His English was atrocious, no one understood a word he said, and the prices on the clothes were never marked. You asked and he looked at it, looked at you, then wrote something down on a piece of paper and either you said yes, or you said no. He wrapped everything in brown paper parcels with string. It felt like a secret to be walking down the stairs with that old-fashioned package then coming home and seeing what you'd really got, outside the fluorescent strip lighting of the cluttered, smoky, meat-smelling room. Often there were stains you hadn't noticed and sometimes they wouldn't come out. But then you could get a little jacket with the label CHANEL PARIS inside it.

I arrived at university in a crêpe de Chine cocktail dress and created an instant, sensational impression. Now life begins, I thought, and yes, it did.

At the low-lying concrete campus on the outskirts of the medieval 'city' of York (it was no bigger than a town), I gave the appearance of being a worldly sophisticate, a Londoner-born, brought up in the heart of the city, confident, full of self-assurance and originality. Inside – fear, uncertainty, social awkwardness. I was told I had an aloof charisma, wandering around the man-made lake populated by ducks and other water birds, empty fields stretching to the horizon. But all I felt was an aching loneliness of perpetually grey skies and beyond them in one direction the Pennines, bare, brown denuded hills and, heading east, the North Sea.

In some ways it was a disastrous choice, influenced solely by a teacher who had merely recommended the excellence of its English department and knew nothing more. I was city bred. The furthest distance I had travelled from London was the hour-long journey to Brighton, and I had only seen cows sheep horses pigs chickens in pictures. A field was generally green, sometimes yellow at wheat time. The great outdoors was the distance between the bus stop and the front door, and parks laying themselves down flat as if for a rest, and not getting up again.

I did not know how to explain the refugee parents, my mother's felt waistcoats, the claustrophobic atmosphere of Benson Court, Mrs Prescott, Gilbert and his joints and sketch pad, and my nervy anxiety about open spaces and fresh air. My clothes acted as a kind of carapace, an armour with which I protected my inner, soft body. But the way I dressed made someone stop me on the covered walkway beside the lake on a windy late autumn day and ask if I would be interested in joining the drama society. Not as an actress but as a costume maker. I could not sew, I said, surprised. But sewing didn't really come into it, just scouring junk shops, so it was me who devised the outfits for a famous production of *The Winter's Tale* which would live on for many years in the memories of those who took part in it for the enormous amount of sexual tension it released, along with silver bangles, floating scarves and other campery.

It was through the drama society that I learned how to manage the tricky manoeuvres of the divided self, the inner longings at war with inner panic. Gay men gave me the courage to be Vivien, or rather to develop her from scratch, from the materials at my disposal. I became, I suppose, a gay icon. A gay man's fantasy fuck. And if they were going to have one final experiment with the opposite sex, just to make absolutely certain before committing themselves to boys, it would be with me. I got very tired of floating scarves and silver bangles, but quite comfortable with taking my clothes off and being examined with the slightly repelled curiosity of one who is looking at a physical example of another species.

One summer day at the end of my second year, I was lying in the bath smoking a cigarette when a tall, thin, blond boy from the biochemistry department barged in, desperate to take a leak while returning a textbook to one of my flatmates.

The choice was his, not mine, instant and decisive:

So there you were, lying next to that vase of poppies on the wash-stand, and you had a slant of red across your breasts from the stained glass panel in the window. Everything was covered in steam and you were smoking a cigarette with your wet fingers, lipstick on the stub and splashing the water with your other hand. You looked exactly like a Modigliani painting I once saw. The whole room smelt of red and what was going through my mind was who is she and what is she thinking?

An unlikely pair, but many couples are.

Alexander Amory. He seemed the most extraordinary person to be chosen by: cerebral, opinionated, self-confident. He was, I now think, rather shallow, but in a very complicated way. Sometimes he could be a rigid post, inflexible in the certainty of his ideas, droning on about science and progress, his research into proteins; yet other times he would be lying on the sofa reading, his feet hanging over the arms, lit up by lamplight, giggling over a newspaper article, reading bits out loud, mocking the follies of our politicians.

Mine, he once pointed out, was not what he considered an objective intelligence, and literature was not, he considered, a real subject. You could talk about literature with a hard precision if you extracted from it ideas about political philosophy, for example; whenever he read a book I had the impression of a man putting in a thumb and pulling out a plum, which he would hold up to the light and examine before putting it in his mouth. But as a guide to the perplexity of human nature, he considered it inexact, more or less useless. My own approach he thought hilarious. Somehow I would manage to climb *inside* the books I read, feeling and tasting them – I became the characters themselves. It was too intuitive an understanding of art to be comprehensible by him.

If I was a hothouse orchid which thrives indoors, bunched up by the fire, reading, in winter Alexander would sit for hours in the freezing fog looking at the Canada geese rising from the water of the campus lake, hearing the echo of the beat of their wings across the slushy ice. Then he would come home, blowing on his fingers, and try to write poetry, 'which is your field, not mine, so what do you think, Vivien? You're the expert.'

Poetry was different from the novel's mush, he declared, and his poems were hard work. Clever, metaphysical, something buried in them, like a crack of light showing beneath a door. I admired, but did not like them. I did like it when he tried to describe his proteins. Poetry and proteins, he said, much the same thing. He explained how they resembled dense ice etchings on a winter window. '*Now* do you see?' Sort of.

What I really adored about him was how immensely interested he was in *me*. He had never met anyone like Vivien Kovaks, he said: it was what he perceived as my lack of logic that was the attraction, as if I were an immensely hard sum he were trying to work out, a mathematical equation to be cracked. He was always asking me questions about myself, trying to shed his clear cold illuminating brilliance on every aspect of my personality.

For example: 'Every pair of Fair Isle gloves you buy ends up with holes in the fingers,' he said, picking up my hands, 'and then you have to buy new ones and all because you never cut your nails. Why, Vivien? Why don't you cut your nails? Don't look at me like that, I'm not being judgemental, I'm just fascinated.'

'I don't notice how long they've got till it's too late.'

'Isn't there some deeper reason? That your fingers hate to be trapped in there?'

'No. I'm just lazy and forgetful.'

'Yes, I realise *that*, but why?'

'I don't know.'

'You're off in a dream the whole time and I just have to know what you're thinking.'

But I was thinking how lucky I was to have escaped from

Benson Court, walking along the street holding hands with this tall blond Englishman with his mutton chop whiskers which were all the rage in the early seventies, and the long narrow feet in their suede desert boots, and the fine, already thinning hair, and his blue eyes. For there was something inordinately sexy about the *idea* of Alexander without him being obviously sexy himself. He had saved me from the pallid hands of my gay boyfriends, about whom he had no principled objection, but thought I was unwise to allow myself to be an experimental station in the science of the discovery of sexual orientation.

His father was a vicar in the county town of Hereford; his people were types I had only read about in books and magazines. They emerged from their two dimensions into a fleshy discomforting reality. For example his mother bred a type of long-haired dog as a hobby and showed them at Crufts. The house smelt of dogs, dog food and mildew and they ate small pale meals: pink slices of ham with wide rinds of white fat, boiled potatoes, boiled marrow, rice pudding. After dinner one of his sisters played the cello and another played the viola and everyone nodded along or read the score. I slept in an icy room under an eiderdown and Christ, with his arms spread out, bled wooden blood on the wall above my bed. At breakfast Alexander's father ate a soft-boiled egg with a vivid runny yellow yolk that flecked his beard, and his mother held a dog on her lap, kissing it on the mouth. No one paid any attention. The dog put its tongue on hers – they reached out to lick each other.

Nonetheless, I could not imagine how the child of the vicarage could meet the man with the dusty glasses and the copies of the *Radio Times* with the evening's programmes ticked and circled.

We got the train to London and I took him through the front door of Benson Court. I had never noticed the smells before, of cleaning fluids and charladies' sweat and, inside the flat, my mother's cherry odour. 'I was virtually born in this lift,' I said, as we ascended. The mahogany cabin looked like an upturned coffin. He stretched his hands out to touch the sides. 'This womb,' he said, 'this incubator of you. Tremendous. Well done.'

My parents were struck dumb at the sight of the young English gentleman, the vertical lines at the side of his mouth which deepened when he smiled, his corduroy legs crossed on their cheap furniture as he patiently explained his proteins and what he did with them.

'Does he know?' my father whispered, coming into the kitchen where I was helping my mother put shop-bought Swiss roll on a plate and dusting a wine glass which came with the flat, in case he asked for a drink and one of us would have to run out to the shop to buy a bottle of something.

'The bare bones,' I said. He had asked me about my surname, Kovaks, and whether I was related to the infamous slum landlord. He knew the Sándor Kovacs story, as it had been reported, but he assured me that there was no connection in his mind between the two of us. One thing had nothing to do with the other, he said. This idea that *blood will out* was medieval nonsense, and he should know, he looked at blood through a microscope.

In the late fifties, my father had undertaken the expense and effort of changing the whole family's surname by deed poll from Kovacs to Kovaks. 'Only one letter,' he told my mother, 'and now we're no relation.' Who did he think he was fooling? Himself, certainly. My mother never really swallowed it and kept on signing her name the old way. My father was more fastidious. She can't spell, he told me. I married her and still she doesn't know my name. He laughed, and winked at my mother, who ignored him.

I pointed out the difference in the spelling to Alexander but when I applied for my first passport, for my first ever trip abroad (a weekend in Paris, what else?) he saw my birth certificate.

'K or c, which is it?' he asked. 'I won't give it back until you tell me.' So I had to explain about the uncle, the man in the mohair suit with the leopardskin floozy.

'How did he take it?' my father asked, nervously, peering round the kitchen door, ill at ease with the presence of a stranger in the flat. 'He still wants to carry on with you?'

'Yes, he didn't seem to mind at all.'

'And he knows about prison and everything?'

'Yes, yes.'

'You're certain he understands?'

'*Yes*.'

'OK, then you better stick to him. You never know how the next one might react. Tell him he's always welcome in our home.'

We both began postgraduate dissertations, mine on Dickens' minor characters, what were called the 'grotesques', whom I found familiar from my own upbringing at Benson Court. I was dreamy and lazy and it proceeded slowly, while Alexander raced through his, a disciplined and hard worker, putting in twelve-hour days at the lab and in the library.

He was offered a job as part of a research team, at Johns Hopkins University, Baltimore, Maryland. He asked me to marry him, a formal proposal over dinner at an Italian restaurant with a bottle of wine and the presentation of a ring with a small chip of diamond in it. He didn't want to go to America without me, I was the light of his life, he said, an exotic little black monkey whose fingers curled with pleasure when she was happy and who argued with tongue-tied inarticulate passion about what she cared about – literature, clothes, the colour of a lipstick. Serious and frivolous, exciting and sensual, sexy, incredibly sexy . . . and I cried out, 'Is this how you really see me?' 'Yes!' he said, amazed that I did not understand that this was who I *was* – did I really need him to be a mirror for me?

My father was so worried about the task of giving me away, of walking down the aisle in a rented penguin suit with everyone looking at him, that it made him ill. He began to develop an ulcer, worrying about it.

'You know, I don't like it. I got no baptism certificate like we got for Vivien when she was born. She has the papers, I don't. It's not something you should do, if you haven't got the papers. They can hold it against you.'

He put the wrong stone in a necklace, the blue sapphire instead of the diamond, the first time in nearly forty years of loyal service with the same firm that my father had made a mistake. His boss, Mr Axelrod said the wedding was getting to him. He was sick with worry, 'and personally,' Axelrod said, 'I think it's psychological. And where's Hereford anyway? Hertfordshire, I know. But Hereford I never heard of. What's she got to get married for? She's far too young.'

'I told you, the boy has a job in America, in a laboratory.'

'Is he going to find a cure for cancer?'

'You know what? That's exactly right. He's on a *team*, I tell you. A team for curing cancer.'

'A team is what you have in a football game or the other one, cricket.'

'Yes, well this is another kind of team, a science team. And by the time they've finished, all the illnesses will be stopped dead, *just like that*.'

'So what will people die from?'

'How should I know? Maybe we'll live for ever.'

'You mean I got to put up with you, working here for all eternity?'

'What, you're going to give me the sack now, just because I got everlasting life?'

I had to walk down the aisle all by myself; my father was going to vomit all over my dress if I put him through this ordeal. So I, alone, in a grey satin gown, strolled towards my groom, as he stood in his new suit, his hair cut close to the nape of his neck, his cheeks shaved, a pale gold knife, standing there.

It was done, and my father collapsed and fanned himself with his hymn sheet. 'Berta,' he whispered to my mother, 'all our troubles are over. They can't touch us now.'

'Please, Ervin,' she said, 'don't go boasting of this to your brother.'

My parents bought us the honeymoon as a wedding present, which was touching because they had never been on a holiday themselves, had barely left London in nearly forty years, let alone been abroad, apart from where they came from. But how could they find a hotel, and where? And what about the travel arrangements? Their idea of what a honeymoon should be like was from the television; they knew there must be cocktails, glasses of champagne, sunsets, almost certainly some kind of beach, or at least a sea view. Apart from the Thames, they thought about a cruise, but it was too expensive; they considered Rome, but no sea view there. They were adamant about that sea view. They had only seen running water outside their bathtub when they made their own tumultuous crossing of the English Channel in an overnight sailing before the war, spending every minute below deck and occasionally looking out with a brief, terrified glance through a porthole to the rushing black sea. But they knew that the sea didn't have to be like that. You could have a palm tree, for example, though they couldn't decide what grew on it: dates, coconuts, bananas?

After many nights of discussion my father decided to take what was for him a huge step: he turned to the only people they knew who could assist – the neighbours, who were delighted, especially the longer-standing residents who had watched me grow up, playing noisily alone in those carpeted halls, pushing the button of the lift in mischief, running around the communal garden in my imaginary world.

Gilbert, who had taken my virginity and was delighted to be passing me on to a husband, convened a meeting in his flat to decide on our destination. The ballerina was there, the plutocrat husband, the BBC announcer, an orthopaedic surgeon who had just moved in, and other interested and opinionated parties. Ten altogether, not including my parents, who had never once set foot in any other flat in the building; they had no idea that other people lived this way under the same roof, with coffee tables, dinner services, paintings, rugs, ornaments, brocade curtains, chintz-covered sofas, bookshelves, sideboards, tassels.

After intense debate – and two pots of coffee and a decanter of wine which my parents didn't touch, but ate the foil-wrapped chocolate liqueurs instead – they chose the French Riviera, specifically Nice, the Hotel Negresco, and a brochure was sent for and the prices noted, my parents with hands on their chests, like they were about to have heart attacks, screaming with shock at the tariffs. And then letters, telegrams, money orders: three nights booked in a room with sea view and balcony, breakfast and one dinner included.

'Oh, yes,' said Gilbert, 'she'll like it there.'

'The place you are going to is renowned,' said my father. 'That's all you need to know. Renowned.'

'For what?' asked Alexander as we got out of the taxi and walked into the lobby. 'Vulgarity?'

'Well, I like it,' I said, looking round.

'What? What do you like?'

I liked everything: the wood-panelled bar, the heavy chandeliers, the tapestries, the crystal whisky fountain, the atmosphere of decadence and luxury and inertia. I liked the creepy child in a tiny mink jacket lounging in front of the sculpted floral arrangements; the severe blonde women in tweeds and pearls sipping cocktails in the velvet club armchairs; the names of the dishes on the menu held on a gilt easel outside the dining room.

And most of all I liked our reflection in the mirrors that we passed: the young English lord in the white open-neck shirt and a petrol blue linen jacket, and his dark wife with the persistent shadow on her upper lip, her raisin eyes, her sallow complexion offset by a slash of scarlet lipstick. Her cream bouclé wool jacket, short navy crêpe skirt, two-tone shoes.

'You're in your element here,' Alexander said, 'now you're dressed just right for the setting.'

We went for a walk along the Baie des Anges. I'm married, I thought. I'm Vivien Amory. I'm free. And yet I still didn't fully understand his attraction to me, however close he held the mirror.

'Why were you so very certain when you came in on me in the bath that time? How did you know from the very start?'

'We were getting too stringy, we Amorys,' he said, putting his arm around me and kissing the top of my head, while passers-by smiled at us because we so obviously had the white phosphorescent gleam of a wedding still about us. 'Every generation an Amory would marry a tall blonde and we got longer and whiter until we started to look like worms. When I was going up to university my father said, bring down the height can you, and get some red blood in our veins. So it was you, there you were, in the bath. Of course you weren't at all what he had in mind, but I can't help that.'

'What did he have in mind?'

But he just started laughing.

Mid-afternoon. Benson Court is quiet. The ballerina wakes from her afternoon nap, it's not her day for lunch in the Fountain Room, and the plutocrat is writing letters in the study to his mistress. Gilbert is at work scratching with his pen at a piece of paper, *malicious* slashes; he'd rather poke the eyes out of the prime minister himself, he hates them, fat or thin, they are all liars and crooks. My father is still in Hatton Garden, looking through his magnifying eye at diamonds, and who knows what thoughts pass through his mind during those long hours he spends at his bench with the cold lumps of carbon?

I am trying to read a book. A book I read already. Sometimes I weep, suddenly, and wipe my eyes on my sleeve. The memories of Nice are worn down to thin panels of beaten gold. His blue eyes looking out at me from beneath the blond lashes as he died, eyes now locked up in a box. And the box is in a hole in the ground and some metamorphosis of Alexander is taking place, he is being recomposed, back into proteins, and the proteins feed the soil, and the yew trees of the churchyard and the dandelions and the ornamental roses at the gate. The earthen mound above his body gently subsides. Soon his ribs will be crushed under marble.

He died. He died on the second night of our honeymoon, a ghastly accident. You take a misstep, you turn your head the wrong way when you cross the road, you gargle with bleach instead of mouthwash, it's just ridiculous the doors that are slightly ajar between life and death. Life's extreme fragility is all around us, as if we are perpetually walking on floors of cracked glass.

That beautiful boy was dead and would not be alive again. I couldn't believe it, standing looking at Alexander, of all people, inert, silent, perpetually incommunicative. I was still wet inside from his last act, up in our honeymoon bed, our clothes scattered across the floor and the red lizard high-heeled shoes tumbling over and over the roiling sheets.

I'm glad I still have a photograph, because he left such a short, shallow groove in the world. Yet many years later, after all the things that happened since his death, and long after that, sometimes before I go to sleep I still see his face, the small blue eyes, the thinning hair, the narrow smile. I turn towards an empty sleeve.

I returned home alone, to the claustrophobic flat and its boiled cabbage smells, my parents more shocked than me, if that were possible, more frightened, as if a policeman might suddenly appear and arrest me for somehow being implicated in the murder of a real Englishman.

'You know,' my mother is saying, 'during the war you never knew if you would get to the end of the week alive, the terrible bombing.'

The ivory Chinaman with the ebony fishing rod, yellow with age, broken and mended invisibly by my father's expert nimble fingers, looks at me with two tiny ebony eyes. Simon used to say all kinds of things in my head and then he fell silent for many years. Right now he has found his voice, saying: *She's up to something, pay attention.*

'Really? I thought that was mostly in the East End.'

I lit a cigarette. I was smoking a lot since I got back from Nice, and the joints of my fingers were nicotine stained, my nails bitten down to raw skin. My mother waved the smoke away with her hand; both my parents thought it was a 'filthy' habit' but I kept filling saucers with my ash and my reddened, lipsticked stubs.

'No, no, no,' she said, 'it was everywhere. I think of it a lot now because of the Irish bombs.'

'I suppose so.' I held the smoke in my lungs as long as I could. The burning of my tissues gave me a masochistic pleasure.

'Yes, it was a horrible time, you know, horrible. You had to look after number one.'

'Mmm.'

'A woman who thought to bring a child into the world had second thoughts in such a time.'

'I suppose she would.'

Her words murmured like the sounds of Benson Court itself: the coughing pipes, the floorboards' creak, the doors along the hall opening and closing, the panting ascent of the lift and the accordion pleats of its metal cage opening and closing, the life and soul of the building. And this room, with its brown leather sofa; its faded wallpaper on which one could barely make out the pattern of bamboo; the oak floorboards covered in cheap rugs; the empty walnut sideboard containing no bottles, decanters, or dinner services; the velvet curtains even more faded than the wallpaper – nothing indicated that the flat was a home and not a cheap rooming house, except the framed colour photograph of me, in my grey academic gown and mortarboard, clutching the rolled-up certificate which was my degree, taken with Alexander's camera, and to the right of me a Canada goose attempting to mount a female of the species in the grass beside the artificial lake.

The Chinaman closed his eyes and went to sleep, having alerted me to the presence of a subtext in the room.

'If you found out you were pregnant, for example, you might want to consider your situation quite carefully.'

I looked up. Her head was still bent over the brown sock.

'Yes, you might ask yourself if you would even get through the whole thing, if the baby would die with fright inside you, because of the bombing all the time. It wouldn't want to come out at all.'

'Who did this happen to?' I said.

'Who?'

'Yes.'

'Did what happen?'

'What you're saying.'

'I'm not saying nothing, just an observation, that's all. *Horrible* food we ate during the war, no fresh fruit. A little bit of meat. Your father found it hard to do without butter, and no lemons for his tea – that was the worst of it, I think, for him. The coffee was atrocious, too. Just chicory, I think.'

'We were talking about babies.'

'Oh, yes, we were. If a person is expecting a baby and it's not a good situation, they need to consider what to do.'

'You mean abortion? Wasn't that illegal during the war?'

'Yes, of course it was. It was a very serious crime. A person could go to prison for this.'

'So what did people do?'

She shrugged. 'They did what they did.'

'And why are you telling me this now?'

'Oh! Just to remind you that some things need looking at from all angles.'

'Why remind *me*?'

She looked up, finally, from the brown sock. 'Are you stupid, Vivien? I am not stupid.'

'But I'm not—'

'Is it me you lie to, or do you also lie to yourself?'

I got up and left the room, stood for a moment in the hall, leaning against the door frame, and experienced that strange sensation I felt as a child, of sudden elongation, of my feet being too far away from my head, or perhaps the other way round. One is not oneself at all, at all. I was able eventually to reach my room, to lie down on the white candlewick bedspread across from the *Swan Lake* picture. The cygnets stood on tiptoe with tiny waists and slender calves. I put my hands on my breasts and squeezed but they were tender and my belly was distended.

Possessed by another living thing that clung with force to my insides, I looked round at the walls that I had once so willingly imprisoned myself in, and felt the cage door clang shut. An interior tenderness throbbed painfully. The *thoughts* were back, like hammers in my head. I touched my breasts tentatively with a finger and thought of a warm, wet mouth, sucking. Fear, panic, desperation. And I had nowhere to go but where I was already.

My mother came in later, when it had grown dark and my father had returned home and settled himself in for a quiz show, writing down the answers and ticking off the correct ones.

'You want something to eat? Soup?'

'No.'

'There's a place on Tottenham Court Road. I pass it sometimes. I see the girls go in and I see the girls come out again. It looks very nice, clean, hygienic, healthy. But look at you, you're white as a sheet. Are you frightened? Don't be, I won't let anyone hurt you. I'll be there all the time, I promise. I did it all alone, no mother to help me. But don't worry, you will have *me*.'

Her face was very near mine, her cracked skin and nut-brown

hair with its few white strands. I was her third try at a child, she had cancelled the previous experiments.

'Did Daddy know?'

'Him? You think he could have lived with such knowledge? Every night he would expect a policeman. Go and have a bath, dear. You'll feel better. Tomorrow we will telephone and make all the arrangements.'

I soaped my body with Camay. The shower curtain had a pattern of yellow ducks on it; I felt that if I stayed there long enough they'd peck out my eyes.

My mother came in and sat down on the edge of the bath. 'It's nothing,' she told me. 'Really quite a simple little procedure. Don't be anxious.'

'My life is awful.'

'Don't be silly,' she said. 'No one is trying to kill you.'

I went to bed and lay beneath the covers. I heard the door handle turn, she came in and sat next to me on the bed and sang an old lullaby from my childhood.

'*Loola loola loola loola baby, do you want the moon to play with? Or the stars to run away with? Loola loola loola loola bye.*'

'After this,' she said, 'you have a fresh start. You'll see. Of course it's a great shame about Alexander, but let me tell you, life is very hard for people like us. No one should make you believe it is easy. It is not, not at all.'

'What do you mean, people like us?'

'The outsiders.'

'I'm not an outsider.'

'You think?'

During the whole of his interminably long life, until his death at the age of eighty-six, I felt I was a stranger to my father – I don't mean he didn't love me, I know he did, but the limited means he had of expressing any form of affection had to find their way though so many obstacles in his personality that it was easier for him just to sit and look at me over his black dusty glasses, when he thought I was as intent as he usually was on the TV screen.

He came home from work each night, his eyes aching, and turned on the set, and ate what my mother put in front of him, and after a while, he seemed to notice my presence.

'Vivien! What are you still doing here?'

'Daddy! I live here.'

'Of course a father gives his daughter a roof over her head. I mean, why do you not have a job yet? You think it's a disgrace to work?'

'No.'

'People who don't like to work go to the bad, that's my experience.'

'I know who you're talking about.'

'Who? Who am I talking about?'

'Unc—'

'*Don't mention that name in my house.* Anyway, I didn't mean him, I meant the layabouts I see on the television, not to mention the ones who got jobs and don't want to do them, the miners, for a start.'

'No politics,' said my mother. 'I'm putting my foot down right here and now.'

My parents had brought me up to be a mouse. Out of gratitude to England which gave them refuge, they chose to be mice-people and this condition of mousehood, of not saying much (to outsiders or even each other), of living quietly and modestly, of being industrious and obedient, was what they hoped for for me, too. And whatever Uncle Sándor was, he was no mouse. If he was anything he was a rhinoceros, coated in the mud of the river, goring and grabbing. Even while he slept, if he turned over a huge shoulder, the earth shook.

'Who was that man, Daddy?' I had said, after my father had finally slammed the door after the surprise visit in 1963.

'No one. Forget about it.' But I persisted.

'Daddy! Who was he? Tell me, please, Daddy.' And I climbed on his lap which was an action I rarely dared take because it either made him angry ('I can't see the screen! I'm missing everything, get out of the way!') or he buried his face in my hair and smelt it, and said to my mother, 'Isn't she just good enough to eat?' 'Yes,' she replied, making for the umpteenth time their little joke about me, 'with chocolate sauce and ice-cream.' For years I thought that maybe they did mean to eat me. You couldn't be sure with them, perhaps it was an old Hungarian custom to cook daughters and serve them for dessert, like the old witch in my picture book who captured Hansel and Gretel in her gingerbread house.

Even knowing what Sándor had done, knowing not long after,

in fact, from the news on TV from which they could not shield me, I was still fascinated by my father's reaction. I knew my daddy had a hot temper and bore age-long grudges against people I had never met, who had died before I was born, but nothing had ever before roused him to this level of volcanic rage. And never before had I heard him pronounce whole sentences in a foreign tongue, which I thought at first was Hungarian, and wasn't.

'What am I going to say when people ask if I'm related to him, Daddy?' I asked, when I was about to go to university. 'Don't you think you should tell me a bit more? You say he lied when he said he was your brother . . .'

'Just don't you ever utter a word about that man,' said my mother. 'Nothing should pass your lips.'

'I wasn't thinking of telling strangers our business, of course not, but don't you think I have the right to know? It's my family too.'

'Family? He stopped being family years ago, before you were ever born,' my father said.

'Aha!'

'Oy, look what you made me say.'

I started laughing. It was not easy to get one over on the old boy; normally he constructed an impenetrable screen of words.

'Is he a cousin, then?'

'A cousin you can cast off, who knows a cousin?'

'Closer than that . . . so he *is* your brother!'

He didn't say anything, and I knew that for the first time I had defeated him.

'Think what your poor father has had to put up with all these years,' my mother said. 'Knowing that *that man* could bring down everything on top of us. We kept him away as much for your sake, you know, Vivien.'

'He's poison,' said my father. 'Always was. He was never any good.'

'Did you flee to England together?'

'No, no, he didn't see what was coming, like we did. We were smart, we read the papers, didn't we, Berta? We paid attention and we weren't so vain as to think that we could charm our way out of the horrible things that were happening. We knew that once a man gets a political idea into his head, then you need to move out of his way, because a man with a political idea will soon enough be a man with not just an idea but a gun. And a man with a gun and idea – well, you just run until you're out of breath, and he can't see you no more. But him! Even after the war he still hung on. He stuck it out until '56. Fool.'

'But what happened to him during the war?'

'Well, he had a hard time, I'll give him that. But that doesn't give him no excuses.'

'OK, but what . . .'

And my parents, who believed in God in a mildish fashion, as long as he was a God that left them alone and didn't pry into their affairs, or insist they could not watch the television, an undemanding God of no particular denomination, received at that moment a miracle. For the phone rang, which it did only a few times a year. It was the landlord's agent to say that workmen were coming round to replace a broken lift cable and they were not to be concerned or ask them for identification, or call the police like last time.

After half an hour of delivering paeans to the family who owned our flat, those great benefactors who expected no gratitude, indeed liked to stay as far away as possible from their properties, in their own villa in the south of France, it was obvious that the subject of my father's brother, the notorious slum landlord, could not now be raised. The momentum was lost.

I went to bed thinking about him and concocting some imaginary meetings between the two of us, in which I at last got to find out who exactly my parents had been, back in Budapest, and were they made this way or had fortune changed them. These daydreams were mildly pleasant and gave way to peaceful sleep with colourful shadows dancing inside my head. But then I went to university, got married and forgot about my uncle until I was back in my childhood bed, with many of the same old thoughts returning.

If you are unemployed, if you face every morning the desolation of the days, you may find that not even reading can be stretched out adequately to cover all of the hours, because being without work, and largely friendless, and thrown back on your own cranky parents for company, has a strange effect on your mental state. You become aware of how long a day is, and your own responsibility to fill it from your own resources and how shockingly limited they turn out to be, what a sham and fake you are, how you fooled your husband, who believed in you, who thought you cared about thinking as much as he did.

So you find a constant companion in a pack of cards, and lay them out on the table in endless games of patience until you are so sick of the aces and the twos and the suits and the kings and queens and bloody jacks, all the black and red and red and black, that they swarm in front of your eyes and rise up to fling themselves at you, with their smug royal faces, looking sideways at their own edges.

I bought a second-hand copy of the *I Ching*, an ancient game of fortune telling which was in vogue at the time, and tossed coins between a closed nest of my hands but it never once turned out any good. The *I Ching* failed to predict correctly what the future really held for me – that only a year or so later I would be kicking myself for not having used my time profitably, finished my thesis for a start or at the very least read all of Proust and Tolstoy instead of playing with coins and Chinese hieroglyphics. But in the presence of those great intellects I felt all the more worthless and insignificant, and would shut the book and crawl away under the bedcovers, not getting up until my mother knocked on the door and said, 'What? Are you going to spend the whole day stinking in bed?'

So I walked.

South to Oxford Street I tramped, to wander the halls of Selfridges with no money in my pockets. Down to the underpass, coming up at Marble Arch and down again to Hyde Park to watch the swans on the Serpentine and listen to the cranks and crackpots standing on their soapboxes at Speakers' Corner and sometimes east and west, along Marylebone Road between the railway stations. My head had nothing in it, *nothing*. Sometimes I found a bench and sat down and fell asleep. When you start falling asleep on benches you know you're in trouble.

'Like Mrs Prescott,' said my mother. 'That's who you turned into, you understand? Maybe she had a sorrow too. But watch out, all this walking will drive you crazy, like her.'

What do you know about grief? I thought. You haven't lived. You've *never* lived. You have no idea. You don't know what it's like to wake up every morning and see the light through the curtains, feel the sunshine tentatively casting patches on the walls, your spirits rising at the wonder of there being a new day, then remembering what you know: that there is *no new day*, just a dead repeat of the one before. For never again will you half listen to him talk about his proteins, or gently probe him about his childhood in the vicarage. You won't walk together in Hyde Park and you won't get on a plane and fly high in the air together and descend into the new world. *You won't you won't you won't.* He won't kiss you. He won't insist that you put on those red lizard shoes with the high arc of the heel, the *ache* he called it.

He won't make you tea in the morning and bring it to you in bed. You will never find the record he wanted of Glen Gould playing the Goldberg Variations and watch the pleasure in his face as he unwraps it. You won't cut his toenails, because his back is too bad to bend, after sitting over a microscope for many hours. You won't ever again read a new poem about geese, because there will never be a new poem. He will never see his child's face, and nor, of course, will you.

(Was it deep grief, or just the devastation a person feels who comes home to find themselves burgled, the telly gone, the flat trashed.)

Go and find a job, my mother said. A girl who had a degree from a university could have any career she chose, if she should want such a thing as a career, because a degree, this was like a special ticket you showed all the top people, and at once, as soon as they saw it, they knew you were to be let inside. This was my mother's opinion. A person with a degree (especially one from that York University), a person who knew a lot about Charles Dickens, was at the very top of the tree. My mother didn't know exactly what openings were available, but she was certain that whatever they were, they were mine for the choosing, and it was my own wilful obstinacy which prevented me from getting one.

I went twice a week to the library on Marylebone Road to read the appointments pages in *The Times* and write down in my notebook the addresses of positions I could apply for, and sent off my minimal curriculum vitae which had a blank employment record; I had never had a job, of any kind. I sent away to be a researcher at the BBC, to become an editorial assistant on a literary magazine, to publicise books at Faber and Faber. I didn't even get an interview.

One day I swallowed my pride and applied for a job selling postcards in the shop at the National Portrait Gallery. My letter came straight back.

I got so angry I rang them up. 'Why won't you even see me for the job?' I said. 'I know those postcards. I know the name of every writer who has a portrait in the gallery. I know the Chandos portrait of Shakespeare off by heart. I could describe it blindfold.'

'Really?' said a sharp voice at the other end of the phone. 'There were one hundred and sixty-nine applicants for this position, and fifty-two of them had degrees in art history.'

Everything in me was yearning and longing to pull myself out of the mud, and still I stuck. I was jealous of myself. I was afraid that if I lost the knack of being the person I was only a month ago, who was engaged to Alexander, then I would be trapped as Vivien Kovaks for the rest of my life and I would have to marry someone in Benson Court and spend an hour every evening visiting my parents, up and down in that lift, forever ascending and getting nowhere. Or worse, I'd get my own flat, and be Mrs Prescott. Maybe her clothes had eaten into my soul.

The library was full of people with colds and men with nowhere else to go. Signs on the walls prohibited spitting. I don't see people spitting at all these days, let alone any signs warning against it, but people did spit then, spat into handkerchiefs, and a bluish-brown pall hung in the air beneath the fluorescent strip lighting, choking the lungs of non-smokers. A man in stained tweed trousers, fresh coloured in his complexion, who arrived at noon with a pint of milk and a tin of cat food in a string bag, was warned by library staff to keep his hands on the table at all times, whatever the subject of the books he was studying .

But libraries have a serendipitous quality to them. They lead you on. Standing with my fingers in the card index, I saw in the K section, a familiar name, my own. Kneeling on the linoleum floor by the metal shelving I began reading a short, rather sensational work, which despite its arresting title – *Kovacs, the King of Crime* – was an investigation into slum housing in west London. A small inset of photographs in the middle revealed my uncle, taken through the window of his silver Jag, his bulbous face staring past the glass, enrobed in shadows. Next to it was a reproduction of an article in the *Evening Standard*, with the same photograph, this time captioned:

IS THIS THE FACE OF EVIL?

I examined the features: a heavy-set man with a pendulous lower lip and a fat neck, a profile like Alfred Hitchcock above an exuberantly knotted tie looked back at me. I could just about recognise him as the same uncle who had called at the house with the golden bar of Toblerone and the West Indian girlfriend, but there, on the mat, years ago, he had been full of life and colour, in his bright-blue suit and sparkling wrist. The uncle in the book had a black ink smudge eating away part of the side of his face. The dots of the photographic reproduction didn't do him any favours, either, making him appear pockmarked, while I remembered his skin as pale and smooth, pungent with expensive aftershave.

It was a very unfortunate picture. The glass of the car window already cast him in shadows, but reproduced on the cheap shiny paper of what seemed to be a vanity press imprint he reminded me of old murderers and houses where bodies were found under the floorboards.

According to the author, my uncle was a complete bastard, a cheap thug and greedy, grasping bloodsucker. Not just a slum landlord, but a racist, who let his black tenants live in unspeakable conditions. And not just a slum landlord and a racist, but a gangster, a man who employed local heavies to beat tenants who could not pay up on rent day. And not just a slum landlord, racist, thug and gangster, but a pimp, a man who kept teenage prostitutes in houses all over west London. A girl said she had given birth to three babies and two had died of bronchitis from the chronic damp and condensation. Another child fell through a rotten stair and broke his back. A father of seven was late with the rent: my uncle's goons beat him with chains. And my uncle got up in the morning, shaved, splashed eau de Cologne from Jermyn Street on his Hitchcock face, put his feet into calfskin Lobb shoes and walked past the ormolu clocks and gilt furniture of his Bishops Avenue mansion to his Chippendale desk which was surrounded by unopened packing cases containing all the luxury goods he had carelessly bought on credit and never even looked at.

The account of my uncle's revolting crimes chilled me to the bone, the heart freezes. I had not really understood the extent of it. The interviews with his victims were heart-rending. The photographs of the squalid interiors of his houses were loathsome. Someone testified he'd seen better in the POW camps in Burma, yes that bad, and the book recorded that my uncle burst out laughing when he heard this, which demonstrated the callous disposition of a psychopath. I turned to the final page:

> And with the arrest and subsequent conviction of Sándor Kovacs in 1964, one of the darkest periods in the history of west London came to an end. The government's policy of urban renewal promises new, sanitary housing at affordable rents for all. A modern Britain is in the making, one in which the shadows of the past, of unscrupulous foreigners squeezing profits from the poorest and most vulnerable, are fast being banished for ever. A new dawn, a new equality. The reign of Sándor Kovacs, his henchmen and his kin, had come to a final end.

There was something about this account that I did not quite like, though I couldn't put my finger on it. Knowing what we do now, about the slums that sixties social housing erected over the slums that they destroyed to make way for them, it seems painfully obvious that the schemes of political visionaries are always doomed to disappointment but I was also struck queasily by two words: 'foreigners' and 'kin'.

For there remained in my mind that black girl with the nylon leopardskin coat and the mock-croc handbag with the gilt clasps, and the bar of Toblerone, the heavy weight of it in my uncle's hand as he tried to give it to me, as if it were a gold ingot. And I could see his hand-stitched suede shoes, and the way he looked at me, eagerly but also with sorrow and nervousness, and my father screaming, my uncle laughing. And these events were more real to me than the Sándor Kovacs in this book.

We were at a wedding once, here in London, after we got engaged, a society occasion, someone with whom Alexander had been to school. While he was on the dance floor leading about the groom's sister, a woman leaned across on her elbows, already sloshed, looked at my place card and said, 'I just have to mention that I knew your father. And I must say, I do think it was awful what happened to him.'

'My father? How could you have known my father?'

'Well, darling, he knew absolutely everyone. It was such rubbish what they said about him in the papers. People were quite happy to shake his hand at the time, I mean, it was anything goes, you could rub shoulders with who you liked and who cared? I knew some very nice people who were quite fascinated by him and would have taken him up in a big way if only he had managed to jump through the right hoops. Anyway, he was always perfectly charming to me.'

'But you couldn't have met my father, he never goes out.'

'Well, not *now*, perhaps, but at the beginning of the sixties you bumped into him everywhere.'

'And where was my mother? Did you meet her?'

'Well, you know I never really heard anything about her, he didn't say much. I rather had the impression that she had died. But perhaps that's wrong. To be honest, I don't think I ever quite asked. One always assumed that he was on the loose, sexually, I mean. And despite being rather an ugly man – do forgive me, he was always rather amusing about his looks – one found him quite attractive, though in a coarse way. Well, I adored him, I could have spent hours with him. Not that we ever went to bed, but a girlfriend of mine did. Anyway, do tell me, what is he up to now?'

'I'm sorry, but could you tell me who you think my father is?'

'Why Sándor Kovacs, of course. Who else were we talking about?'

This woman, bright, loquacious, lit by crystal chandeliers, on the other side of a table littered with demitasse cups and silver coffee spoons, was a fragile, brittle blonde, the type who smokes too much and spent too much time in the sun in Cannes in the fifties and sixties, skin driven into ferocious grooves and whorls on her face and neck. Mrs Simone Chase, she was called: 'My older sister came out with the groom's mother, we seem to have been mixed up with that lot one way or another since before the war. Except they have better luck getting their marriages to stick than us. I'm a gay divorcee.'

She put her cigarette out in the pool of coffee in her saucer, and looked around to see if there was any more to drink.

'Bloody petit fours, aren't you sick of the sight of them? Wherever you go there are petit bloody fours and they're always identical. It's not as if anyone ever touches them.'

'Sándor Kovacs is not my father,' I said. 'My father's name is Ervin. He works in Hatton Garden mending jewellery and putting old stones into modern settings. He lives with my mother in a flat off Marylebone High Street.'

'Good heavens, are you absolutely certain?' She looked up at me; her hair, a fine gold mesh helmet hardened with lacquer, stood away from her scalp and her face beneath drooped under the burden because after she had stared at me for a few moments, her eyes fell to looking about the table for more wine.

'*Yes*,' I said, with unbecoming vehemence, being too young, too green, to have mastered nonchalance, and certainly not sang-froid.

'But, darling, he told me all about this little girl, a dark-haired thing, he said, very dark. And even mentioned her name. Began with a V. What could it be but Vivien, surely not Vera. Could it have been Veronica? No, it couldn't because I remember quite plainly that he said you were named after Vivien Leigh, so you see it has to be Vivien. I can't have got it mixed up.'

Kovacs is a common Hungarian name and Sándor Kovacs is not my father and I was not named after Vivien Leigh.'

'I find that quite odd,' she said. 'And you've never heard of him?'

'Of course, I've *heard* of him. But only on the news.' I looked around. Alexander was still moving effortlessly round the dance floor with that upper-class grace of his. 'What was he like?' I said quickly.

'Well, as I say, frightfully coarse, and he wore the most extraordinary clothes, flashy watches, terribly *nouveau riche*, but they all were, they had money to burn and they were showing off like billy-o, that crowd. You know, the fat blonde starlet and her cockney husband, what were their names? I don't remember at all, now. Bethnal Green bingo kings, that type. What they didn't say much about in the newspapers, because of the scandal, was that he had a great liking for coloured girls . . .'

'Why was that a scandal?'

'Because of *who else* they were sleeping with, darling. Some of whom are in this very room, but I shan't name names. Not after all this time. Thing about Sándor is that I don't think I ever saw him in public with a white woman, though he did sleep with them when he got the chance, and quite well-bred girls, too, but he was more of a trophy hunter, in that respect. You felt there were notches on the bedpost – and with coronets, if he could manage it, but he always kicked them out in the nicest possible way the next morning. A friend of mine said he had the most awful scars on his back, terrible really, the war. Ghastly. The coloured girls he dragged around with him made him even more beyond the pale, at least in my set, but you know when you met him, you couldn't help but notice that he had terribly kind eyes. Or at least I thought so. A beautiful brown, like rather good chocolate. Personally, I think he was a public benefactor.'

Alexander returned to the table.

'Who are we talking about?' he said.

'Sándor Kovacs,' said Mrs Chase.

'Ah, yes,' Alexander said. 'A fascinating study.'

'People said he was evil, you know,' said Mrs Chase. 'But I don't. Never. People talk a lot of rot, don't you think?'

'Yes,' said Alexander, coldly.

In the state I was in, the early summer of that year, 1977, that dreadful grief and boredom, failure and worthlessness, I decided that I would go and find my uncle. Why not? I didn't have anything else to do. The more I thought about him, the more I visualised that photograph, and those words on the page – *Is this the face of evil* – the more I found myself pondering questions that were beyond my limited philosophical reach. I had never met evil, only read about it in books, in the plays of William Shakespeare, but even Macbeth was a person of flesh and blood, who was spooked by a dagger, floating in the air.

So I looked up my uncle in the phone book and there, to my surprise, he was.

The mornings lightened, summer began and I woke earlier and earlier. The silence of the city punctuated by stray cars. Then the gathering moan of traffic along the main arterial roads, trains arriving, departing at the stations. Clatter of heels on the pavements outside my window, girls walking to work in offices. The dustman's cart grinding its brakes, the electric motor of the milkman's float. London in the morning.

My father had already left for the day. My mother was sitting in the kitchen in her brown dressing gown, drinking milky coffee. Her hair was all haywire. She looked heavy and old, and I saw the first twisting of her hands that would be the rheumatoid arthritis which was about to begin its additional torment of her body.

'You know I think I will paint that stool,' she said. 'We got it when we came here, but it is very chipped. I'll do it while I still can.'

'What colour?'

'I don't know. Maybe green.'

'Then make it an emerald green, or a grass green.'

'This sounds *very* bright.'

'We could do with some brightness round here.'

'You think we are a little drab?'

'Yes.'

'Maybe you are right. It always seems enough work just to keep it all clean, never mind you worry about what it looks like.'

She sometimes got little jobs in shops, serving behind the counter, but my father always found an excuse to talk her out of them. A very handsome Spaniard with an oiled black quiff once took an interest in her. I think he just felt she needed some flattery, to cheer her up; he encouraged her to buy a real silk scarf. After that, my father became very fussy about domestic cleaning, and would run his finger over surfaces. 'Berta, look at this, the house goes to rack and ruin with you at work.' So she gave up the job and spent her mornings on her hands and knees scrubbing linoleum, and in the afternoons she knitted things no one would ever wear.

My mother's green period would last ten weeks, all that summer. Once she touched the top of my father's nose with the brush, and laughed at him.

'Berta, what you lost your mind? I got to send a doctor for you?'

'Don't make such a fuss, here's a turpentine rag, rub it off, if you're so fussy.'

'And what are you going to do today?' she said to me, as she boiled the kettle, looking out through the window to that other flat, whose blinds were still drawn and whose occupants were seldom seen.

'I'm going out,' I said.

'Oh, I'm pleased to hear this. Where do you go so early in the morning?'

'For a walk.'

'More walking. You're very thin, you walk and you do not eat. Is there still pain, down there?'

'No, no pain.'

'So just in the heart. I still have this pain from what I did, and twice it was, for me.'

I ran out of the kitchen and out of the flat, turned up the High Street, crossed Marylebone Road and went into Regent's Park.

The park was ringed by white palaces, lions roared in the distant zoo. Crossing the road, I came almost at once to a boating lake, with birds – geese, like the ones Alexander had studied and written his poems about. You could walk from north to south through London's parks, you could pass through Hampstead Heath, Parliament Hill Fields, Primrose Hill down to Regent's Park to Hyde Park, St James's Park, Green Park – the parks reached almost to the river, and to the west the great open spaces of Richmond, Clapham, Wandsworth. One park had deer, and another a picture gallery; parks with theatres, open air concerts, zoos. This was my nature, these mown lawns, bandstands, boating lakes, ice-cream vans, cafés that closed in winter.

The birds were making a big noise in the early summer morning, and they demanded my attention. I sat down on a bench to look at them and think about what Alexander saw. Their small eyes watched me, their webbed feet padded across the grass, they clustered round crusts of bread. You couldn't imagine what they were thinking, he said, because their brains were in their wings, they had compasses in there, and maps. They knew exactly what they were doing.

'Young lady, excuse me, this is my bench, every day I sit here.' And he was just standing there in a mackintosh, with a leather folder under his arm, his hair grey and thin, his face white, the lower lip trembling, all the weight in the barrel chest and the shoulders, straining against the cotton of his shirt, his legs and feet like those of the water birds, a superfluous under-structure. My uncle.

I never saw prison pallor before. Nothing he would do would

ever return to him his old complexion. Jail had rendered him monochrome, his voice faltering as he looked at me and his hands holding his leather folder tightly, pressed against his belly. I saw now the same nose as mine, the same fleshy nostrils which he shared with my father and which were their legacy to the next generation, not a big nose, a flat podgy nose. Everything else I got from my mother. And he was of a totally different build to my father, with small feet, which was strange because his hands were swollen, like rubber gloves filled with water.

'OK,' I said, my throat closing on the word. 'I'll move along to make room.'

He sat down, unbuttoned his mackintosh and unzipped the leather folder, which held inside it a pad of lined paper and a loop containing a gold pen. I couldn't take my eyes off it. This was the Sándor Kovacs I knew all about, with the flashy trinkets, the platinum and diamond life.

'Nice, eh?' he said, holding it up to show it to me. 'It's what you call Cartier, the *very* best.' (He rolled his r's like my parents.) 'They make watches, all kinds of things, but only in the finest materials. What do you think?'

'It looks very smooth to hold.'

'Exactly. Quality workmanship. That's how you tell something is expensive, not how much it cost or what it is made of.'

I could smell him, he was so close. The same scent of expensive aftershave, masking a sweet sick odour. My third blood relation.

He started writing, slowly, his meaty hand moving through a sentence. It was painful to watch him.

'Yes, yes,' he said, looking up at me, 'I write very slow. The slowness is not in my brain, but the fingers. I got frostbite during the war, some of the flesh is a bit not right, this is why a good pen is a must, or I drop it.'

'I see.'

He wrote for a another minute or so, then stopped, rubbed his fingers.

'You come to this park often? You a regular?'

'No, I was just cutting through.'

'I come every morning. I get restless and don't sleep too good, and I get up in the dawn and come for a walk here, sit by the lake, me and the birds. We watch the sun come up over London. Well, I watch, they got their own business to attend to. Very beautiful the what-you-call it, the wet that comes down on the grass.'

'The dew.'

'Yes, dew.

He bent his head back to his writing. *I acknowlege I was not a better son*

'Excuse me, there's a d in that,' I said, unable to help myself, the little know-it-all.

'You say a d?'

'That's right.'

'Where is this d?'

'Before the g.'

'Show me.'

He handed me the gold pen and I wrote it out for him. When I finished, he spelt it aloud. A C K N O W L E D G E.'

'Yet when I say it, I don't make a d in my mouth.'

'The letter g can be tricky that way.'

'Thank you, that's a help. I don't spell good at all and as for my writing, well, look, you see how I make too many loops?'

'What are you writing?'

'My memoirs.'

'Are you writing your memoirs because you're famous?' I said, waiting for the moment at which I would reveal myself as his niece, who knew exactly who he was, because I wanted to hear first what he told me, what *he* had to say about himself. If he was contrite, if he offered himself up as a repentant sinner, or if he had concocted excuses for his crimes.

'I was, once.'

I gave him an excuse to lie. 'An actor?'

'No, I was in business.'

'Retired?'

'I gave up my profession some time ago, but I had a few golden years, everyone is entitled to them, if they can get them, and to cherish the memory, keep it bright.'

I thought of the Toblerone in the gold box, the gilt knick-knacks, the gold tooth I could see at the back of his dental work, and understood, with the surprise of pity, that this was as golden as it had got for him, and how short the years had been, seven altogether, between him escaping from Hungary and finally the arrest, trial, imprisonment.

'So what was your line of work?' I asked.

'Property, and entertainment.'

He doesn't remember me, I thought. Why should he? I was just a little girl, and now I was a grown woman, or that was how I thought of myself.

There were several moments in this conversation when I could have told my uncle who I was, and there were times too, I later understood, when he could have revealed himself to me too, for it turned out he recognised me at once, and not because he had a good memory, but because my father had gloatingly gone to see him in prison: three visits in which photographs of me arriving at university, graduating, and engaged to Alexander were pushed across at him, so he could feast his eyes on the success my father had made of himself, through me. But I didn't know that, at the time.

Nor did say – I am Vivien Kovaks, your niece, the little girl you came to see once. I couldn't find the words, even though the words were simple. He was so . . . I don't know. When I had looked at the newspaper in the library, and when I read that book about him, he was an idea, not a person, just a set of opinions about slum housing. When I had imagined this meeting there was a speech, in which I would announce myself, and I had made up his reply as well, but it turned out that in real life he wasn't opinions, he was flesh and blood, and fingernails and nose hairs.

And I now understand that he believed he could prepare a good impression, he wanted to defend himself in the court of public opinion, *my* opinion, prove that he had a case. He didn't want to plead for special mercy because he was my uncle, his brother's brother. He badly wanted me to know that he wasn't the face of evil, but something more complicated altogether.

'I have many memories,' he said. 'That's what I'm writing, I want to put everything down, so there's a record, so they will know.'

'They?'

'The world, of course, and any other interested party.'

'Who might that be?'

He hesitated. But then he turned to me with those watery eyes which had once been the colour of bitter chocolate and had faded to fawn, the lip wet, the chin shaking.

'My brother.'

When he turned up on the doorstep and they screamed at each other, I was struck dumb by his existing at all, appearing out of a void (and he had once been in a void, as I was to discover, a terrifying emptiness, as close to death as death itself, like death, darker than it, and irradiated with fear). That my father hated him was obvious, the bespectacled gnome who laboured twenty-five years not to be noticed in anything he did, and this crude gangster, this mobster appears out of the past, from a time that seemed more and more like a hallucination than the real past. But the words 'my brother' were quite strange for me to hear, as an only child, and I felt a slight shock of envy that there was once something between them, an intimacy between siblings that I had never experienced.

'So what do you plan to do with the memoir when you've finished it?' I said, not daring yet to go towards that brother word.

'I get it published, of course. I want that it's a book, with my name on the cover.'

'How much have you written so far?'

'Eleven pages. How many do you need to make a book?'

'I don't know. Quite a lot, I think.'

'That's the problem. Still, I got a lot to say.'

'You should finish it, then.'

'It comes slow, very very slow.'

'Do you do this all day?'

'No, just in the mornings, here in the park. I can't stand to be alone in a room. A room I don't like, especially if it's a little one.'

His eyes started to water again.

'I'm not crying, I got an eye condition. Two day ago I trod on my spectacles, I can't see too good to write until the optician makes me another pair. I'm waiting. But I don't want to miss a day, no. How do I know how long I got left in life to say everything that I need to say? You can't waste, waste is terrible. Do you understand that? Do you, dear?' He turned to me with the expression of a man who has lost the power of speech and is trying to communicate something urgent with his eyes.

'Yes, I know, it *is* terrible.' My own life was nothing but waste.

His face altered, looked puzzled.

'You married, courting?'

'I'm a widow, my husband died.'

'*What?*' He slumped back on the bench, shocked. 'How is this?

A young girl like you? What a shame, terrible shame. What makes you a widow?'

I told him.

'What a story!'

'Yes.'

'He's dead from a piece of steak? Choked to death in a restaurant on your honeymoon?'

'That's right.'

'Nobody could do nothing?'

'They kept slapping him on the back, but it didn't work.'

'My dear.'

He moved his arm as if to take my hand, but I pulled my elbows in to my sides. I didn't want him to touch me.

I remember returning from the bathroom where I had combed my hair and reapplied my lipstick. He always hated cold food; his father took an age to say grace, the vegetables were tepid and the gravy congealed, so he would not wait for me. I saw him sprawled back on the chair, his legs kicking and thrashing and a fist banging on the table, as if he were trying to attract attention. His eyes rolled back in his head and his mouth open, a big black O.

'What is it, what's wrong?' I cried.

But he just turned to look at me with such a stare of accusation.

A waiter started to bash him on the back, uselessly pummelling while Alexander shook his head furiously and stabbed with his fists at his abdomen, just under the ribs. The plate was pushed towards the salt, his entrecôte, with a corner cut away, and *pommes frites* scattered across the tablecloth. He lunged at the edge of the table, then laid down his head on it, tears welling up in his eyes. The waiter went on slapping and hitting him.

I saw the hairs on his arms silver under the many lights, the white cuff, with its twenty-first-birthday cufflinks, the wedding ring still unfamiliar and slightly loose on the finger of his left hand. I watched him going under, I watched as he saw the surface of life closing in over his head, going down into blackness. And as I went on watching, his eyes closed, the brain died for want of oxygen, the heart stopped.

It was so accidental. You walk into a bathroom while an unknown girl lies in the bath, next to a vase of poppies, and she reminds you of a painting you once saw, and three years later, because of that, because of *her*, at the age of twenty-four, you are dead. Not dead for a year or so, but dead altogether. Death by choking, on a one-inch piece of steak, unable to communicate the instructions on how to do the still unknown Heimlich manoeuvre.

'It's a terrible thing,' my uncle was saying. 'I saw myself people who died and I couldn't do nothing for them. Still it doesn't leave you alone, thinking what you might have done. So now what happens to you?'

'I couldn't go to Baltimore. I didn't have a job there and I couldn't afford the flat we'd rented even if I did. I came back to London, to stay with my parents for a while.'

'You got a job?'

'No.'

'You got a profession?'

'I have a BA in English literature, and I was doing a thesis.'

'An educated lady I been talking to all this time. You read lots of books and I never asked. You know all about that racket.'

'Which racket?'

'Books, how you write them, and get them published.'

'No, I only know about Dickens, Shakespeare, people like that. I don't know much about contemporary authors.'

'I saw a movie of him, years ago. Henry Five with Laurence Olivier. I didn't understand too much, the English they spoke back in them old days is too hard for me, but he was some king, eh? Very nice. Mind you, nothing like real life.'

'I don't know a lot about real life,' I said.

'So? I don't know nothing about Shakespeare. We each got our own limitations, yes? Am I right?' He smiled tentatively.

There was a great hue and cry on the lake, a terrible flap of wings and a lot of birds making a big fuss. Perhaps they heard what we could not, a bomb going off in the underground caverns of the city. There had been bombs the year before.

'These ones are geese,' he said, pointing to the ones with the black heads. 'I know because they got a board there with pictures of everything, and a description underneath.'

'My husband wrote poems about geese,' I said.

'Geese? You can write a poem about such a thing? I never knew. I thought poetry is about love.'

'You can write a poem about anything you like.'

'But why a goose?'

'He was trying to get to the very bottom of them, to enter, as it were, the soul of a goose.'

'A bird has a soul?'

'Well, Alexander believed they did. He thought about them a lot.'

'What is to think?'

'All kinds of things. He kept lots of notes. About the velocity of the air against their wings, the lightness of their skeletons, the weight of the beak, what they needed to do with their eyes. Flight, migration, water, navigation – the science of being a goose expressed in metaphor.'

He took another look at the geese. He kept his eyes on them for a few moments then shook his head. 'Now, you see I look at a bird, I just see a bird, you see something else. This is why it is important to listen to intellectuals, a man like me can pick up very useful information though I don't know how I can squeeze any use out of these birds, except roasted, with potatoes, or made into a soup. You write poetry yourself?'

'No, I just parse it.'

'What is parse?'

'You take it apart to see how it works.'

But he had lost interest in poetry. He was formulating the plan. Plans came to him extremely fast, that is how the brain of a businessman works – ideas strike like lightning, they flash and dazzle and illuminate. You see what was darkness a second ago, and the genius of a businessman is to hold on to it, to keep it as a picture inside his brain and elaborate it, to go on imagining what you saw.

'Say, I just thought. If you got no job, how would you like to come to work for me?'

'In what capacity?' I said, startled. How low my fortunes had sunk, to be asked to be my uncle's rent collector.

'I thought maybe you help me write my book.'

'How could I do that?'

'I buy a tape recorder, a typewriter. I tell you everything, you get it over right. All the words spelled with the letters in the order they should be. No mistakes. You play back, you listen, you write it all down nice.'

'And you'll pay me?'

'Pay? Of course, I pay. What do you think I am?'

'And when would I start?'

'Soon as you like. Come Monday.'

'Here?'

'No, you better come to my house. We have to have electricity for the tape recorder.'

'All right.'

'I am Sándor Kovacs,' he told me, and I saw in his eyes that his heart was flooded, which surprised me at the time.

'Pleased to meet you,' I said, trawling around in my mind for a name and coming up with a girl in school who had a smooth waterfall of blonde hair. 'I'm Miranda Collins.'

'Meeranda,' he said. 'Meeranda. I don't know this name. From what language does it come?'

If you try, if you have a profound willingness to let yourself go completely you can enter the mind of another person. It takes a certain habit of thought, honed by many years of reading in the way I read, that (scorned by Alexander) immersion in books, so that they are not so much inside your head; rather, as if they are a dream, you are inside them.

There is a trick I often play when I am bored, or waiting, on a bus or a train, or in airport departure lounges, a knack of predicting when a person is going to stand up to buy a newspaper or a cup of coffee or take some papers out of a briefcase. I also have a bizarre ability always to know what time it is, without a clock or wristwatch. Alexander once told me that it was a logic which passed at the speed of light, going too fast to be monitored; and I was pleased when I heard this, because I had worried that it was a form of mental disturbance. A few times until I reached the more settled shores of my thirties, marriage and my daughters, I really worried that I was crazy, that my parents had driven me mad or I was just born this way, or that it was the closed air of Benson Court.

Now, I don't think I was ever mad, I just possessed the only child's overactive imagination. Whether you always get people right when you try to imagine being them, well, that's a separate question, but the more you practise it, the more interesting life becomes, though also harder to bear because you understand how quickly most people reach their own limitations, how impossible it is for them to fulfil your ardent expectations of them.

So I think now, thirty years later, about my uncle making his preparations for my arrival. What it must have meant to him to know that at long last I was coming to his house, the little girl he had once seen clutching the edge of an open door, the child now grown up and with her own sorrows and heartbreaks. Every time I go to Harrods I see him moving up in the lift to the third floor. His ghost must dwell in that place; I hope it does.

He loved entering early in the morning, just after the uniformed men in top hats and overcoats would open the doors to the first shoppers. He knew he was safe there, in what he called *the finest store in the world*, where you could buy anything you wanted, even a cat or a dog; fish, birds in cages. Sometimes he would spend a whole day just looking at all the beautiful things he had once owned before he went to prison, and had treated far too lightly, feeling that they were like water that fell through his fingers; but the pleasure was in holding them for a moment, until something else caught his eye.

Walking through the halls he smells the perfumes, he watches the beautiful women in their spring dresses and their high heels. He sees a young lady with red hair, a dimpled chin and black patent leather shoes on her high-arched feet turning, and catching the eye of the man who is watching her. For a moment he thinks she's going to scream and call for a security guard, but she doesn't; she smiles to herself, because she understands that she has been acknowledged, even by a creature like him: an old man with a pendulous lower lip. And she is a respectable woman, too, my uncle can tell this at once. If we were introduced, he thinks, he would kiss her hand, like he once kissed Shirley Bassey's, and there he is, standing there among the face paint, all of him yearning, longing, just to put his mouth lightly to her skin, like a queen.

On Sunday, he rested and thought. He was thinking about why I had given him a false name. Why Collins? Maybe Collins was my married name, but Miranda? Many people he knew used aliases for all kinds of reasons, but he didn't expect them from a young girl, unless she was running away to London to leave behind mothers and fathers and husbands, people she didn't want to find her.

And various maybes turned themselves over in his mind, until he found, at last, as I would discover later, the most likely explanation: that I was spying on him for someone else.

I see him in bed that night with Eunice.

'Spying? Who for?' she asks him. He is leaning against the cane headboard, his eyes watering in the light from the bedside lamp that she bought for him, a china base in the shape of a little gleaming black boy holding aloft a red silk parasol, which was the lampshade.

'The newspapers, maybe.'

'Sándor,' she says, rubbing hand cream into her skin, massaging it all the way up to the elbows, 'the papers haven't been interested in you for years.'

'Well, that's true,' he admits, knowing that only Eunice would say it to his face, a bold and no-nonsense woman who did not engage with fantasies, only reality. Which is what he admired about her.

He couldn't wait for Monday, though, to see me again. That I know for sure, and I was excited, too.

*

My parents wanted to know where I was going. I told them I'd found a part-time job, off the books, working for a man who had a private library, cataloguing his collection, and they believed me, relieved to have me out of the house instead of moping, crying, sleeping. My mood had changed completely: I had something to live for again, my own intense curiosity about the man who was supposed to be the face of evil but had the nostril hairs and shaking lip and the faded eyes. There were a thousand questions I wanted to ask, about my mother and father and about their past in Budapest as young people without a care in the world, before they became the reclusive refugees who hid behind their front door and were timidly grateful for any kindness. After all those blanks and silences I had grown up having to take for granted, I was going to get the answers on a plate.

I knew that I was going to meet a monster, a true beast. The crimes spoke for themselves, but the beast was housed in the body of a man in early old age. Whose fingers felt pain when he held a pen. With a spelling mistake.

He was going to tell me his confessions, or what his exculpation of his sins would turn out to be, and I would need all my wits about me, more than the woefully thin experience of life that comes from growing up in Benson Court and going straight to a windy concrete university not eight years old. So I wished Alexander was still alive, for he threaded together his fingers and explained (he got this from his father the vicar) that there were absolute distinctions between right and wrong and you could achieve them by logic and clear thinking. There was a vast literature on the subject, which he had dipped into in his teens, when he was slipping away from the control of theology into the boundless sea of atheism and required a new moral code, one which had not been handed down on tablets of stone.

Logic. Which nobody in my family had ever considered to be a trait worth cultivating or a methodology with any discernible purpose to it. You operated on instinct and emotions, mainly fear and cowardice. Principles were for other people, the kind who had sideboards and cut-glass decanters and documents with their names on that nobody in a uniform could quibble about. They were a luxury, like fresh flowers in vases and meals out in restaurants; you could aspire to be one day the sort of person who had the status and disposable income to afford a principle, but the foundations of your existence were distrust and, if you were endowed with brains, cunning.

This inheritance was all I had at my disposal in the coming meeting with my uncle, the fiend. And books. I thought of him as Fagin, who fed on the flesh of his gang of street kids, except I had always had a certain sympathy with that doomed gent, who seemed less cruel than the one who shut up Oliver Twist in a coffin to sleep at night. At least his boys had freedom, laughter, a marketable skill, pickpocketing.

The house was a narrow, tall early Victorian terrace off Parkway near the tube station, a dirty, windy, dishevelled area of London, one of its neighbourhoods where spring comes later and winter earlier. The houses are worth a great deal now, but then you could buy them cheap. They held unconventional pets, and the cats and dogs looked hungry and disoriented. It took Sándor some time to get down the stairs. He opened the door white and panting, dressed in a maroon zip-up cardigan and velvet house-slippers with a crest embroidered in gold and blue thread, the kind you steal from a hotel.

He looked at me, as if I was the police, scanning me for symptoms of search warrants.

'It's me,' I said, 'Miranda, you told me to come.'

'Yes,' he said, 'I know, don't worry, I didn't forget. I got all the goods. Come.'

The hall was lined with doors, each with a number. My uncle had returned to property in a small way; he owned three houses in Camden, letting out the rooms and living off the rents. I had no idea how you could fit so many flats into the ground floor of such a house and opened my mouth to ask him, but he pushed me forwards, up a flight of stairs, past a bronze-green vinyl wallpaper, framed hunting prints and a smell of fresh paint. It wasn't at all what I expected. This was not a slum, it was a good house, nicely decorated, by which I mean nothing was offensive. It was bland, but bland is often OK. Bland is better than condensation, leaking roofs, dry rot, broken stair rails, blocked toilets, faulty boilers that blow up and kill people.

'This is it,' he said, turning the key in the lock. 'I hope you like the furniture, a lady friend chose it for me.'

'Cane,' I said, cautiously. 'It's nice.'

'A tropical feel to it, she tells me. And look, turn round – see what is here.'

This great gift, to a man who had been staring for many years at prison walls, was a mural, a picture of a sunset on a Caribbean island, the kind of thing you see in Jamaican restaurants in Brixton and Notting Hill where they serve jerk chicken and dishes made of goat.

'What do you think?'

'Marvellous!'

'See how he does it so clever that it looks like you could walk into the wall and find yourself sitting on the beach, drinking rum punch from a coconut. You like it? I see you are smiling.'

'It's lovely. Where would you like me to sit?'

'Anywhere you like. No charge for sitting.'

I sat down in one of the cane chairs: not the one that was obviously his, the wicker throne, the chair with a back like a peacock's tail.

'You want coffee?'

'Yes, please.'

'Please, this is a word we don't hear so much these days. You must be well brought up. What is your family's business?'

I had practised all of this the night before, drawn up for myself a simple biography, based, as it happened, on the blonde-haired real Miranda whom I sometimes talked to on the bus going home from school.

'Picture framing.'

'That's a good enough trade. Skilled. A person who works with their hands, am I right? Nimble fingers, your father has?'

'Yes, he does.'

'And good eyes, too, he must have.' He smiled cynically, and I thought he was starting to wink at me but thought better of it. 'Now for the coffee. You see how I make it the old way in a saucepan with the grounds? I can't stand the kind that's new, in a jar. Revolting. You want to eat something? Here.'

He had bought a cake.

'I wanted to get something fancy, but I spend so long choosing the tape recorder and the typewriter that I forget to go down to the food hall. I got this one from the corner shop, I don't know if it's any good. Battenberg it's called, go on, have a slice.'

'I do like cake, but not that one.'

'I know what you mean. It sounds German to me, too, but they say it isn't, it's just a name.'

'You don't like Germany?'

'I never been there. About that place I have no opinion. A street is a street and a house is a house and a field is a field and a tree is a tree. Who walks around is a different matter. Next time I buy a real cake, then you'll see what a cake is. About cakes I know absolutely everything. It's my special subject, you might say, an appreciation, like some people appreciate art and music – but with me it's pastries.' He cut a slice of cake and chewed it nervously, the moist sponge stuck to his gums and he washed it away with strong coffee. 'OK, let's start. You like a cigarette?' He held out a packet of Benson and Hedges in their expensive gold box. Mine were the cheapest available, Players No. 6. 'In the old days I smoked Balkan Sobranie Black Russians, a very good flavour, but there was a long time when the supply was not available, so I started smoking these. An OK smoke, but nothing special.'

I took one, and lit it. It was extremely smooth, I missed the rasping, throat-constricting rush of my Players.

He had arranged everything on a table by the window. The tape recorder, the typewriter, a pile of typing paper.

'You seen something like this before?' he asked me, as we looked at the tape recorder.

'Yes, but I haven't actually used one.'

'*Actually*. Now this is a real English word. I never use it myself but I heard other people, maybe I will start, it makes me sound less like a bloody foreigner, do you think?'

I noticed how much he seemed to need to impress me. I'd never met a monster before, maybe this was what they were like, but I found him pathetic. The mural, the cheap cane furniture, the absurd cane peacock throne, the tall house with its view over the street, to other houses, dirty and poor, the pink cake and marzipan stuck to his gums, created the impression of mediocrity, and the man with the glittering wrist on which diamonds flashed, and the suede shoes and the West Indian girlfriend with the nylon leopardskin pillbox hat seemed like an old story that a child is told at bedtime and forgets in the morning.

'Are we ready?' I said.

'Yes, yes, of course, but who is going to operate the machine?'

'Do you want to?'

'I don't know how. I looked at the book that comes with it but I can't make anything out of it. See.'

The instructions were daunting to me, as well. A diagram showed various manoeuvres you needed to make, to get the thing going. 'It's a bit baffling,' I said.

'I'll leave it up to you. You have an intellectual's head.'

'I don't think that's going to be any use. Let's try pressing this button.'

'OK.'

So I pressed Play and my uncle started talking.

'The day I arrive here, which is 14 December 1956, this is a day I remember in every detail.'

'Is that where we're going to start?'

'Of course, that's the beginning of the story.'

'No, no, no, I mean the beginning of your life.'

'My *life*? This is not what we are discussing.'

'What, then?'

'My career.'

'But if a book is to be publishable, it has to be more than chronology, it has to shed light on the human condition.'

'Look, miss, I just want to tell you a few facts, facts that got missed out and the public is not aware of.'

'OK, it's your story, not mine. But facts aren't as interesting as the inner truth.'

'*Truth?*' cried my uncle, in a hoarse voice. 'Miss, people who like to hear the truth don't know nothing about the truth. Truth would make them sick if they knew it. Truth isn't nice. It's for grown-up people, not children. You think truth is something I give away, like pennies to a beggar? A man holds on to that until his dying day.'

'So what is it you want to record?' I said, coldly. 'A fairy story?'

'Yes, that's it, a fairy story that people will pay attention to. Because only that kind of dreck is good enough for them, it's all they deserve.'

'Contempt for the reader is not a good start.'

'What do you want from me?' he said. And the old Sándor Kovacs was suddenly there, the beast – I knew this because I felt intimidated.

'Your story,' I said, finding it harder than was reasonable to get these two small words out.

'Story?'

'Yes.'

'And what's *your* story?' He looked at me with those faded brown eyes which now sent out points of gold fire that pierced my heart. I could hardly bear to return his gaze. I could sense another's flesh and the spirit prowling inside it.

'What?' he said, almost shouting, 'what's wrong with you?'

'Nothing.'

'You sick?'

'No, no, carry on.'

'You don't look good.' A hand lifted for a moment, then fell back.

'I'm fine.'

'OK.' He sat back in the cane peacock throne like an exhausted king. Once, when he was very rich, he had had a chair with lion's feet for arms, painted gold. Someone told him it came from a palace in Italy, from the old times. 'So why are you upset all of a sudden? Is someone in your family ill, for example.'

'Well, you know . . .' I said hastily, to cover my revulsion.

'What?'

'My father is not what he once was.' This ambiguity struck me as enough to throw him. It was a trick of my mother's to create a slight misunderstanding that left an uncertainty in the mind, in order to change the subject, send you haring off down the wrong track without ever saying anything with a proper meaning.

'What is his illness?' Sándor said, looking like a man who has just been given his own death warrant, which struck me as strange because they were supposed to hate each other, but all passions, I now understand, are forms of attachment and if my father was to die then these intense feelings would be a ghost, howling for a body.

I lowered my voice to a doctor's murmur. 'You know.'

Cancer, he thought. I saw it in his eyes.

Ervin, the little shit, dying! And soon, he Sándor, and the young girl in front of him would be the last of the Kovacs. At that moment, he suddenly knew I had come as a spy for his brother. That maybe Ervin, at last, at the very end, was using the instrument of his daughter to make amends. That one brother had given the other permission to tell the truth about the past, the story which had begun in another time, another country. For he was the only bridge left between the generations – he, Sándor, would be immortalised by telling this story, sending it on, into the future, this only way we live for ever, the dead speaking to the living.

'All right,' he said, sitting up in his peacock chair, opening the iron box in which his past was held, 'let me start with a fact. I was born 27 February nineteen hundred sixteen. That's my birthday. I'm sixty-one.'

'Where?'

'It was a village, in the Zémplen Hills, in the east of Hungary, near Tokaj, where they make the wine. You heard of that wine? Beautiful, very sweet, the wine of kings, they used to call it. So now you have a fact, no, more than one! Are you happy now?'

'What was the name of the village?'

'You won't believe this but its name was Mád. It's true. And it wasn't a crazy place, it was beautiful.'

'Tell me more about it.'

It had been many years since he'd thought about the village; somehow it got lost. Yet here it was, it came back instantly, when he called for it.

'Quiet, peaceful. The air fragrant, a lovely smell over everything, the grapes warm in the sun when they were ripening. Plum trees in blossom, I remember them very well, in the orchards, beautiful flowers they had in the spring, then fruit, so sweet. The best plums you ever tasted in your life – you know my father lifted me up in his arms so I could reach out and pick a plum for him to eat, and then I picked a plum for myself, ach, those plums.'

'What did they do with the plums?'

'Nothing, they didn't do nothing but eat them, maybe make jam and a *kuchen*, a cake all the women made, you put the plums on top of the dough with plenty of sugar and put it in the oven, a big iron oven, not like the modern gas cooker. The grapes, that was what was important, that was where the money was. The vineyards.'

'They made wine in the village?'

'Of course, wine, that was the whole business. But not just any kind of wine, not the wine you drink in a tavern in Budapest, it was holy wine, because these were Jewish winemakers. They made the wine that got sent east, to the Ukraine and Russia, to the Hasidic Jews, to make their blessings. A ruby-red wine, always.'

'Did your family work in the wine trade?'

'Yes, my father, God rest his soul, he worked for his own father who was one of the merchants, he helped him run the business side of things, the paperwork for shipping. He wrote the letters to the rabbis in Ukraine, in Yiddish, you understand. And also he wrote the letters to the Russian authorities in Russian, Cyrillic, the two languages he knew and also, of course, Hungarian. So he was quite an educated person, a very gentle soul. Not like me, eh?'

'You say you had a brother.'

He had been talking non-stop for several minutes. I saw I could wind him up like clockwork and off he would go.

'Well, you know until I was four years old I lived in heaven,' he said. 'It was a very special life we had then, the neighbours, the Christians, everyone got on fine, some of them were Greeks, because the Greeks were also big in the wine trade in Hungary in those days, I don't know if it's the same today. Everywhere you looked there were beautiful fields, the vineyards, and hills with trees on them. Flowers. Everything quiet, except for the drays carting away the wooden barrels, going east. If I could have one moment in my life to live again it would be when I was four years old because the next minute my mother, who had got very big and fat, went to bed and out of her belly came an old man, a little old man, my brother Ervin. You want to see a picture?'

I had never seen any photograph of either of my parents before their arrival in London just before the war. Framed portraits, held behind glass in silver frames, of their parents, pictures taken in photographers' studios, were kept in their bedroom and the images had faded to speckled pale milk-chocolate mist, evaporating towards the deckled edges of the print.

'Here,' he said, and took from an old enamel box, decorated with sunflowers, a brown envelope that smelt of must and sweat and, faintly, blood.

I recognised my grandmother, just about. At her knee was a sturdy boy with a thick lower lip, hair plastered back under a glassy layer of pomade, and what I'd call an *adventurous* expression. In her arms, wrapped in a shawl, my father peered out beyond the white wool, with a face that at a few months old already seemed like it was looking around for his glasses.

I burst out laughing.

'You think it's funny? My life came to an end when he entered the world. Ervin. Oy. What a nasty child.'

'What was the matter with him?'

'He was a screamer. He screamed, he whined, he would never let go of our mother. You know one time he found a pot of glue like they use to paste the labels on to the wine bottles, everyone had this stuff round the house, and he paints himself in glue and goes and runs at our mother and presses himself against her, so they can get totally stuck. It took her days to get the glue out of his clothes.'

'Was he jealous of you?'

'Who knows? He was crazy. Full of phobias. Nothing ever happened in his life to make him the way he was, not like me, with me it could have gone either way. The circumstances could have been different.'

'Are you still in touch?'

'Maybe we should stop it and play it back, to see how it sounds, make sure everything is working.'

'OK,' I said, breathless from all the revelations, about which I knew *nothing*, absolutely nothing. My father was born in a village? Him? With plum trees and grapes?

I pressed the button on the tape recorder marked Stop and then pressed the button marked Play again, but nothing happened. Silence.

'Try the volume knob, maybe that's the problem.'

Still nothing.

'What's the matter with this? Here, look at this book again.'

I looked.

'Oh. It seems you have to press two buttons simultaneously, not just Play but also Record, both together.'

I pushed my finger down hard on the two buttons. Another light came on.

'Say something.'

'My goddam brother Ervin. The little screamer, ha ha. That enough?'

Then his voice. '*My goddam brother Ervin. The little screamer ha ha. That enough?*'

My uncle had never heard this before. He knew he did not sound like an Englishman or a man with an education, because he never had an education, not the kind I had, but when he heard his voice coming out of the tape recorder, for the first time he understood why no one believed anything he said in court. The voice was guttural, it was coarse, it was hard even for him to make out some of the words.

I could see he had had enough. He was tired and didn't want to talk any more. He looked as if he had torn off a chunk of his soul and handed it to me, as if he had given me his liver, or his kidneys. He didn't look good at all.

'We'll start again tomorrow,' he said to me. 'A fresh start.'

He had the money all prepared in an envelope, with my name on it.

'I pay you forty pound a week, but each day is be one payment. Like the lady in the *Tales of Arabian Nights*. She always kept the end of the story for the next night. Eight pound is not enough to live on. You'll come back tomorrow this way.'

'Of course I will come back tomorrow.'

'Maybe if my life story takes long enough you get the money to buy a little car, that would be a good start for you in life.'

Because my parents never answered any questions about the past – *that's finished, it's over and done with, here you are in England, that other place has nothing to do with you, stop bothering your head with this rubbish, no no no* – I learned to stop asking, and eventually I forgot all about wanting to ask. Suddenly, a treasure chest had opened and out spilled all these precious objects. I was full of everything my uncle had told me; it was not only my parents who suddenly acquired an additional dimension (time) but me too. In my past there were rabbis and plums and grapes and wine. Everything was different now. I felt like I'd eaten a horse.

I couldn't go home at once so I went to see a film, then wandered along Bond Street, looking at the impossibly expensive, dull, grown-up clothes in the windows which I did not want to buy, but I was interested in watching others go in and come out with carrier bags, and speculating what might be inside them. This exercise calmed and soothed me, it was a neutral space between home and my uncle's flat. When I got back to Benson Court my parents were finishing fish fingers with tomato ketchup and baked beans off a tray in front of the TV.

'Did it go good?' my mother asked me. 'You got a respectable employer?'

'Don't let him take advantage,' said my father, 'just because he's paying you under the counter. He's not such a nice person, to break the law.'

'She doesn't pay tax,' my mother said.

'Exactly. They can arrest you for that.'

I sat down in an armchair next to them and we watched the news.

'I have to say, I find this lady quite attractive,' my father said. 'What do you think, Berta?'

'She should wear a hat. It will make her stand out more, like the Queen when she's in big crowds.'

'Good point. Maybe I'll write a letter.'

'That's an idea, but where would you send it?'

'To her house.'

'Or drop it off, it would save a stamp.'

'You can't just walk up to the front and pop it through the letterbox, can you? Aren't there policemen guarding her from assassins?'

'What assassins?'

'The Irish.'

'Oh, yes, those barbarians.'

'Vivien?' my father said, turning to me. 'What can you tell us about this? You are out more than us.'

We all knew there would be no letter, stamped or unstamped.

'I'm hardly out at all,' I said.

'Such a nice woman she looks,' my mother said. 'Margaret, a lovely name.'

I didn't like the hair or the dress or the teeth or the mad eyes. 'She's barking,' I said. 'Look at her, she's like someone you talk to on the bus and think they're quite nice until they say something which makes you realise they're an escaped loony, or something.'

'Where,' my father asked me, 'did you arrive at such a nasty opinion?'

'What opinion? It isn't an opinion.'

'It's a point of view.'

'No it isn't, just a feeling.'

'A *feeling*?' said my father. I knew exactly what was coming next, and he opened his mouth and said it. I could see his red tongue moving around the cavern of his mouth. 'Ideas are bad, but when they attach themselves to feelings, then you have *disaster*.'

'She must have picked it up from one of her friends,' said my mother, standing to draw the curtains.

'About this pleasant lady, they have feelings. *Some friends*.'

My parents did not believe in friends. 'I had a friend once,' my father said. 'He borrowed my bicycle and took it off to go joyriding in the countryside. The paint was scratched when he got back. He never told me he was leaving the city on it. After that I said to him, "you and me are finished".'

This incident took place in 1935. The ex-friend was sent a letter of dismissal, in which my father laid out the terms of their divorce, involving the return of stamp albums etc., and the location of particular cafés where he was no longer to stop by after work for coffee and cake, the whole city in You and Me zones. It was his most successful letter: begun, finished, signed (Ervin Kovacs), posted, delivered.

'I would forgive him if he apologised,' my father said. 'My arms remain open.'

'He could at least have sent a reply,' said my mother, agreeing. 'There was no call to ignore you, not after such a letter.'

I went to my room and tried to read but my head was full of thoughts of the chimerical world of my forebears and I looked for a long time at the map of Hungary in my atlas. I wished more than ever that Alexander was still alive so we could sit down with a bottle of wine and I could tell him everything, and he would once again steeple those long pale fingers and nod and think for a few moments before pronouncing on the situation. A view which I might have initially resisted, but certainly respected, and I doubt if I would have rebelled against his opinion, but secretly I would turned over in my own mind some other ways of seeing things.

For while I had decided at a young age to become my family's intellectual with the university degree, to cope with all their crazy grudges, the rages and sulks, their shouting, their obsessions and compulsions, that did not mean I was at all rational myself.

When I was a child, I had the book which told the cautionary tales of Struwwelpeter, Cruel Frederick, Little Suck-a-Thumb, and the Inky Boys, because my mother had had it when *she* was little, like me. So I knew all about fairy tales, forests and witches. I had been to all those terrible places in the dark and, like the Babes in the Wood, had nearly lost my way in there. I was never really certain of my moral bearings.

The next morning I was back in the cane chair, having mastered how to operate the tape recorder. We began again from the beginning. Sándor told me a second time about the plum trees and wine, and he remembered all kinds of things he thought he had forgotten, like the synagogue which had animals in it, lions and griffins above the Ark, 'a beautiful blue it was inside', he said, 'you know that colour called royal blue? That's what it was. A holy place, but you know very fascinating for a small child because of all the decoration. And on the outside, two windows and they always looked to me like a pair of eyes, brown eyes, dark ones, taking notice of everything. It was already over a hundred year old when I was living there.'

During the trial, in 1964, and what was said about my uncle, and my suspicions that we were related, I became aware that there might be a reason other than thrift that my parents did not cook a turkey at Christmas and give me a stocking to hang at the end of my bed and fill with presents or that there were no chocolate eggs at Easter.

'Look,' my father said, when I confronted him before I left to go to university, 'when we came here, to England, we had a choice – the choice was between the Jewish refugee agency or the nice ladies from the WRVS. And your mother looks at one, and she looks at the other, and she makes a decision. I backed her up to the hilt, and see how it turned out? No one bothers us! It was the right thing to do, in my opinion. You, you're English. None of that other stuff has got nothing to do with it.'

So on a fairly superficial level I understood that my parents were Jews, but that didn't make me one, any more than the fact that my parents had discovered, just before I was born, that I was entitled to be baptised under English canon law and had gone to the local church and had me dunked in the holy water, which would later partially assuage Alexander's parents' misgivings about me and allow us to be married in the chapel at Hereford Cathedral. My parents had me baptised because you got a piece of paper at the end of it, and there was nothing they liked more than official documents with their names on them which they could show the authorities, if called on to do so.

But religion has to go deeper than that to lodge itself in your soul, where it counts, and neither Christianity nor Judaism did, but I was still fascinated, and shocked by what Sándor had to say about my father's upbringing. My parents were both city types who kept off the grass because – 'who needs grass?' They had never been on a motorway, but they admired the idea of them. And now it turned out that my father knew all about orchards and vineyards and horses and that Mrs Prescott had been quite right about my peasant shape. Square hands, broad feet, there they were.

The process of interviewing Sándor first gave me the ability to listen without interrupting, to use my ears instead of my eyes. Sometimes I asked my uncle a question, but mostly I stayed silent. I let him talk, I found a way to steer him as if he were a ship, a little way here, a little way there and that way he went on talking, he couldn't stop. Later, he would tell me that he felt as if he had swallowed a snake, and the snake was eating him up from the inside. Whatever he swallowed, the snake swallowed, so he got no nutrition. He needed me to get it out of him. The snake was now emerging from his mouth, tail first, inch by inch. Its head was buried in his intestines. Maybe this was what caused his terrible digestion, he suggested, smiling sadly.

'You need first a little history lesson,' he began, 'to understand what happens with us.'

'OK, I'm all ears.'

'You study history?'

'Of course.'

'But just your kings and queens of England and France, not real history. Now listen, during the First World War, when I was a baby, we were out of the way of everything. Some of the young men went off to fight for the emperor, but everything really passed us by. The explosion in the village was the row my father had with his father, this was already 1922, when I was six year old and Ervin was two. You know there was a little communist revolution we had in Hungary? Yes, that Bela Kuhn thinks we should go be like Soviet Russia, and he makes a big racket like those people always make who get ideas in their heads that buzz around like bees so they got to let them out through their mouths or they would go mad with all the noise in there. Except he starts meddling in the business of private citizens and they saw what was what and they got rid of him, sharp. Of course how were we to know that sometimes a cold can be replaced by a cancer? You can't predict.

'Anyway, my grandfather was a very religious man, he had a beard that smelt of tobacco and those curls that come down in front of your ears, and he thought that any minute now the Messiah is coming back to earth, so what does it matter what this rabble in Budapest thinks, because they're deluded. But my father, he gets hold of books. Not politics, he's not interested in that, he starts reading about other religions, the Christians, our neighbours, because in those days everyone gets on fine, as I said. Particularly the Greeks, we always liked the Greeks. Then he starts with the Muslims, the Hindus, the Boodists, everything under the sun. He's always sending away to Budapest for books and at night he reads them, while my mother is washing and cleaning. Always his head is in a book, and he starts talking all kinds of crazy things about Allah and Booda and Shiva. No one knows what he's saying. My mother holds her hands over my ears when he starts. I remember that, her hands, smelling of lye soap from the laundry.

'Finally, this got too much for my grandfather. He was a terribly religious person, for him there was only one thing that mattered – the first commandment. You know that one?'

'Thou shalt not kill?' I said.

'No, no, that's not the first, the first is – I am God, I am in charge over you. There is only me, no other. You hear? This is the big message as far as my grandfather is concerned, so when his own son starts talking about Jesus and Booda and Shiva, it was like his son has become a Nazi, though that was later, he doesn't know anything about it then, this is years before all of that business.

'One day they had a row in the street, in front of everyone. The whole village stopped. It was an epic match between father and son, I was trying to listen to it, but my mother's hands were clamped over my ears and I was wriggling to get away from her, because I was a strong boy. My little brother Ervin puts up such a scream, about nothing, some piece of bread and honey he wants, so what with my mother's hands over my ears and my little brother's squawking there's so much din I can't tell what's happening. But then my grandfather picks up a piece of horse dung from the street – and this, you must remember, is a most fastidious man, who washes his hands all day and says a blessing over them, he has nothing to do with animals, just grapes and paperwork – and he throws this piece of shit at my father.

'Oy, my mother is screaming, Ervin is screaming for his bread and honey, I'm trying to get out the door to get a better view because the people are standing in the way, grown-up people, and all I can see is through their legs, when they don't keep shifting about. I want to see what my father does next. Is he going to throw some shit at my grandfather? But he doesn't do nothing. He just stands there, and he starts shouting at the people who are watching, calling them dirty fools, ignorant. He walked off down the street in such a hurry, and no one followed him except the dogs. He went off into the orchards and disappeared under the trees.

'And then we left the village, my birthplace. I never saw it again. We moved to Budapest, that was us and the Zémplen finished. Now we will have a cup of coffee. And biscuits. Or you want a piece of German cake? Sorry, still I don't get to the place where they sell the good pastries.'

'No, thank you.'

'I don't blame you, it's horrible. Make sure everything is working.'

I rewound the tape, and his voice came out of the machine, '*. . . on the outside, two windows and they always looked to me like a pair of eyes, brown eyes, dark ones, taking notice of everything . . .*'

'This is me?' He felt that he was looking at himself in a mirror. When he did that, he saw his bulbous face, the hanging lip. The tape recorder told him what his voice sounded like and it depressed him.

'Is someone knocking at the door?' I said.

'What? Yes, knocking. I go see who.'

He held the door open only a few inches. I couldn't see who was on the other side.

'Oh, you,' he said, sarcastically. 'Yet another visit.'

'That window's still broken.' The voice on the other side of door was high and sharp, but not feminine; the words came out like metal arrows from the unseen mouth.

'What's the hurry? The fresh air will do you good. You should always sleep at night with an open window, I keep meaning to do this myself.' He turned and winked at me.

A short, abrupt laugh. 'Then you can whistle for the rent till you've done it.'

'Oh, oh! Threats. You hear that Miranda? Go and drive your choo choo train, I'm busy.' And he shut the door in his face.

'Is that boy sleeping with a broken window?' I said, eagerly, having found, I believed, an irrefutable sign of my uncle as the evil landlord.

'A lucky child to have a window. He has ventilation. Sometimes I slept in a hole, just a hole.'

'Well, that's there, wherever that was, and this is here, in London, and you have a responsibility as a landlord. There are laws. You can't—'

My uncle looked at me, his niece who went to university and studied Shakespeare and had admitted that she didn't know about life, and thought it was time that I heard some facts about laws. He didn't want to keep me in ignorance because in his experience people who were ignorant were easy meat and he did not want that for me. He wanted me to know how to stand up for myself, not to be a victim, because it was his opinion that if you wanted deliberately to scramble a man's brains and drive him out of his mind with total nonsense, you started out for practice on the intellectuals who were the easiest meat. An intellectual had *no idea at all* how to look after himself when times got rough, because he believed that thoughts were more significant than deeds, whereas my uncle knew it was the exactly the opposite.

'Yes, laws,' he said, quietly, at first so as not to scare me, but he did scare me because white foam started coming from the corners of his mouth. 'You talk to me of law? And where is the law that a landlord who rents rooms must make a profit?'

'The law shouldn't be there to protect the powerful, it's supposed to protect the weak.' I was not political, at all, like my parents I had never voted, but such ideas were the stuff of student life, you could not avoid them

'Oh, oh, oh, I see, I get it now. Socialism. Listen, you're going to start hearing about socialism soon, when we get to that part of my story. You won't like what I have to tell you.'

'I'm not interested in party politics, but anyway that wasn't socialism, it was communism.' Or so Alexander said.

'Same thing.'

'No, it *isn't*. Communism is total rule by the state, what I'm talking about is laws that will protect the—'

'My profit? Is there a law to protect that? No, just the scrounger who tries to sponge off me, for *him* there is a law. For me, nothing.'

'Why on earth should there be a law to protect your profit? Everyone has the right to have a roof over their head, profits aren't a right.' It was a new experience for me, moral indignation.

'Oh, so you don't want that a landlord makes a profit? You think he is a charity? Why a charity? Why should a man be a charity? A charity is full of people with nothing better to do because they don't need no profit, they got everything they want already and they start up a charity. Fine, let them be landlords and I'll find another business, but for now, a young man comes to me, he says he hears I got a room to rent. I tell him the rent, he says, yes, I agree, I pay this rent. Why is this rent £6? Because the government tells me I can't charge any more than £6. It's the law, your law. So when I can't make no profit on £6, still he wants a window fixed, not tomorrow, not today, he wants that the window never be broken. If I had a *profit*, I would fix his window.'

The expression on my face was one he recognised, which he had seen many times before when people looked at him. He knew it well, a mixture of fear and contempt, a queasy nausea at something you don't want to touch, and if you really have to, you take a piece of paper and pick it up between your fingers and wash your hands afterwards.

Politics didn't come into it. The man really was Fagin, and now perhaps I would have to reassess my previous evaluation of that Victorian villain.

'I'm sorry, I frighten you,' he said, his voice trembling. 'Don't pay any attention. You must understand, I am not a violent man. I just raise my voice a little, sometimes.'

He was sweating, and he took a tissue from the box on the table and wiped himself. Purple blotches broke out over his skin. The eyes were milky and looked at me with fear.

'OK,' I said. 'Let's continue.' I had heard enough and I knew what kind of man my uncle was. Everything my father had told me was right, in this once-in-a-lifetime instance, to be grudgingly acknowledged. The plan was, I would finish out the morning, collect my £8 and that would be the end of the experiment. I didn't consider that my uncle was *evil*, that was sensationalist nonsense, he was just a deeply unpleasant person, a creep, and I didn't want to have anything more to do with him. Satisfied with the information he had already given me about my family's antecedents in the village, I knew that anything else he could tell me was to be paid for with a price too high – a kind of contamination by someone in whose presence I could no longer bear to stay. My parents loved me and they did the right thing, protecting me from this horrible relative.

But he wouldn't leave it at that, it was too important to him that I understood.

'No. You tell me first, why do you care about these laws?'

'Because they are fair.' I was pleased with the simplicity of my answer. Alexander would have approved of this short definitive, cutting sentence.

'What does it mean, fair?'

Everyone knew what fair meant, it was the basis of English society, the English instinct of judging right and wrong; every immigrant understood it, as soon as they stepped off the boat. Fair play, and all that. My parents subscribed to this commonly held opinion. A Nazi party could never take hold here, my mother once remarked. People would laugh.

But what was fairness, exactly? I had taken for granted that I knew what it meant and later that day I would look the word up in the dictionary, to be sure. 'I'm not sure it's something you can define,' I said, 'but I suppose it's a matter of respecting others.'

'Respect must be earned.'

'Why?'

'You have to have qualities inside you that can be respected.'

'Such as?'

'Strength, brains. In the jungle a lion is respected by all the other animals.'

'That's not respect, it's fear.'

'Same thing.'

'Could you respect, say, that boy who just knocked on the door?'

'That one?' he started laughing. 'Listen, he is not a bad kid, but respect? What's to respect? He's twenty years old and wears a leather jacket that stinks.'

'Why not? He's another human being.'

'So what?'

'So he deserves respect.'

'Why?'

'For who he is. Just that.'

I shook my head. 'Oy, Miranda, you are just beginning your life. Believe me, where I come from—'

'It doesn't matter where you come from. It's all the same.'

'It is *not*.'

'OK, let's get back to the tape recording. Maybe if you listen you will hear a different point of view.'

'All right,' I said, coldly. 'Where were we? You left the village. What happened next?'

'What happened next? We came to Budapest, me, my father, my brother.'

He must have felt that we were best in the past, me and him, not the present, for back there he was an unknown quantity and had something he knew I wanted, that mysterious life which was lived before I was born, by people who would not take me back into that life, who denied me this gift. And he was starting to enjoy some of these memories, which returned him to a very agreeable period, when the future was just a series of doors you opened, and no unpleasant surprises on the other side.

He didn't understand that we were finished, it was all over by the second morning.

'My father has made a total break with his father, with the village, everything, the wine trade,' he went on. 'So we take the train to the city. I never been on a train. I never saw a place bigger than Tokaj. You know what a place Budapest was in those days? You ever seen it?'

'No.'

'Don't go. It's a shit hole. But then! *Then* it was a city. A river running through it, the Danube, with the bridges across it, and all the beautiful buildings. You know it's two different cities, Buda and Pest? Well, I became a Pest boy, and the way I started I finished, always a pest. A pest. You get it?'

'Yes.' My uncle noticed I was smiling a little and felt relieved. He believed that there were two types of people, the ones who take offence like a match to hay and it burns fast and bright and fierce and short: this was him. Then there are those whose flames bank down into glowing embers that smoulder for years: that was my father. He hoped I was like him, hot and hasty but it doesn't last. He was right, that's exactly how I am, whereas my father never forgave, never forgot, always bore a grudge.

Then he went on with his remarkable story, and I confess that despite my dislike for this vile man, I was reluctantly drawn deeper and deeper into his world, to me like a film or a novel in which I was becoming engrossed. He was a fantastic talker, he could bring every moment alive, he had the seducer's gift of the gab. I could picture with my inner eye his description of the arrival at the railway station, and all the people he saw – only at the synagogue on the high holidays had he seen so many – and everyone walking up and down as if they had urgent business they had to see to, jumping on and off trams and running around like dogs and cats. A whole city alive! His mother was holding my father in her arms, because he fell asleep on the train and when she tried to wake him up he started up with his screaming, and so she had to carry him and he fell right back to sleep and never saw what Sándor saw, that first hour in Budapest.

'You sure this machine is working OK?' he said, after this long passage from his life.

'Do you want me to rewind and check?'

'Yes, let's make sure.'

I pressed the button and let the tape whir back for a second or two. '. . . *with the bridges across it, and all the* . . .'

'It's working fine,' I said. 'Where did you live and how had your father got an apartment and a job?' We had another forty minutes to go, so I might as well squeeze all the information out of him that I could, before I left. I thought that when I went home I might make some notes, just for myself, no other reason.

'Ah, this I never found out, I just know he wrote letters, a lot of letters, and some he got replies and some no answer, but in the end he got a position with a firm that made hats, as a clerk, you understand, and bookkeeper, but he got to be in charge of the export department, because he spoke Russian.'

'What kind of hats? Millinery?'

'No, no, no. Fedoras. In those days every man had a hat. These was good quality hats and they exported them all kinds of places. Now when they took him on, remember this is 1924, they think they're still going to be exporting hats to Russia but they don't know that first of all, the Russians don't want no hats, except the kind the workers wear, caps, and second, even if they wanted a fedora, they want one made in Moscow, and not a capitalist hat. My father tells them all this, after he gets nowhere selling hats to the Soviet Union. Now he was very quick with languages, like me by the way, he learns German, studying every night with a book and going out to cafés and listening, because in those days a lot of people spoke German, and soon he sets up the German export department. By this time he looks just like a Hungarian, no beard, nothing. The firm was in the Erzsébetváros, the seventh district, and that's where we got an apartment, in not a bad building. And this is where I start my new life as a city boy.'

He told me how he had to stop speaking like a village child. 'I wanted to be a Magyar, like all the rest. This was very important to me, to be Hungarian, not a Jew. To speak their language, not Yiddish which we spoke in our childhood. And my father, he was not that interested in being a Jew any more, either. At work he sold hats, at night he read all the religions, and he liked the Boodists best of all, he said they were nice quiet people who never did no one any harm. Of course my mother paid no attention to any of this, and she kept all the Jewish rules like she always done.'

'And what about your brother, Ervin? How did he get on?'

'Ach, well he was a city child from the word go, because he was a mamma's boy, and a mamma's boy is no good in a village. Now he was also a pest, what a pest he turned out to be! I'm laughing just remembering him. When he started school, I remember, my mother had to stand outside the classroom while he was screaming at her not to abandon him, the little baby. But the funny thing is, you know, me – I was the one who ran wild in the fields and spent all day running under the vines and going to the stables to see the horses – but once I got to Budapest, it turned out I liked school, I was not a stupid person. I came top of my class in many subjects, including mathematics which was always very easy for me, the numbers just jumped around in my head, they were like dancers, and if I closed my eyes I could see them holding hands with each other and then when they held hands they turned into different numbers. I never understood that it was just me that did this in my head, I thought it was everyone, but other boys, they were very slow with numbers and you could always cheat them, like that trick with the three cups and the dice.

'Ervin, he was something different. Ervin was no good in school but with his hands he was very skilful. His hands were always busy with something, always making, and painting his pictures.'

'Painting *pictures*?'

'Yes, what's the big surprise?'

'I don't know, you didn't make him sound like an artist.'

'I didn't say he was an artist, I just said he painted pictures. That doesn't mean they were any good.'

'What were they like?'

'Well, you know, he'd take a bowl of fruit, and he made a picture and somehow he makes it like he wants the fruit in his picture to be more like the fruit in the bowl than the fruit is itself Like he's in a competition with nature. That's what I told him, and he got angry with me, and my mother was angry too, because she said, how can you be unkind to your baby brother? You should encourage him. But that was her, she was a very soft woman, motherly. What time is it?'

'Eleven-thirty.'

'OK, now we stop, you got to start the typing. You leave here one o'clock, prompt. I got a visitor coming.'

I sat down at the table which overlooked the street, and the children playing, the dogs whining, the cats sleeping, a rag and bone man passing with a horse-drawn cart.

My uncle went into the bedroom and lay down. I think he fell asleep. I began the laborious task of transcribing the tape on to the typewriter, half a sentence at a time, rewinding every half-inch or so. His voice echoed through the flat – and beyond the bedroom door the same voice was lightly snoring. Listening the first time was interesting, but listening again, I started to notice how he made a sentence, and that guttural accent which grated on me when I first heard it started to get inside my own head. I could hear a mind recreating the past out of its mysterious material.

But it was tiring, as well. When he woke up, I was calling through the door, 'It's one o'clock, I'm finished, I'm going now.'

'Wait,' he said. 'Hold on a minute, there's someone I want you to meet.'

Hurriedly he got dressed and emerged from the bedroom in a blue suit, pink shirt and purple silk tie, his hair slicked back and his skin smelling of that expensive scent he wore. I had never known a man who smelt of anything but soap. Alexander's skin smelt of himself, and the fibres of his clothes, and his mouth of toothpaste.

'I look all right?' he said.

'Very smart.'

'I'm expecting a lady. A man should always dress up for female company. You don't want to give them no disrespect. Come on.'

'So you do understand respect, after all,' I said, as we walked downstairs past the hunting pictures.

'That's different.'

'Where are you meeting her?'

'She's waiting in the hall, you'll see her. She's always bright and early, that's Eunice, all over. Yes, here she is.'

'Eunice,' he said, 'I want you to meet Miranda, the person I was telling you about, who is helping to write it all up, everything, like we discussed.'

'Pleased to meet you,' she said and held out a blue leather glove.

That was the first time I saw her, and felt that fine-boned hand in mine, like a silver fork. She was a beautiful woman then, and more elegant than anyone I had ever known, in a navy suit with a white blouse, the navy leather gloves with three buttons at the wrist, and her hair a shining helmet of blue-black waves. Under it, her dark eyes looked at me as if they were taking a photograph to be blown up and examined later, with a magnifying glass.

'You hear that?' Sándor said to me, as she spoke. 'You know where she comes from?'

'Wales?'

'Exactly, Wales, like Shirley Bassey. Tiger Bay. Same place. What do you think about that?' And he give Eunice a kiss on her face, so I would know that she was his special friend, his lady friend, very different from the little tart he took to our flat.

'I got you a present,' he said to her, 'I show you when we get there.'

The sun struck her hair. She looked like a black lacquer ornament. They walked off down the road together in the warm spring sun, arm in arm.

As I watched Sándor and Eunice walk down the street, the voice of the boy who had knocked on Sándor's door said, 'Who are you?'

I turned round. He had come out of his flat and was sitting on the step with the door open behind him, smoking. My first impression was of a sharp face with blue eyes, very short dark hair pushed back from his forehead, fingers drawing the home-made cigarette to his lips, and a red mouth with a lecherous smile. A twenty-year-old with the edgy, cocky, sexual confidence of someone who knows that he must always look out for number one, because no one else will do it for you.

I didn't know how to answer his question; it would take some thought. I was startled to be addressed.

'While you're remembering, do you wanna come and sit down?'

'Where?'

'Here, on the step, if it's not too hard on your arse. Nice arse, though, from what I can see.' He laughed. It came out short and quick and without pleasure or humour.

But after the hours upstairs – the dust of the Kovacs past, the old soiled memories, the faded photos, the frozen sunlight – I laughed too. And of course I was not without an ulterior motive and wanted to know from the mouth of one of his own tenants what kind of a man Sándor was these days. Here was a person with a grievance against my uncle. So I sat.

'Do you want a roll-up?' he said, offering me a tin with tobacco. 'I can make it for you if you like.'

'No, thanks, I've got my own cigarettes. How long have you lived here?'

'Few weeks.'

'Is it all right?'

'*No*, it's not all right. The old man's a shyster. He can smell a pound note from ten feet away.' He rubbed his fingers together as if they were feeling money, a disagreeable gesture. 'So what were you doing up there in his flat?'

'I work for him.'

'Doing what?'

'Paperwork,' I said.

'Right.'

I lit a cigarette and we sat for a few minutes, smoking in silence, as people passed on the street. As if my pores were full of my uncle, I tried to expel him with each breath. When I got home I would have a bath and soak and dream amongst the yellow ducks, try to think about what, if anything, the future could hold for me. A black cat squatted and urinated against a tree across the road, then snarled at the legs of a passer-by.

'Do you want to have a look at my window?' the boy said. His fag had gone out and he put it away carefully in his tin of tobacco. 'Come on, I won't bite. Though I like biting.' His laughed again, quick and hard, showing a row of small, sharp teeth.

I was curious to see how my uncle had managed to squeeze so many flats into the house. I stood up. 'Go on, then, show me.'

The door was at the back of the hall. A room that had started out in its youth large and handsome and well proportioned, with high ceilings and elegant cornices, had been hacked up like butcher's meat, chopped into several diminished slices with one third of what had been a substantial sash window overlooking the garden.

'Freezing, isn't it?' he said. 'I'll put the kettle on. You can see what's happened: the glass in the top pane had a diagonal crack and I think, "what happens when you push it with your finger?" and it fell out. Look, there it is.'

The garden was dark and overgrown with weeds, self-seeded saplings, branches fallen in the winter storms. No lawn or path. On the ground a transparent triangle pressed down hard on the nettles and dandelions and dock leaves, a strange three-cornered section of reflective green glaring back at the sky which dropped some clouds on its surface. And the window was left with a triangular hole, through which the early summer breezes blew.

The room wasn't much: a single bed, an enamel-topped table with a hotplate and an electric kettle, a small, hard armchair upholstered in maroon velvet plush, stained brown on the arms, a plywood chest of drawers with a row of five or six books, all horror stories. Jammed between the bed and the window was a small glass tank containing some tropical fish in fluorescent colours.

'What are those?'

'My fish, of course. Do you want to have a go at feeding them?'

'Not really. Why did you bring fish with you? This place is hardly big enough to stretch your arms out.'

'I didn't bring them. I've got more at home but the tank's too big for this room so I had to start again. It's a hobby, I like looking at them. They're good. And quiet, too, no mess.'

'What's happened to the others?'

'Someone's looking after them, they're all right. But what about my window? Can you get him to fix it?'

'I don't have any influence.'

We were jammed up together next to the tank. I could feel his breath on my neck. 'I think that blue fish fancies you a bit. Look at the way he's swimming round and round in circles, you've got him in a right state, he's not used to female company. In fact, you're the first person he's seen apart from me since he left the shop.'

The claustrophobia of the tiny room, his physical presence next to me, the sight of the forearms with their dark hairs and his hands with their long fingers pointing at the tank, his odd, arousing smell, of musk and lemon and leather, disturbed me. My breath felt trapped in my chest.

'Are you off?' he said. 'You haven't had any tea yet.'

'I've got to go.'

'I'm going out myself, I'll walk along with you, if you like.'

I couldn't stop him. It's a free country and anyone has the right to walk down the street.

We set off along Parkway to Camden tube, passing the pet shop, where he said he bought his fish. The cages in the windows were full of downtrodden creatures.

'If you could, which would you have, a parrot or a monkey?' he said.

The parrots were of many colours and had tiny primeval eyes. I couldn't see any monkeys there, but their hands disturbed me.

'A goose,' I said, 'a Canada goose.'

'That's a bird but it's not a parrot.'

'No.'

'My go. I'd take the monkey. I'd let it sleep in my bed. It would have to be female obviously, you don't want a monkey's dick sticking into you in the middle of the night. But no monkey business with the girl monkey, just to cuddle.'

'You're in need of a girlfriend, it seems,' I said, teasingly. His nonsense was soothing after the menacing hours spent with my uncle.

'I've got a girlfriend,' he said, and his face seemed to acquire a little colour.

'Where does she live?' I asked.

'She's back home, where I come from.'

'Is she coming to London to be with you?'

'Don't think so.'

It seemed like an unsatisfactory arrangement, and I wondered if she even existed. 'So perhaps she's no longer your girlfriend?' I said.

'No, she is. What's your name?'

'Miranda. What about you?'

'I'm Claude. Go on, laugh, everyone does. My mum got it from the pictures. There was some actor who played a Frenchman in a film she saw, but he wasn't even French, she just thought he was.'

'It is quite funny. Haven't you got a middle name you could use?'

'Yeah, Louis. Aka Louise, as they called me in school. So as you can see, I'm screwed either way. I'm stuck with Claude. You learn to live with it.'

He was taller than me, and he walked fast with his shoulders hunched down and his hands in his jeans pockets, as if his head was driving forward through the air, pushing it back. His name was his face, and he challenged anyone to deal with it, as an ugly person learns to inhabit their body, make it something arresting and interesting.

We descended the escalator at Camden tube station and waited on the platform. 'I start work here next week,' he said, lighting his little cigarette. 'As a trainee guard.'

Rats ran up and down on the rails. The train came with a blast of cold air drawn along the tunnels, the noise filling all the narrow space. We came back up at Bond Street to a fine sunny afternoon, the wind dropping all the time. The sides of the streets pushed you forwards like the arteries drive on the blood, in endless circulation.

'My window,' he said, 'what about . . .' But I was slipping away into my own privacy, remembering what Uncle Sándor had told me: of the brothers' childhood in the village, and coming to Budapest, and my father being good with his hands, and my uncle good with his head. I didn't even know what that city looked like. I was not curious about the place my parents came from, except I knew it was cold, dark, hard, evil. There were squares and cellars where they shot people. In the last months of the war people hid where they could, up or down. In 1956 the people rose up against the Soviets and were crushed. I couldn't picture it and had never wanted to, until now.

Then I found that we had lost each other in the crowd, for I was on my own on the pavement, so I turned up towards Harley Street, though I thought I caught a glimpse of him outside a pub, watching me, as I hurried along the street.

Shocked and embarrassed was the mood of Benson Court when I returned home from my honeymoon a widow. The residents felt it must be their own fault, sending us to the Hotel Negresco, signing a death warrant, as the ballerina put it, theatrically crossing her hands across her breasts and holding her head to one side, when she stopped me on the stairs to offer her condolences.

I went to see Gilbert. 'You've been in the wars, haven't you, poor love?' he said. 'Come and have a drink.' The mantelpiece was full of invitations to parties, and the floor was covered with half-read books.

I told him about my attempts to find a job, and all the applications I had sent off but he said, 'Oh, applications darling, don't you realise that that's not how it works at all?'

'How does it work?'

'Silly girl, contacts!'

'I haven't got any contacts.'

'Yes, you have, lots of them. Starting with me. Do you want me to see if there's anything on the paper?'

'A job on *The Times?*'

'Probably not a job, but maybe some freelance work, I could certainly see about that. What about book reviewing, for example, do you think that might suit?'

I could be a book reviewer, a literary critic for the newspapers, and I would go to parties and meet interesting people and make friends, and get a flat of my own somewhere! I had a sudden passion to read books again, a need for their deep nourishment. But didn't I need to work for *The Times* to be entrusted with a book to review? Would they give me a book if I wasn't paying national insurance and tax and had other numbers? My father had numbers and cards. Morris Axelrod gave them to him. No, Gilbert said, I would be what was called freelance, and freedom was already embedded in the word, so it was for me.

Humbly grateful, I agreed to let him take out the pictures he had drawn of me at seventeen, and we looked at them, and he asked if I still looked like that, with my clothes off. I wasn't sure. The girl in the pictures had a body that looked like a stem that is budding limbs. She was embryonic. My feet had calluses and faint scars now. My eyes seemed totally different. And I thought, Shouldn't we talk about what time has done to *you*? but he was familiar and kind and I knew he couldn't harm or hurt me, his pale chest would be warm against my cheek. So we went to bed, but most of the time I was trying to think of something else. Halfway through, his grandfather clock chimed eleven. I was lying there, counting the beats in my head, and further away, across the city, Big Ben joined in, that cracked bell.

Next day he came home with a book for me to review; a novel about a limp young woman who falls for rugged men who are not interested in her. 'It looks pretty drossy,' he said, 'but apparently she's popular and they'll give it a good spot. Do you want to come round for a drink tonight?'

'No, thanks, I think I'll make a start on the book.'

'Suit yourself.'

I lay on my bed reading the book, which was very sappy, in my opinion. I was summoning all the cruelty of the first-time reviewer trying to make her mark. To be intimidated by the author's fame didn't occur to me, for in my arrogance I couldn't understand why someone who had, according to the author biography, a double first from Somerville College, Oxford, should lower herself to write such tripe, when she had the example of Virginia Woolf and George Eliot. I certainly wouldn't, if ever I were to write a novel, which was bound to be of the highest literary order. There were definitely those in whom the serious demands of great art only revealed their intellectual limitations.

No one had ever written such an incisive account of the failings of a novel. No one had ever defended literature so honourably from its own practitioners. This was a start, a start in literary journalism which I hoped could turn me, by osmosis, into a *writer* of books, as publishers admired my stinging prose and invited me to lunch to ask if I would like to write a novel myself. But the end of the next day, the review was returned to me with a brief note: 'Next time, try writing in the English language.'

I rang up the literary editor. 'What's *wrong* with my review? I spent two days on it.'

'Yes, I can tell. What does "the surplus value of modernism" mean? No, please, don't tell me. Listen, dear, all we want to know is what the subject is, a bit of an idea about the plot, who the characters are and whether the author has pulled off what they set out to do. That's it. And if you could make the review interesting to read, obviously that would be a help.'

'But no one in literary criticism, now is—'

'As I say, if you want to review books, you need to know what a book review is. Just go and read a few, will you, and give me a ring in a couple of weeks. And could you post the book back or drop it off, if you're passing. I need to give it to someone else.'

I seemed to be going backwards in time, and nothing I could

do would reverse the direction of my life. My work was no good, once again I was sleeping under the roof of my parents' flat at Benson Court, and some sleeping was even in Gilbert's bed. Soon I would be back in the jumble-sale hand-me-downs my mother bought me and which still hung in the wardrobe.

I saw a man kiss a woman on the nose as they were holding on to the rail on a lurching bus, and she smiled at him, and he reached around and kissed her again on the ear. I saw buckets of flowers in florists' shops, and bouquets being created to give to someone who was loved. I saw women with briefcases streaming up the steps of Oxford Circus underground and walking north up Regent Street to Portland Place to the doors of the BBC. Everyone was in motion with things to do and places to go and people were falling in love, making love, having brand new thoughts that no one had ever had before and everything went on. New goods arrived in the shops. People were making money in their jobs to buy them. They were renting flats, buying houses, and above all they were kissing each other on London buses, and everyone and everything was busy while I was sitting on the bench in the communal garden watching the flowers very slowly grow before my eyes. But at least they grew.

The man I had loved was dead and I was no longer even certain that I had loved him, or if it had been a child's game, the impersonation of a grown-up woman who shared a flat with her boyfriend, got engaged, got married, went on honeymoon. The more I tried to relive them, the more fake my memories felt – I was no longer fully certain whether the events they recalled had happened to me or to a character in a film or book. I didn't believe any more that I had ever left Benson Court, gone to university, met Alexander and married him in the chapel of the cathedral; it seemed impossible that I could have managed a series of such unlikely manoeuvres. Only the abortion remained real. It had to have been, my mother was there.

When, one morning, I sat down to breakfast and my mother poured me a small glass of sweetened orange juice, and I bit down on it and heard the crack loudly rend the surface and saw my parents look at each other with meaningful nods, I decided that I had better go back to being Uncle Sándor's secretary, for there, at least, there was £40 a week, and the completion of a story that remained kind of interesting to me: of who I was and where I had come from, the shadow land before I was born.

'You didn't turn up – six days in a row I waited,' my uncle said, when he came down to open the door. 'I bought a fresh cream cake, and you didn't come. I sat and waited. I don't like waiting. The cake spoiled.'

He looked sick. He skin was even whiter than I remembered and his hands were covered in white, flaking patches.

'I'm sorry,' I said, 'it was unavoidable.'

'Why is this?'

'I was in a pub and a bomb went off.' There *had* been a bomb, in a pub in Islington, a small ineffective bomb that had been on the evening news, with no one killed but a cat that fell asleep on the abandoned holdall and was blown sky high, its tail wound round the best bitter pump and its eyes flung out into an ashtray. The insertion of myself inside this event seemed, as I spoke, yet another indication of my detachment from reality and my increasingly desperate attempts to get back to the concrete world of here and now which were no more than self-dramatisation.

'What! You were hurt? How? What did they do to you?' Again, I noticed that impulse to raise his arm and touch me, and again I flinched, and he noticed this too, and the arm lowered to his side.

'I wasn't hurt, no one was, apart from a cat.'

'Yes, I heard about it. So if you weren't hurt, why didn't you come?' His eyes were watering again and he wiped them on his sleeve.

'I was in shock. What's the matter with your eyes?' I said, changing the subject.

'I don't know, maybe glaucoma, it makes you go blind in the end, but the optician says is something else.'

'Do we have to stand in the hall?'

'No, no, of course not, come upstairs. Please, and I'll make you good strong Hungarian coffee. And you should eat a piece of cake, the sugars and the fats are good for you when you have a shock.'

We reached his flat and sat down in our old places, him in the cane peacock throne, me mastering the tape recorder.

'So where were we?' he said.

'In Budapest.'

'Yes, Budapest. What do you want to know?'

'What did you do when you left school?'

'Here, eat. I just got the Battenberg, I wish I had a better class of refreshments to offer you.'

'Don't worry, I'm not hungry.'

'You *should* be hungry. You're too thin.'

'I lost a bit of weight recently.'

'Then definitely, I'm getting a real cake, for tomorrow. OK, first you must understand that the time I left school in 1934, it was when the Jewish quotas started to come in so I tell my father, why do we need to be Klein? This was our name, you know, in the village, but it is the time when a lot of Jews were changing their names, Hungarianising them, why not be something else? My father doesn't care what name he has. My mother does not express an opinion. Ervin, my brother, is still at school and is not asked. So we became Kovacs, a very nice *echt* name. It was my doing, the name change. So from Sándor Klein, now I am Sándor Kovacs and I go looking for a job.'

I could see that all the time he was talking he was watching me, and for the first time I began to wonder if he knew who I was. This was the earliest suspicion, but I was too interested in the story to pursue it, because it was a revelation that my name was only a few years old, and that we were something different before. That I was the very first of our Kleins to be born with the name Kovacs.

'You want more coffee, a smoke?' he said.

'No, thanks. Tell me about your first job.'

'My first job was a good job, in a real estate office. This is 1934. People already don't like the Jews, but what can you do? Maybe we are not so likeable. What do you think?'

'About what?'

'About the Jews being not lovable.'

'I don't have an opinion,' I said. 'Please continue.'

'OK,' my uncle said, smiling slightly and giving me a benign and even gently pitying look that I could not decode. 'I was only eighteen. Now I'm going back to the time that without doubt was the very best of my life, because even when I lived high off the hog in the house in the Bishops Avenue, I was beset by nightmares, I admit. The job is all day renting apartments, all over the city. I get to know Pest like the back of my hand, every street. We had some marvellous flats on our books. You know the buildings they put up had stone faces on them, yes, the faces stuck out into the street and looked at you. Some of them were knights from the old times, but nearly every building was decorated. So by day I run around the city on my bicycle, showing tenants flats, but at night, this was when I was truly alive. In Budapest we have cafés, still, to this day, but nothing like the cafés before the war. Palaces, they seem to me, with waiters in beautiful attire . . . this is the word?'

'Attire, yes.'

'The cafés were full of wonderful people, journalists, writers, politicians, crazy people. Ladies in their fur coats and fur hats, and the fur casts a shadow on their face like lace. *This* was my education, not university, in the cafés of Budapest. Nothing is like it here, in England. When I first arrived, I looked for the cafés, I go to the Kardomah, only housewives and in the evening they close.'

'What were you reading at that time?'

'When?'

'In Budapest in the thirties.'

'Reading? Me? Nothing, I wasn't reading nothing.'

'But why did you want to be among the intellectuals?'

'I like to hear them talk. I like to study what they say. To pick up tips. You see if you listen to the intellectuals you learn how to bullshit, and this is very important in my line of business. Do I offend you? I remember now you are an intellectual yourself.'

And now we were coming to a part of Sándor's story where he had to make a decision. A little girl had stood with her small fingers clutching the frame of a front door, looking up at her uncle, while her father screamed abuse at him in a foreign language. He wanted to give her chocolate: he was not permitted. What would follow, the tale of his crimes, his terrible deeds, which he had every intention of defending himself against, these accusations – that was one thing; but he wanted that little dark child, now a young woman, also dark, with a faint shadow on her upper lip, to know that her law-abiding father was a hypocrite and a prig. If it alienated me, he didn't care. Someone had to know, Eunice knew, but no one in the future would consider *her* opinion – for Eunice, the beautiful girl, was just a coloured woman who worked in a shop, with a son who was in prison.

He knew from court how some people's opinions had more weight than others, and the girl in front of him had a degree in poetry from York University. Which was not Oxford or Cambridge, admittedly, but still very good, he'd made enquiries.

'OK, look, I tell you about the cafés,' he said, and his brown eyes looked straight at me, those eyes which could be dead or alive according to his mood but were always alive in these pauses, as he took a mouthful of strong coffee and thought about what he was going to say next. How do you play it? Farce, the best way.

'I don't earn too much in the office, I have work, but this kind of work is not going to make me a millionaire. To be a millionaire I need my own business, you don't make yourself rich if you are at someone else's beck and call. I have a lot of energy, but I can't see an opportunity. Now comes the time when I see one. Listen, Miranda, never in my life was I a good-looking man. I never looked like no movie star. But for some reason women like me. They like to talk to me, I am easy with them, and this makes them easy with me. That is the way it is. I meet a lot of young ladies in the cafés, all kinds. Some single, some married. Some working, some not. I have a lot of acquaintances. A young man who is easy with people, who has energy, who knows the city very well, who has a knowledge of empty apartments, this person has an opportunity. You understand?'

'No.'

'Ach, I have to spell it out. The ladies I meet, sometimes they want money for a hat, sometimes they want money for the rent. On the other side of things is a man who has a wife, and the wife is sick or pregnant, or just had a baby, or she don't like doing things in the bedroom. These two people are destined to meet, if only someone bring them together. But where do they meet? Not his place, not her place. But I know where there is empty apartments, and I have the keys. So this is how my business starts.'

For all these years I had thought of him as a slum landlord, a rampant capitalist exploiting the very weakest. But he was more than that: his greed fed on human flesh.

'You were a pimp.'

'Very ugly word. In Hungarian we call it *strici*. No one used this word about me in Budapest, this is first time I hear it, from you.'

This wasn't really true. He had been arrested for living off immoral earnings, but I kept my mouth shut. I just looked at him with a cold disgust. He really was the dregs. I saw my parents' point.

'OK, Miss, er Collins, you want to finish?' he said coldly, seeing that I was no better than anyone else, a person of limited understanding and imagination.

'For today?'

'No. Finish altogether. You don't like to sit and drink coffee with a *pimp*? You want to find another job? Go and be the editor of *The Times*, if it suits you better.'

He couldn't have chosen a more cutting taunt. 'I didn't say anything about leaving, I—'

'Let me tell you what a pimp is, what he does, a pimp is a man who—'

'Look, we really don't need to discuss this. I'm just a secretary.'

'No, no, you are more than this. A secretary takes a letter. This is no letter, this is my heart I tear out of my . . .'

But he saw that he had gone too far. This was the second time I thought, Maybe he knows who I am. Still I didn't say anything.

'What, what?'

'Never mind, why don't we just go on?'

'Go on?'

'Yes.'

'Talk about pimps, if you want, but I first—'

'I won't type up this part of the tape, you know. I don't type my questions or anything I say.'

'Well, just so you understand, I know pimps, in my time, and no girl ever did any good with a pimp. My girls ran their own business, I just bring them the clients and provide the room. I take a management fee. Everyone understands this. The rules are obvious to all of us. I don't force them into nothing or feed them drugs.'

'Yes, yes. Continue.' The shock of this revelation still jangled my nerves.

'OK, let me tell you about my brother Ervin. You can hear about his way, the honest clean way that is his road, not mine. The first girl he meets, he gets engaged to her. A girl with a limp, and a stick, but a very nice person. I always liked Berta a lot better than him. He got an apprenticeship in this jeweller's business and he is very, very lucky to keep the job, because my father, by now, has been sacked from the hat company. Business is bad, they drop workers, they have two Jews, one Jew has to go, under the race laws that came in, and since the German export department is not a department you want to be run by a Jew, bye-bye to my father, after fourteen years with this company. And by the way, it's the same with me, I only work for a little firm, they can't take no Jews at all any more, but I am someone who knows how to keep his head above water, and more and more my business is putting together girls and apartments, because I still manage to know what apartment or room is empty and I still manage to have the keys, because I don't do things the official way.

'Now my father can't sell hats, all he does all day is read his books. Word gets round about me, and how exactly I manage to keep my head above water and bring home money for the rent for my parents because without it, you can be sure they would starve. Ervin can't stand it. He has a job! He is a respectable person! He has a fiancée! Every night he comes home and starts picking fights with me. He never says directly what his problem is, he just says, Why is there no milk? Did *you* drink the milk, Sándor? You selfish sonofa— Now, my mother loves both her sons, equally. She cannot stand that any bad blood should come between us. I tell her, Mother, he keeps his way, I keep my way.

I'm twenty-two year old, time I move out, get my own apartment.

'Oy, she cries when she hears this. But I say, listen, I get an apartment on the same street, I see you every day. So this is what happens, I get my own apartment, not an apartment, a room, but a good room, very good. They are on Sip utca, I am on Dob, just round the corner. Every day I go to my office, which is the café at the Hotel Astoria.'

'Your base of operations,' I said. The story was getting very interesting now.

To have a picture of my parents, in the few months before they left Hungary, and were photographed outside the front door of our flat, just before they slammed the door.

'Yes, lot of different people come here in the evening. I see everyone.'

'Did your mother know what you were up to?'

'This is the thing. Ervin keeps threatening me, I tell, I tell, he's screaming. He means he is going to tell my mother how come I still have money in my pocket and nice suits. "Why?" I ask him. "Why do you want to tell her?" "So she knows," he says. "Know what?" "What a brother I have." "Why do you care?" I ask him. "I have a reputation," he says. What reputation? He works in a back room in a jeweller's shop. I wiggle it out of him in the end, it's this girl, his fiancée, Berta, he don't want her family to find out.

'Well one night, I bumped into him on Karoly Korut, on the way home from work. I tried to be friendly, I said, come and have coffee with me at the Astoria. So we go, we have coffee, I try to make nice with him. After we finished our coffee I buy him a drink. He don't drink, Ervin, usually, but I say, let's have a glass of Tokaj, to remember our childhood, so he agrees, then we have another glass, and for the first time I ever see, he is mellow and rosy. This girl I know comes in, she sits down. Ervin goes to the toilet to take a wee. I say to her, this is my little brother, be nice to him, and I give her a few notes.'

He started laughing and took a tissue from the box and wiped his eyes.

'Why are you laughing?' I said.

'I'm just seeing Ervin in front of my eyes, as he was then.'

'What did he look like?' I said, eagerly, I think I had so much forgotten myself that the mask was lying on the table and behind it was just a young girl who doesn't know about pretending.

'He is not a big man even now, and then he was little and thin. His cuffs come down to his knuckles because he was mean and he thought he would still grow, though he is eighteen already, so he don't have to buy a new jacket. All his clothes are too big for this reason. He always remind me of that animal, what you call it, the one with the shell on its back?'

'Snail?'

'No, bigger.'

'Tortoise?'

'This is the one. An old man's face he has already, sticking out over his shirt collar. Anyway, I go off to do some business and I see them leaving. Later in the evening she come back to the Astoria, and she tell me everything went fine, but he is a virgin, so there is not much work for her to do. It's all nice and quick, and now he goes home.'

You think your parents are there just to love and irritate you. You see them as satellites spinning round your sun and you try to run away across the universe while they chase you. The time before I was born – the city where I had never been, the country that was just a coloured shape on the map – was newsreel land, black and white, one-dimensional. Time is such a strange thing. Here I am, walking home across Regent's Park carrying a new dress, and the year 1977, when these events that I am describing took place, is almost as distant as 1938 was from then. Was it real or imaginary? My father, as a young man, having sex with a prostitute after all his talk about his prescience in leaving Hungary. Could there be a more ridiculous proposition?

'You OK? You want a glass of water? I don't want to happen to you what happen to your husband.'

'No, I'm fine,' I said.

'I thought you were swallowing your tongue.'

'Go on, please, I'm all ears.'

'Few days later, my mother comes and knocks on my door. She is in a terrible state. Ervin is emigrating, he is leaving Hungary, I got to come to our apartment immediately. OK, I say, let's hear what he has to say. Now this is a time in Hungary when it is not that the noose tightens, it is rather that now we notice for the first time that there is a noose on our neck. Ervin taps his spoon on the glass of tea he is drinking and says that suddenly, there is a danger for Jews in Hungary, he and Berta have to leave at once.

'"Tell him not to go," says my mother. My father just sits and says nothing. "Well, Ervin," I say, "tell us how you see things going here in Hungary." Then he begins with a big story about what is happening in Europe. Germany he talks about, and the Soviet Union.

'"Seems to me like you been reading newspapers," I tell him. "You must have been sitting in the cafés." When he hears this, he goes berserk and takes a pinch of sugar from the bowl on the table and throws it at me. I'm laughing. "I'm sweet enough," I say, "without your sugar." But it took all night for Mother to calm him down. So now it becomes known, through the neighbourhood, that Ervin Kovacs and his fiancée Berta are leaving Hungary, fleeing the Jewish persecution. But in the cafés it's another story. In the cafés, Ervin Kovacs is leaving Budapest because he is terrified that his fiance will find out he slept with a prostitute.

'And this is the story of my brother. Next thing we hear, he is in London, a refugee. Refugee from what? Gossip.'

So that was it. All those years living behind closed doors, the timidity, the obedience, and the terror that Sándor formed in my father's mind: not only that he was a gangster, a slum landlord, a liver off immoral earnings, but that he knew about the worm at the heart of the marriage, the little lie that it was based on.

'But he was right, wasn't he?' I said, thinking of all I knew about what had already started in Europe and what was not to get any better, but worse.

'About what?'

'Leaving Hungary. Getting out when he did.'

'Right, but for the wrong reasons. I still can't give him the satisfaction.'

'Because if you had left at the same time, things would have turned out differently for you.'

'How do you know how things would have turned out?'

'I mean, the war. You would not have been in Hungary during the war.'

'True.'

While I was transcribing the morning's tapes, seated at the table overlooking the street, Sándor was in the bedroom, spending a long time getting changed. I heard taps running, the slapping of his face, and the whiff of a strong eau de Cologne filled the flat. When he emerged, he was no longer in his zip-up cardigan but a blue suit, not unlike the mohair one he had worn on that visit to our flat long ago, with two-tone matching leather shoes, in blue and black.

'You're all dolled up,' I said. I preferred him like this, in full colour, rather than the monochrome man in the mac. He was born to a jazzy tie and spats.

'Of course. Today is the day that Eunice and I go dancing.'

'Ballroom dancing? Foxtrots and things?'

'Yes, and also tango. We take lessons. These shoes, these are special for tango. You have to buy them at a particular place, a shop on Shaftesbury Avenue. You can't wear any old shoes, it's out of the question.'

'What happened with that boy's window?' I said, as we got down to the hall.

'What boy?'

'Claude, the one who lives there.'

'Why do you care about his window?'

'Under the law—'

'What is it with you? I try to explain, you never understand. It goes in – what's the expression, one eye out the other.'

'Ear,' said Eunice, who was waiting in the hall. She was fabulously turned out, in a short beige satin dress that came to just above her knees, with those excellent legs brown and shapely in fine sheer nylons. Mine were like milk bottles.

'This girl,' Sándor says, 'has led a very sheltered life, not like us, eh? She wants me to fix a window that a boy broke himself.'

'It was already cracked,' I said.

'What do you know about it?'

'He showed me.'

'You have been in there, with that lout?'

'Yes, why not?'

'Some people don't know who their friends are,' Eunice said, with a knowing expression.

How could I have known that Eunice did not like or trust me, though we had barely met? She was madly in love with Sándor, he was the love of her life, this wildly unlikely combination of the Budapest shark and the black girl from Tiger Bay, with the Welsh accent; the immensely dignified, terrifyingly correct woman with her intense dedication to grooming – the hair, the fingernails, the make-up, the eyebrows; the sharp gaze that noticed a loose thread or a hanging button or a grease stain; the ramrod back (formed in early lessons at Miss Halliburton's School of Deportment in Stockwell, for which she had saved every penny from her wages).

Over the course of many years she had worked her way up from Saturday girl to an extraordinarily trusted position as manageress of the Seymour Street dress shop behind Marble Arch, whose clientele were drawn from the mansion blocks off Marylebone High Street, in fact the ladies of Benson Court, among others – a shop which had opened in the early 1950s when clothes came off the ration and West End women click-clacked on high heels, swishing their ballerina-length full skirts, Yardley-scented, fuchsia-lipped.

Sándor took her to the finest places, where a waiter in a black coat wheeled round a dessert trolley and she picked from all its numerous temptations a little coffee mousse and ate it with a silver spoon. He bought her trinkets, an Omega watch, a Colibri lighter in its own velvet pouch. He treated her like a queen.

And when, the first time she saw him naked, she touched in pity the places on his back that still gave him pain, the marks of the whip. '*Oh, Sándor*,' she said, '*you and me were slaves in the land of Egypt*.'

Then I appeared. The deceitful niece who was spying on her uncle for reasons neither of them had fathomed yet, and with whom she sometimes thought, after what Sándor told her of our sessions, that he was falling in love. *Why*? She did not at first understand, until one night when he moaned in his sleep and wept, and she saw the tears on his face as he was sleeping and realised that it was all because he was a man without a child, who knew that one day he would be nothing but bones in a box and nothing going forward into the future, except me, my memories of him. I was danger. I had the power to hurt him. She knew all about that.

'But she's not had our experiences,' Sándor went on. 'She has led a sheltered life at the university, with books, talking about things you know the way the thinkers do. She doesn't know. How could she know?'

'What people know is what they know,' Eunice said, looking at my stained blue silk dress and my denim jacket.

'Say,' said Sándor, 'maybe she should come with us.'

'To dancing?' Eunice said, opening her eyes wide, so that the whites encircled the irises altogether.

'Yes, why not?'

Have you ever seen a cat swish its tail?

'She can't go dressed like that. It's out of the question, she'll make a show of you.'

'No, that's true. We can get her something in your shop.'

'I can't afford to buy dresses,' I said, in a panic.

'Don't worry, I pay,' Sándor said. 'Come, Miranda, come and see life. Which you tell me you don't know about.'

'And we, dear, know too much,' Eunice said, linking her arm through his, and looking at me with the Persian cat face.

'Something nice for a young girl,' Sándor said, looking round. 'Expense no object. Eunice, it's up to you.'

It was the first time I went to the shop on Seymour Street, a shop I had passed without paying any attention, on my way to some more important destination, without looking, and without seeing the parade of rich women who passed in and out through its wrought iron door.

Eunice in her element.

'This is lovely for her,' she said, her fingers expertly running through the rails and coming out, lightning quick, with a green silk dress. 'It will match her eyes,' she said. 'And it has a nice shimmer. Not too ostentatious.'

'Beautiful,' Sándor said, 'try it on, go ahead.'

'What about shoes?' Eunice said, next. 'You can't wear those plimsolls. Have you got anything at home?'

Under the bed, still in their box, was the pair of red snakeskin platform-soled shoes that I had worn only once, the night Alexander died. I could not forget how after we had made love he went on looking at them while we were dressing to get ready to go down to dinner and he said, 'Get more shoes like that.'

Sometimes at night, after my parents had gone to bed, alone in my room in my nightdress, I put them on, and looked at them, and all sorts of weird ideas came into my mind, memories, thoughts, feelings, that I had no words for. But they gave me a perverse comfort, this bright emblem of our little marriage, this exquisite point, dancing in the darkness above his grave.

'I do have some,' I said. 'I could go home and get them, I don't live far from here.'

'We'll wait,' said my uncle and it was only as I was walking down the street that I thought that I should not have told him my whereabouts in case he put two and two together and started to think I might be Vivien, his niece. And I was so green that I never thought that it was absurd to think that a man like Sándor Kovacs would buy a young girl an expensive dress unless he had some reason.

We weren't going far, just three stops on the tube, but my uncle had a phobia about the underground. It was not just the prison years in an enclosed space, and not even a morbid terror of tunnels. A narrow earthen passage somewhere in the Ukraine, he wasn't sure exactly where, had fallen in on him some time in 1942. For a several hours he was buried alive and this was not the worst thing that happened to him during the war, but it was a time that he relived repeatedly in nightmares, whereas the other experiences had passed from raw shock to a sealed metal box inside his heavy chest, where they stayed, undisturbed.

No, what bothered him was something more practical: the fear of falling. That in the moment he stepped on to the moving stair which took you down into the tunnels, as his right foot stepped forwards and his left foot followed, and his right hand grabbed for the moving rail, his eyes looking downwards – all these actions together, if not scrupulously coordinated with split second timing, which he didn't feel capable of, especially with the clouded vision, would cause him to lose his balance and plunge down to his death. It was a prison legacy: fear of the iron steps.

'He can't do it any more,' Eunice whispered. 'I've tried to help him, but he panics. He buys his ticket, then he has to throw it away. As soon as he starts looking down, he gets the sweats.' So we took a taxi, a black London cab, in which I had only ridden on one previous occasion in my life, when my parents and I set off for Paddington station for Hereford and my wedding, my father's hands shaking as he handed the driver two pound notes.

I sat on the tip-up seat, with Sándor and Eunice hand in hand together opposite me, the spun nest of blue-black hair and my uncle's heavy shoulders in his best suit.

We were going to a place I knew nothing about, a large room above a shop selling ironmongery in a street off Sussex Gardens, near Paddington station. You rang a bell in a side door and an invisible hand admitted you. People were arriving, some of them holding their dance shoes in paper bags, others already dancing as they skittered up the street, on their toes.

'Look at those little beauties,' my uncle said admiringly, as a pair of young black girls rushed past up the stairs with hair haloes round their heads like the saints in the old pictures.

But Eunice dug her silver nails into his arm, to remind him that a woman her age doesn't like too much attention being paid to the young things coming up.

'Help me, Miranda,' my uncle said, laughing. 'Speak up in my defence. You know how it was for me. Every time I see these girls I feel like I'm a new man. I remember when I first arrived in London from Budapest and saw these little queens show off their goose-bump skin and they smiled their big smiles, and scream and jump around like crazy beans. I remember thinking, *now* I'm in a city.'

Eunice snarled.

'Darling, you think they look at me? Not a chance. Anyway what do I want with them when I have you, my dearest? It's just to look, a man can look, can't he?' He winked at me.

The silver talons dug more sharply into his arm, but he just turned to her, laughed, planted a kiss on her cheek.

We climbed the cobwebbed and dusty stairs, the air smelling close and warm, of deodorants and powerful cheap scent. I saw my uncle suddenly in his element, dressed in his gangster's suit, walking up the steps of a tenement, his meaty hands clenching in his pockets, his fingers longing to fiddle with cash, notes, loose change rattling in his palm, and so we ascended, him panting, clutching Eunice as though she was a stick or a cane.

The sounds of people and music were rushing towards us and we entered a room where dapper men in suits and more two-tone shoes, and women little and – sixteen-stone ladies balanced on fat feet plunged into high heels, and brown twigs with no hips to speak of – were smoking, talking, drinking cups of tea from a metal urn poured into paper cups, holding them gingerly with their fingers. An uproar, and in the background, still turned low, the orchestra of Victor Sylvester, playing 'Hernando's Hideaway' on a stereo with large box speakers.

A woman passed in an electric blue sequined gown and matching shoes whose sequins had been stuck on the white silk with glue and they fell away from her as she walked, leaving a trail like blue dandruff. 'Look,' Eunice said to my uncle, giggling, 'she needs a broom tied to her bottom to sweep them up.'

'Oh, she don't care,' said Sándor, 'she thinks she is the belle of the ball and why not? Just wait a minute, Miranda, we'll find a partner for you when one of the ladies wants to sit it out.'

'Our tune,' Eunice said, as another record went on. The volume was turned up and the dancers began to take the floor.

If I had a golden umbrella,
With the sunshine on the inside
And the rain on the outside

'A golden umbrella,' said Sándor to me: '*this* I have been looking for all my life. And now I got it.'

My uncle's golden umbrella was a room full of sweat, perfume, hair oil, laughter, gold teeth, Jamaica patties on plates, the tea urn, bottles of rum smuggled from the islands, folding chairs against the walls, the wooden floors, the yellow velvet curtains drawn against the afternoon light, the big gramophone, the piles of records, her cheek against his, his heart beating in his chest like a metronome, his hand on her smooth satin behind, her arms resting lightly on his, his old-fashioned bow when the dance ended, his Hungarian courtesy.

All I could do was watch, and then even watching was not enough for him because he said, 'I want you to dance.' But I couldn't dance. 'You never took lessons?' he said.

'No.'

'Your parents didn't insist?'

'It never entered their heads.'

'What a pity, what a shame.'

'It's too formal for me. I just like to groove along to my own thing.'

'Your own thing? Listen, miss. That is not dancing, it's showing off.'

'Jim will teach her,' Eunice said, 'Jim can dance with anyone.'

They called over a small, dapper man in black patent shoes and a suit with a wide chalk stripe.

'Jim,' Eunice said. 'How is life treating you? Easy, I hope?'

'Not so bad, yet not so good,' he said.

'How's business?' Sándor said.

He was a slow individual, not stupid, but in his speech, which was at variance with his flashing patent shoes, so it took him a while to formulate an answer.

'The customers are no good,' he said, finally.

'What's the matter with them?' Eunice asked.

But he had nothing further to add. He sighed, and tapped his shiny feet to the music.

'I expect he means they steal,' Eunice said in a whisper.

'They just started now, all of a sudden?'

She shrugged.

'Jim,' Sándor said, turning to him, 'do you have a problem I can help you with? The office is open.' He laughed, but Jim just stood there, his mouth shut.

'I'll get it out of him,' Eunice said. 'Between me and Jim there's no secrets. Never has been.'

'Listen,' Sándor said, 'this is my – my secretary, Miranda. A very, very clever girl and the two of you have something in common.'

'What's that?' I asked.

'Reading.'

'What do you read, Jim?' I said sceptically.

'He reads the papers,' Eunice said, 'he has a newsagent shop.'

'Oh, I see.'

'She reads *books*.'

'Well, they're all print,' Sándor said. 'Words, same thing. But can you teach her to dance, that's the question?'

Jim looked at me. 'I'll give it a go,' he said.

'They're starting up with the tango,' said Eunice. 'That's hard, maybe she should sit this one out.'

'No, I'll show her,' Jim said.

A man with short legs and a long trunk, wearing purple trousers and carrying a double-sided crocodile handbag over his shoulder, raised his hands. Everyone broke apart from their partners and formed a line.

'Who is he?' I whispered.

'It's Fabian,' said Eunice. 'Our teacher. He's all the way from Argentina.'

'What's with the handbag?' I asked, and she giggled.

'No, no, you mustn't mention that. It's not what you think though, he isn't one of them.'

He reached forward and picked one of the women to instruct, a lanky girl with a morose horse face.

'Watch what we do. Ladies, I want you to pay special attention, what I'm saying is for your benefit.' We all pushed forward to take a good look. The horse-faced girl looked terrified.

'I don't want you to go forward when I am trying to lead you. I am leading, I will control you,' he said to her, turning to us, with each sentence. 'Don't be so analytical, just concentrate on taking big steps. All ways of thinking pale into insignificance if you just take big steps and leave the thinking to me. When you dance you embark on an adventure, you cannot predict what will happen to you, or where you will be taken. And finally, I want to remind everyone here of something: it is not necessarily the best-looking girl who looks best when she dances the tango. Do you understand? Do you get it? It is the girl who agrees to follow, to be led.'

The horse girl smirked. Already she was prettier, we could all see that.

'OK,' he said. 'Has everyone understood? I want you to find a partner and make a start.'

Jim stepped forward and took me in his arms. He was not much taller than me, and smelt of rum and aftershave. 'You just follow what I do,' he said. 'It's easy. OK?'

We began to move. 'Follow,' he said. '*Follow.*'

And to my surprise, I could do it.

'Look,' Sándor shouted to Eunice as we passed them, sitting down on one of the wooden benches, Eunice fanning herself with a small tortoiseshell fan she'd taken from her handbag. 'See, this one she does fine. I told you.'

Eunice tossed her head. 'Yes, Jake the Fake,' she said. 'A good effort.'

Fabian walked round looking at people's shoulders and feet. He pointed at me.

'See this girl? This is a girl who knows what to wear for tango. These shoes will give her the ability to dance, even if she has no natural aptitude.'

Everyone was looking at us. The crowd of faces were smiling at me, the young white girl in the crazy high red lizard shoes and the shimmering dress from Eunice's shop and her short partner, eye to eye.

Jim held me tight, he took good care of me. I felt alive again, that I was not a person who only existed within the pages of a book, a papery individual. Not happy, for the music was very dark, but it gave the darkness of my own life, the sadness, the physical ache – its real meaning. We are born to suffer, we can't avoid pain. All we can do is enter it, and turn it against itself. And that's what tango does.

'Smile,' Fabian ordered. 'Show some teeth.'

'By the way, what was Jim's problem?' Sándor said to Eunice, as we stood on the street waiting for a taxi. 'Did you find out anything?'

'Oh, poor Jim. It's skinheads. They have started coming into his shop every day and throwing things around.'

'What are skinheads?'

'Bad boys.'

'Why do they throw things around in his shop?'

'Because they don't like the coloured people.'

'I know the type from back home, their heads are full of poisonous substances. Destroyed. What can we do for him?'

'He needs a security guard, someone who will stand at the door and keep those bad boys out.'

'Protection. Easy. I'll call Mickey.'

'I don't like Mickey. Keep him out of it.'

'How can you dislike that boy? He's harmless, and my oldest friend here.'

'He drags you down, Sándor, to his level. You could have been an important businessman without him, and respectable.'

'Oh, Eunice, you don't know about business. Come here, give me a kiss.'

I watched them. I saw her laugh, and turn her face to him, and the unspeakable tenderness with which he touched her lips. I don't know how long we'd been there, my feet in my red lizard shoes were bloody, a ruby liquid seeped through on to my toe-nails and outlined them in red. The clouds were a painted rag in the sky over Paddington and the pale outline of the rising moon was visible between the buildings. We were a little past the longest day.

'That's a lovely dress,' my mother said, when I came home. 'Where do you get that dress?'

'I bought it from a stall on Portobello Road market.'

'No, no, this is a new dress.'

'It isn't.'

'It looks like no one ever wore it before.'

'Maybe they bought it and didn't like it. I don't know.'

I was being blocked in the hall, in front of my bedroom; her back was to the door. She stood for a moment, then said something to herself in Hungarian, which she rarely did, a fragment of a thought, her eyes distrustful, then she let me pass.

'I don't want you to be unhappy,' she said. 'Not my daughter.'

'Well, I *have* been unhappy.'

'I know that.'

'So can't you just leave me alone?'

'Did your employer give you this dress?'

'Yes,' I said. 'That's what happened.'

'What does he want from you?'

'Nothing. He's just rich.'

'Don't let him take advantage of you. I don't think a romantic affair with an older man is good for you at all. Your heart needs its rest.'

Sometimes I came across her sitting alone in the kitchen, thoughtfully drinking a cup of strong, scalding hot coffee, a dribble of it on her chin. Her eyes were focused on a fixed point on the wall, as if she were trying by some means of teleportation to budge it. But when she heard me in the doorway she put her hand up to her hair and ran her fingers through it. It was heavy, coarse and dry, like mine. Then she stood and moved to the sink to rinse out her cup, wiped it with a tea towel and put it away in the cupboard, as if it were evidence of something.

I didn't understand her then, I don't think I do so any better now, years after her death. I asked her once, 'Why did you marry Daddy?' And inexplicably, she said, 'He used to sing me American songs.' 'What songs?' 'From the films.' 'I don't believe it.' 'Well, yes, I know, but he was different in those days.'

If I regret how many lies I told her, it has to be remembered that her form of lying was silence, secrecy. She hid behind what she pretended was her poor mastery of the English language. It's true she wasn't very expressive, but her hands were full of subtlety, and she rarely used them to touch another person. She was tactile, but just for objects.

'Can I get into my room now?' I said.

'Of course. When have I ever been able to stop you doing anything you set your heart on?' And she turned away, and watched me enter, and I heard her still standing there, breathing, on the other side of the door.

'Still I don't have a cream cake for you,' Uncle Sándor said, when I arrived next morning. 'Tomorrow, definite. I get a chocolate gâteau, wait and see. You'll be amazed.'

Did I enjoy the dancing? I told him I did. And would I like to come again, next week? Yes, perhaps. The afternoon and early evening in the room in Paddington was the most untroubled time I had spent since Alexander died, and I loved the new dress. Sometimes you put a dress on and it becomes you, it is your flesh and blood and that is what had happened to this one, instead of my body rejecting it.

'We have to find you a handsome young partner,' he said. 'Jim is only a short-term arrangement.'

We spent the morning on the last moments of my uncle's carefree life as a pimp in Budapest, where he was popular, successful with women, and able to find ways and means of supporting his parents, my grandparents. I enjoyed listening to someone who was voluble, who didn't excrete small constipated pieces of information, under great pressure. Out it came, there was no stopping him, he was a man who loved to talk. I asked him about my grandmother, and he described a hard-working soft motherly woman, practical and good with her hands, but also somewhat star-struck, who adored the cinema on the rare occasions when she had an opportunity to go (perhaps my father used to accompany her and there he learned his American songs); she would collect pictures of Hungarian film stars from magazines and paste them in an album. My grandfather had become too cerebral for her, and with the freedom of a city she had stopped being a rural person,: she was now at the centre of the modern age. I asked him how old she was, around this time, and he said that she was born in 1896 so she was in her early forties and still strong, ebullient, but deferring to men in most matters. And since his father was lost in his comparative theology books, this meant that it was Sándor who was the head of the household.

She had a music box, he remembered, which she bought not long after they arrived in Budapest, at a shop on Rákószi út, and when you lifted the lid a lady doll and a gentleman doll popped up and danced to the waltz of the city, the famous tune 'The Blue Danube'. They only opened it on Sunday mornings, he said, and they all sat there, him, my grandparents and my father, and sometimes my mother was there too, once they were engaged. What happened to the music box? I asked. But he didn't know. It wasn't there when he came back at the end of the war, perhaps someone stole it.

We were now drawing closer to episodes in his life that would cause him immense pain to remember. During his trial, when my parents tried to send me out of the room when the news came on, there were oblique references to his wartime experiences. It was conceded that, as a refugee, he had 'had a bad war' in the words of the reporter, which I didn't understand, for surely all war was terrible and terrifying – blood, death, torture, blitz, camps. But if you watched the films they made, *The Great Escape*, *The Bridge on the River Kwai*, *Ice Cold in Alex*, it seemed it was possible for war to be a chance for heroism and medal winning.

'It's true not nice things happened to him,' my father said. 'Still, they could have made him a better person, and they didn't. He never changed.'

My mother said nothing. It was my father who kept returning to him, as a dog snuffles in the garden, looking for a mouldy old buried bone.

That morning I heard of my uncle's conquests, his many girlfriends, his business deals, his accumulation of money in the bank, his reputation in the coffee houses of the city, and then his call-up papers for labour service, in what was known as a supply unit. It was the army, he said, but an army where a soldier wears a yellow badge and doesn't have a gun.

'But we'll talk about that tomorrow,' he said. 'Today is enough. By the way, the workmen are coming this afternoon to fix that boy's window. Satisfied now?'

I sat at the table and transcribed my morning's work, while

Sándor went into the bedroom and spoke on the phone for a long time to someone he evidently knew very well and to whom he was an indulgent father, but still the boss, the one in charge, who gave instructions, but did not receive them.

'In the middle of the night is best,' he said. 'And no monkey business, just in, and then out. You understand?'

Two small piles of paper were building up, the original and the carbon. 'How many pages do we have?' he asked. I checked. Forty-six.

'Good, and we're not even at the beginning of the beginning,' he said. 'This is going to be some book.'

He gave me my £8 in an envelope. 'Now I'm going to Soho, to Maison Bertaux, where they do a strawberry gâteau like you never seen. You know that place?'

'Is that the one on Greek Street?'

'Exactly.'

'I had a chocolate éclair from there once, it was scrumptious.'

'Well, this will be even better. You wait and see. Don't eat too much breakfast tomorrow.'

'OK.'

Down in the hall, Claude was letting himself in at the front door. He was wearing a guard's uniform and a peaked hat, which cast a partial shadow over his upper face. The jacket was too big for him, it swamped his shoulders, as if it was a child's garment that a parent buys confident he will 'grow into it'. I felt sorry for him that his job should force him to wear clothes of such ugliness.

'You again,' I said. 'Aren't you supposed to be at work?'

'I am, I'm on a course but we're on a wildcat strike so I came home.'

'How can you be on strike? You haven't started yet.'

'Well, it's the union, that's what they said. Anyway, I've got to go and buy a bicycle.'

'Why?'

'To get to work. I'm going to be on the Northern line and the depot where we start is at Golders Green.'

'So why can't you get the tube?'

'Are you thick?' It was true, I had no practical intelligence, my head was full of ideas and feelings. He was standing there laughing at me, under his peaked cap. His eyes were sea blue, as Alexander's had been, but not looking up, sightlessly, trying to bore through the lid of a mahogany box.

'That jacket looks itchy.'

'It is, I'm fucking dying to get it off.'

A workman came up the steps, holding a toolbox and a pane of glass and asked for flat five.

I was very surprised to find that I had some influence with my uncle, for the discussion of the window had been, on my part, more of an abstraction, in order to determine whether or not he was as bad a man as the papers made out. I didn't believe that I had won the argument about the rights and wrongs of fixing broken windows, but thought that this was some kind of personal gift, like the cream cakes and the tango dancing dress – his helpless, eager desire to please.

But Claude, looking at me as the glazier manoeuvred the pane into the tiny room, said, 'You've got him twisted round your little finger, haven't you?'

'There's hardly any room to swing a kitty-cat in here,' the glazier said. 'Call this a flat?'

'Pitiful, isn't it. Do you want to go out in the garden for a bit, Miranda? It's not bad out.'

The afternoons were long, after my sessions with my uncle. I would see a film, or walk in Hyde Park, or come home, shut the door of my bedroom and read.

'How do you get there?'

'There's a door, but he always keeps it locked, I just go out the window and jump.'

The glazier had removed the broken pane and was preparing the putty. 'Look, it's just a little drop,' he said. 'I'll go first then I'll catch you, but I'm going to get changed first.'

He was looking at me all the time he was pulling his arms out of the guard's jacket and replacing it with the leather one which hung on a hook behind the door. Looking as the white T-shirt underneath rode up above the belt of his serge trousers and I saw his stomach, pale, the dark hairs rising up from below, the shadows the abdominal muscles cast across his skin. Looking as he pulled the trousers down, stepped out of them and put on his drainpipe jeans. Looking to see if I was looking at the white underpants. I turned my head away, ashamed.

'Are you coming or what?' he said, half smiling with that sultry mouth, the little teeth biting the lower lip, reddening it. 'Make your mind up. I'm going down anyway.'

I watched him crouch on the window ledge on his haunches, then jump, lightly like a cat, landing on all fours, stand up again and raise his arms.

'Don't worry,' he shouted back up at me. 'I'm good at catching.'

I felt the metallic excitement in my mouth of the unknown outcome. To turn back into the room, walk across the park, sit down on a bench, watch the water birds, then home to Benson Court, or raise myself on to the window ledge, and let myself fall.

'Are you going to be there all day? Are you coming down or what?'

'I don't know, I—'

And then I jumped. I fell down into his arms and they held me, they felt thin and hard, and now my face was against his skin that smelt of lemons mixed with an arousing odour of leather and warm zips. I was held. Then he released me.

Down in the garden, the grass reached my knees, thistles

reared up with jagged leaves and poisonous hairy stems, great tufts of coarse dock grew next to them. The dandelions were in various stages of their development, the sturdy, sunny flowers, then the ghostly clocks. In balder patches, buttercups and daisies struggled towards the sun. Old rose bushes were covered in last winter's brown hips, and blasted red roses lay in tatters on the branches. Ivy was everywhere, and saplings growing up through the branches of a laburnum bush. Lines of mint sent out roots under the ground to colonise and strangle the lavender, which was jutting up its purple spikes. A tabby cat sat on the fence, and under the derelict trees lay the skeletons of baby birds, the tragic record of their first failed flight.

I looked up at the house, to the many floors and the partitioned windows. Sándor's was at the front, he couldn't see me down here. I didn't want him to see me. I didn't wish to be observed by him. Not with this boy.

It had rained early that morning, I'd heard the patter of the drops on my own window pane and turned over restlessly in my sleep. The damp grass had gone to seed and had shot up long pale green curled envelopes you pulled apart with your fingers to examine the tiny, hairy dots inside. It was still too wet to sit but Claude took off his leather jacket and laid it out for me to lie on.

'This is nice,' he said. 'We haven't got a garden at home, just a yard where we keep the bins. What about you?'

There was the communal garden behind Benson Court. Gilbert sometimes took a drink out there in the early evening and fell asleep over a book, and a few ambitious remarks had spread around the building about holding a party to mark the Queen's jubilee, perhaps with a marquee, but nothing had come of it, and we watched the whole thing on TV.

'Yes, we've got a garden.'

'Has it got flowerbeds?'

'It does.'

'What's in them?'

'Just flowers.' I didn't really know their names, apart from the obvious things like roses. When I was little, my mother came home one day with a packet of mustard and cress seeds and together we went out into the garden and I pressed them into the soil with my fingers. We waited for rain and then they came up. We cut the shoots and put them into egg sandwiches which I took to school. But then we tried hollyhock seeds and they failed, the shoots were sickly and died. I kept caterpillars in a pencil box but the look of them squirming and turning themselves into chrysalises made me sick. Then I learned to read, and the garden became the site of imaginary gymkhanas, and invented horses with elaborate names from my child's book of Greek myths.

I lay back in the grass. The triangular section of window pane was near my head like a garden mirror that had formed organically out of the soil, pushing its way to the surface. A few thin cirrus clouds moved quickly above me in the upper atmosphere, heading east towards the coast, running towards the Thames estuary and out to sea. Above the traffic, closer, more piercing and insistent, bird song. I think it might have been a thrush.

'This is nice,' Claude said. 'I like it out here. The yard at our house stank of empty dog-food tins. Me – I can't stand dogs.'

'Me neither.' Alexander's house had smelt of them; it sickened me. 'Where do you come from?' I asked him.

'Ever heard of the Isle of Sheppey?'

'No. Where is it?'

'It's way out east, along the river, in the estuary. It's not even far but no one knows about it, no one ever comes there, no visitors, no strangers. Apart from my mum and dad, they were immigrants to Sheppey. Which is good because then at least you know if there's a road in, there's got to be one out again. Unless you need a passport or something and the police turn you back when you try and get into Kent.' The short laugh, without humour, like a hated dog's bark.

The more he talked about Sheppey, the more I felt I'd never heard of a more dismal place in my life. It was just marshes and prisons and docks and dog shit and wind and flatness. If you shouted, he said, the sound would carry for miles out to sea, but no one ever shouted unless they were scrapping in the street. The population was too depressed for raised voices.

His father came over from Ireland after the war and his mother was from a family of Kent tinkers who settled on the island to sharpen knives and make eiderdowns out of the feathers of geese and ducks, and sometimes chickens which they stole from farms and ponds. She was a bathing beauty for a season, queen of Herne Bay, 1951, but never got any further in the contests. When they were hard up for ready cash, she'd go out with her friend and sell white heather, casting a gypsy spell on it for good luck and they came back laughing, jiggling change in the pockets of their cotton dresses.

A childhood of church Sundays, pushed up the street to Mass by his father's hand in the small of his back. His mother never went, she worshipped other gods with names no one recognised, in a language no one else spoke. The true Romany comes from India, he said, but he didn't know what his mum was. She liked secrets. Still, she was a good mother to him, he missed her a lot.

'What does your dad do?'

'He works on the fruit docks but I think he'll be made full-time redundant soon. That's why they sent me off the island to get a job.'

That was the story, in full. It only took a few minutes and I had a sudden perturbing sense of someone without a history, as I understood it; I mean thick history, the story of how lives get caught up in other people's grander plans. A week ago, I too was a person without a history, but my uncle had changed all that.

'So do you want to go to a party later?'

'Me? Go to a party with you?' I was startled by this proposition. He was just a boy on the ground floor, a victim of my uncle's shysterish tendencies: a leather jacket and a tank of technicolour fish. When he smiled, two vertical lines appeared at the side of his mouth, but he didn't smile much, was just prone to those sudden, abrupt bursts of laughter.

'Yeah, why not? Do you think I'm too common to be seen with you?'

'What kind of party?'

'Too early to tell.'

It started to rain again. A few drops on my face, then the bushes began to bend their leaves under the weight of the drops. The flowers turned their heads upwards to the sky, to drink. I shivered, then sneezed with a force that shook my bones and by this, and suddenly – with a sensation that smacks you on the back of the head like a wakening blow – I knew that I was alive, a person, not a wraith.

'We have to go in,' I said. 'How do we get back?'

'I climb up the drainpipe.'

'I can't do that.'

'Then there's the other way. Come on.'

We stood up and he pulled aside a broken plank in the fence. We pushed our way through into the next garden, which was as overgrown as this one, and across it to another tumbledown fence, until we had passed four houses and arrived at an alley, which led on to the street and back to the front door of Sándor's house.

'So are you going to come tonight or what?' he said, as I turned to walk to the tube station.

'No, I . . .' and then I sneezed again, four quick times, and this involuntary force which took hold of me reminded me yet again that I was not dead but alive. But alive to what end, what purpose? To live? 'Maybe,' I said.

'Good. Eleven o'clock, under the arches at Hungerford bridge, I'll see you there.'

'Don't count on it.'

He gave me a quick, light kiss on the cheek, then jumped up three steps together and into the house.

It was very hard in those days to stay up all night in London, you had to know where to look to find the young vampires, but the people who drove the trains and blew the whistles and closed and opened the doors saw the city differently from those of us who lived above ground. They were always in motion and lacked our mental limitations.

I was apprehensive. I didn't know how to behave or dress. You could not grow up here London without understanding that there was a secret city, a freaky underground that came out like glow-worms after dark, the muscle men, the lipsticked drag boys, the girls with green hair, dyed-blond platinum queens, gold-painted *things* of no obvious sex.

Looking back over that summer, I remember almost everything I wore. I can recount my whole wardrobe, but this night is a blank. I changed and changed and changed until the bed was piled with discarded clothes, mountains of silks, crêpes, velvets, belts, scarves, high-heeled shoes, jeans, bell-bottom trousers, bras and knickers. Deep uncertainty about what to put on has wiped clean the memory's slate and what the final choice was.

Which is strange, because I recall everything else, vividly. I revisit it often when I have trouble sleeping.

At Hungerford bridge, under the arches, where the down-and-outs and alkies lived, fires had been started from ignitable rubbish and the flames illuminated the dripping walls. Only a foot or two inside, the stench of urine smacked your lungs.

And I was hammered too by the sight of him, in his leather jacket, leaning against a wall, marred only by the way his legs bowed backwards in his drainpipe jeans, as if they wanted to retreat while his body was advancing. His legs denied him gracefulness. But other than that, he could have been a model for a Da Vinci head, with hooded eyes, sharp nose and that perfect, sultry mouth.

'Hope you've got your sea legs,' he said, 'we're going on the river.'

'You never said anything about a boat.'

'I didn't know, you never know until the last minute. Then you have to ring up and they tell you. That's how it works, didn't I say?'

But he had said almost nothing. He was a master of knowing evasion.

The vessel we boarded was a dredger. The sound of the machinery churned beneath us as we pushed off from the Embankment, evacuating the river silt. 'Are we allowed to be on here?' I said.

'Not really.'

It was a strange kind of party. There was no music, no drinks, just a restless anarchy on board, a depraved beauty. A girl had painted her lips silver and bared her breasts in the night air, the nipples swollen and purple as grapes. A boy had tied his legs together with chains and padlocks, a punk Houdini. A lot of drugs were available, mainly pills. 'This one's nice,' Claude said, sorting them in the palm of his hand. 'That one you can fly on, but I'm scared of flying. This is the one you want, to keep you up.'

I had only smoked a few joints, at university. The pills made me nervous, with their many chemical colours. I would have preferred a glass of wine but there was no wine, just these alien characters standing on the rusty deck, the sky black, the moon coming and going in the gaps between the clouds.

'Take it,' Claude said. 'Go on.'

I shook my head.

'I'm not carrying you home through the streets because you're half asleep.'

'I don't want to stay up all night. I never agreed, I didn't—'

'Take it,' he said, tenderly, and put his fingers to my lips and parted them. 'You've got really pretty teeth, all white and pearly and straight. Open wide, go on. Go on.' My tongue flicked out and licked his finger. It could not help itself. He smiled. 'That's nice.' He laid the pill on my tongue and it went down easy.

I felt I had been drugged, that even before I took the tablet from him I was out of my mind. It was the night, and the river and the smell of his skin. I was turned on by him. It was bizarre, it was crude, it was so incredibly surprising.

The drug was his masculinity, his poise and certainty, his *sexual* certainty and that there was nothing to know about him. Sheppey Island, Sheerness. The fruit docks. The mother with her knives and feathers. The photograph on a mantelpiece of the swimsuit, a sash and a crown. The father in the kitchen reading the paper. The pulley and the smell of damp vests drying in the heat of the coal fire. That's all.

The dredger pushed downriver. We were going east, towards Woolwich where they were building the steel barrier against the floodwaters. Beyond were the open waters of the North Sea. Everything was sparkling – the starry sky, the crescent moon like a curved silver knife, the lights on the shore – and I felt a solitary weightlessness, as if I was air or energy. No hunger or thirst. The dredger's progress seemed ponderously slow and the silt of the river churning held back my progress – to run along the Thames, to race on water.

'Look at you,' Claude said.

'What?'

'You're really high.'

'Am I? I feel different. I feel good, really good but my mouth tastes like metal. What are we passing now, can you see, how far are we from the sea, which bridge is this we're going under, I don't recognise it in the dark but I don't know the bridges, I'm not familiar with the other side, the roads are wider, I think and it smells different, but I don't go there, only to the South Bank for films and plays and concerts, but nothing else. I know a girl in Lewisham but I never went to see her, we always met in town and . . .' The ongoing rush of banality from my lips alarmed me. How long could I go on talking like this? I couldn't stop, I said whatever came into my head.

But Claude stood, smoking a roll-up, thin and contained.

'How did you get the job with the old man? Doing his *paper-work*?'

'I met him in the park, when I was walking across to . . . and he was by the lake with water birds, I was sitting on his bench and we got into conversation, he offered me some work and I—'

'He's got that dead white look, hasn't he? The kind you get when you're inside.'

'He goes out, he goes dancing with—'

'You know what I mean.'

I had licked his finger. I had allowed him to drug me. He was on the deck of this iron vessel moving implacably through the waters, under a moon turned milky, standing in his drainpipe jeans and leather jacket, his red canvas boots, his hair standing in spikes, his sultry mouth and little teeth, the blue eyes assessing me. I felt I was being made use of, but for what? What? Everyone was using me: my uncle who was transmitting through me his messages to his brother. But was it not better to be used, than useless?

'I know just to call him Mr K, that's what he told me. Like cornflakes. The *special* Mr K.'

'He's had a complicated life,' I said.

'Haven't we all.'

'How's your life complicated?'

'Nothing's ever what it seems. My old grandma taught me that, before she ran off back to Ireland with my dad's wages and the gold watch my mum won in a raffle.'

We were further east now, past the Greenwich Observatory and its meridian, its Mean. From here, all time was a deviation. Above us lay the Isle of Dogs, which was not a real island, like Sheppey, just a lump of land sticking out like a big thumb pressing down on the river. Then the dredger turned back. The hull pointed west, towards Teddington. The passengers were engaged in ecstatic silent dancing on the deck, silhouetted darkly.

Claude put his arm round me and kissed my hair. I knew it was the start of something I could not resist, did not even want to. I was twenty-four years old, a West End girl, the child of Benson Court and its concealed garden, its wrought-iron lift, its ballerina teetering on points in the middle of the afternoon, its secret drinking, its hidden mistresses, its fears and sorrows behind closed doors. On the river, its banks lightening as the sun lay an inch beneath the horizon of hills, I experienced the strange exhilaration of the sailor who has no home port, only the next landfall, wherever that may be, with all its dangers and possibilities. But the sea itself is home, the unsteady, unstable surface, always moving, drawn back and forth under a gravitational moon.

His hands felt my cold breasts. 'I'll *warm* you,' he said.

*

Dawn behind us. At Southwark Bridge a heavy bundle was being pulled from the river. Every night, Claude said, the river police would set out in their boats to look for suicides and find floating corpses or decaying limbs tangled in the weeds by the pilings. Posters went out across the city and usually they were recognised but sometimes after years in the morgue unclaimed, they were buried in unmarked paupers' graves. A horror came over me, and a sadness that a person could have no connection at all to life, could go missing and not be missed. For the whole heavy weight of history that fell across my family, the Kovacs, meant that we were deeply implicated in the world, even though my father thought he could bar the doors and live anonymously. But if Mrs Prescott had decided to leap from stone balustrades in her cloche hat and submerge her Cupid's bow mouth beneath the waters, who would have reported her absence? The pity of it all struggled inside me, against the amphetamine rush of the pills.

But Claude was still staring at the shape on the deck of the police boat.

'Bodies used to wash up on the beach near us,' he said. 'When we were kids we used to steal their wallets and dry the notes in front of the fire. If there were any notes, if you were lucky. You had to hand the rings and the watches in, cos you couldn't get rid of them, not if you were eight like us. Sometimes the big boys would take them off you, but they only ever gave you a sixpence for them. It wasn't worth the bother. You could always get a note changed, especially a ten bob one, you just said it was for your mum.'

'How horrible.'

'What? That we were little tearaways?'

'No, the dead bodies.'

'They did sometimes stink. The fish eat the eyes, you know, and the testicles because they're soft. They were suicides mainly, or sometimes drowned sailors.'

'That was your childhood? Robbing the pockets of the dead?'

'I never said I didn't have a deprived childhood with no flowerbeds or nothing. Come here, give us another kiss, posh girl.'

It was full daylight. The dredger pulled up at the Embankment and we filed off on to dry land. In the early sun, the young vampires looked weary, their clothes torn and their paint smeared across their faces. It was still too soon for the buses to be running.

We walked miles until we found a night café near a bus depot. The city was locked up tight, nothing was stirring. You could walk down the yellow lines in the middle of the street, you could run and rattle the gates of the tube stations, you could howl like a banshee in the middle of Oxford Circus and no one would hear you. Five a.m. The clocks chime and the bells peal.

The café was full of night-time souls and early risers, people with nowhere to go, and a greasy strain fell over everything. The stools we sat on were revolving faster and faster.

'I'll tell you what you're going to like about me,' he said, fiddling with his little home-made cigarette and drinking sweet tea, and his voice came from far away. 'I'm out of the gate like a greyhound.'

'What do you mean?' I said, and my own voice echoed, tapped inside my head.

He laughed. 'You'll see.'

An hour later, in his room I had the simple, straightforward experience of what had been missing since my husband died. For a few moments I lost consciousness, and came round to find him looking at me, the lips wet, the eyes darkened. There was an inexpressible sense of having committed a sin for which I could not be forgiven, though I didn't believe in sin or guilt. But what had I done, who had I hurt? I liked it. I *loved* it. That's all.

It was at our next session that my uncle told me something which would make a deep impression on me. He said that it was his observation, while a slave labourer, that people can bear much more than animals. A horse, for example, its ribs still covered in flesh, suddenly drops down dead in the middle of the road, while an emaciated man in rags keeps going, struggles on long after his internal organs have been irreparably damaged by starvation. Only the ones who lose their minds are quick to go under, but if you can keep your sanity, then you are capable of extraordinary feats of endurance.

It was also of great interest to him to note that in many cases an individual was exactly the same at the end as he had been at the beginning. Beneath it all, he argued, people are concerned with the same things all their lives: sex, food, power, ideas, if that's their interest. A sourpuss stayed a sourpuss, of course, but there were some whose optimism, humour, their pleasure in fun and their indestructible love of life remained intact all the way.

'What about you?' I asked.

'Yes, I was one of the ones who didn't change. I began as a businessman and that's how I continued.'

It is very strange to realise that when you see those old films on television of the toothbrush moustache dictator ranting and the mass rallies, and the stiff-armed salutes and all the marching up and down, and the well-known flag standing to attention, that famous menace and what it would lead to – all of it was happening while people went on buying shoes and handbags and party dresses and gramophone records and ornaments and choosing a new car or a new wireless set, or just sitting in a café eating cream cakes.

And while they were doing all that, the signs were there, on the streets, such as the sign of the Arrow Cross men, the Hungarian Fascists, which my uncle drew for me on a sheet of paper and which looked like this:

I have to keep remembering that he was only twenty-two in 1938, two years younger than the age I was then, the summer of 1977 when I knew him. Like me, he had a taste for and an interest in flashy unusual clothes; he wanted things that were all the rage and he used to mooch around the shops looking for the latest fashions, would go to the cinema and look carefully at what the film stars were wearing and see if he could find copies. A few months later he would march off to labour service in a suit which would not leave his back for a further four and a half years. During that time, he kept sane by picturing himself lounging on the gilded chairs of the Café Astoria, holding court with his girls, dressed in a fine suit. Whenever he slept and dreamed, that's how he saw himself, not a slave in rags. He thought of spats and tie-pins and cravats and Oxford bags and double-breasted jackets and turn-ups and leather brogues and embroidered braces and opera pumps.

My uncle was drafted into Labour Service Company 110/34, along with his father in 1939. The Jews had been placed into a category called the 'unreliables'; in other words, they were not to be trusted with a gun or even a uniform. They wore their own clothes, with a yellow armband. These labour units were under the auspices of the territorial battalion commands within the Ministry of Defence, and commanded by Hungarian army officers, usually NCOs. It was the luck of the draw, fate if you like, whether you got a decent officer or an anti-Semitic sadist from the Arrow Cross.

For the first two or three years of the war they were operating within the Hungarian borders, armed with shovels and pickaxes, building railways, digging trenches and tank traps, and clearing minefields. Routine work. My grandfather, the hat salesman and self-taught expert in comparative religion, was surprisingly adaptable, having grown up in the countryside, and although my father inherited from him his delicate frame and short sight (my grandmother was fleshier, Uncle Sándor took after her), he was scrappy and could go for long periods with no food; he must have had very stable blood sugar.

My uncle, the pimp and Budapest playboy, already at only twenty-three had acquired the double chin that would create a Hitchcock profile later on in life, which would lead the English papers to ask if he was the face of evil. Fattened on cream cakes and pancakes with cherries in the cafés of Budapest, he felt his heart pounding as soon as he picked up his shovel. Everyone had been told to bring a suitcase; Sándor had packed shirts, ties, jackets and shoes, but confronted on the first day of service with a steep hill in the blazing heat, he dumped them. This select wardrobe was returned to the city and distributed to the Arrow Cross men who wore the clothes in the very cafés my uncle had frequented, so he was there, in a sense, though not in person. And the clothes which he left the house wearing that morning in 1939 were the ones he was wearing when he got back to Budapest in 1945, though they no longer resembled clothes, but a kind of fungus excreted by his skin.

In 1943 at Staryy Oskol, a bombed city in what is now the Russian Federation, they cleared rubble. They marched across it for hours looking for somewhere to be billeted and saw no intact buildings. Their diet was black tea and flour soup, and they slept in the open air, warming their hands on cinders. At Pieti-Lepka, a small village near Veronezh, their legs blistered with frostbite, they wandered across rock-hard frozen snowfields and left behind to die what the Hungarian officers called the 'faulty goods' – the injured.

By now they were starting to go a bit crazy. Deep darkness, dread, fear of death.

'Was it fear that kept you alive?' I asked him.

'Yes, that and business, which we'll come to.'

That year they covered a distance of one thousand kilometres from Male Bikoro to Belograd in thirty days exactly, on a ration of one hundred grams of bread a day and hot water with a few carrots floating in it. They were near the Soviet Occupied zone, there was a possibility of escape to the Allies, but my uncle said that he had been warned not to set any store on Russian hospitality.

All the time, my uncle and grandfather marched together. The older man was mostly silent though on some evenings he would go off in a corner and have exhausting discussions about theology with a rabbi from Debrecen. Sándor helped his father as much as he could, but at Zhitomir they both contracted typhus and were transferred to a quarantine camp at Krasno Ceska. People were demented. A man was screaming that his legs had been cut off at the hip. Another said he had to have an alarm clock, would anyone, he cried piteously, give him an alarm clock, he had to go to meet his fiancée at the railway station and if he fell asleep he might not wake up in time to take the tram to the station, and he would miss her.

My uncle's hallucination was one of the strangest I have ever heard of, a physical hallucination. He thought that his body had somehow been divided in half, and that the lower part was someone else. His face, chest, hands, arms were him, Sándor Kovacs, but his groin, testicles, legs, were those of another man, a stranger. He was trying to run from him, but he had no legs to escape with so he clutched at his thighs with his hands, trying to prise them from his torso. Some time in the night, my grandfather died, but my uncle didn't notice the exact moment; he was busy trying to rid himself of the lower impostor. When he came out of his hallucination, his father was dead.

After the quarantine camp, they were all taken for a bath, the first in over three years, and their clothes, the ones they had left home in, were boiled and ridden of the millions of lice that had taken up residence there.

In clean clothes they felt suddenly reborn. They examined their rags for signs that they had once been human beings. Might this flap be a lapel, and was this an indication of a pocket? A piece of cloth bore faint traces of once having been tweed. This man's trousers had once been exhibited in the window of a fashionable department store in 1937, with a ticket indicating a high price. But though the slaves were clean and dry, they were also starving. They ripped grass from the earth and ate it. Men were writhing and dying in their boiled clothes.

At a place whose name Sándor said he didn't know, some Germans appeared and cut off a block of men and herded them into a building which they then set fire to, and as the screaming slaves ran from it they used them as an exercise in target practice. That was the worst, he said, *that* is what I call a crime, not what they write about today in the newspapers or what I see on television.

Yet amongst all this horror, my uncle maintained that he had been kept alive by trade.

'Yes, business was going on constantly. You see, although often we were starving, there were also times when we weren't. Don't ask me about the logic of it, there wasn't any logic. What was, was. We had rations, and rations had value. Now a man is given a can with something in it. If he is starving his natural inclination is to open the can and devour the contents, that's obvious. Or a cigarette, you smoke it at once, what's the point of saving it? But I could see that the minute I had a ration of some kind, then there was an opportunity for trade, and the essence of trade is profit, this is the capitalist system. So when we came to a village and the officers gave us some supplies, I would find a building and I would open a bazaar and sell the food and the cigarettes to the local peasants. Then, you see, I had cash, real money, and with money I could talk to the officers on a more equal footing.

'Now when they gave us the supplies in the first place, we had to give them a coupon in exchange. We didn't know what these coupons were, they were just worthless pieces of paper on which we signed our names. But you see when these noble Hungarians got back home they took the coupons to our families and said that this paper was a deed we had signed which gave the bearer the right to take over our apartment. And if our families said no, then they threatened them with the police. So we sold our birthright for a mess of pottage just like it says in the Bible.

'But not me, no way. I didn't take the supplies, I took other people's supplies and I sold them and split the profits with them, so there was no coupon with my name on it, and this is why, at the end of the war, my mother still had an apartment. And now do you understand why your ideas about what is decent, and respect, and equality are for babies? A boy like that one downstairs, strong and stupid, is the kind who is most like the animal who suddenly lies down in the shafts of the cart and dies, for no reason, because his strength is exhausted. His strength is all he has. I'm not that type, and I hope you are not either. Nor is Eunice, by the way, but that's her story, not mine. Maybe if you ask her, she'll tell you.'

Years later, I tried to trace the route of my uncle's forced march across eastern Europe, but I was frustrated by the maps. The names Sándor gave me, spelled out at my insistence and carefully transcribed, did not appear in my atlas. Names themselves had been altered, as towns and villages changed hands over the generations, from war to war to war, and after all, my uncle was recording only what he remembered. The slaves asked the townspeople or the villagers where they were, or their officers did, and what they were told was often not what appeared in any cartography. It did not matter to the villagers that a regional governor had decided to rename their hamlet after some hero of the Bolshevik revolution.

Other times, my uncle just got the spelling wrong, or he was guessing or the village had been totally destroyed in the war, or was abandoned and left no trace. But over the course of several days, with visits to the British Library, I was able to piece together the course of a chaotic directionless journey east, from Hungary deep into the Ukraine and Russia, culminating in the town of Berdichev in 1944 where for some reason for which he had no explanation and which he anyway didn't care to investigate, so happy was he to go home, Sándor was demobbed and sent back to Budapest.

'Does your brother know what happened to you in the war?' I asked him. 'Does he know what you've told me?'

'Yes, yes, of course he knows. Everything.'

'What happened to your mother?'

'She survived in Budapest. Whenever there was a round-up, she was always in the wrong place at the wrong time, I mean the right place. All the luck was with her. It was amazing. Hers is a story I never even got to the bottom of while she was alive, but she was like one of those balls you see in that game, pinball, the one the teenagers play in the coffee bars, she pings around the city, yet the levers of fate always catch her before she falls and push her back.'

'You went to live with her when you returned?'

'No, that was too dangerous – for her, I mean. I stayed with my girls. They looked after me, all those beauties.'

'And then the war ended.'

'Yes, it did. It was over.'

'So why did you stay in Budapest when you could have come to England?'

'I know, I know. There were plenty of places I could have gone. The Red Cross came and found me, with a message from Ervin, saying he would sponsor me. I could have gone to Palestine, that was another opportunity, or America. But I wouldn't leave my mother, and she was sure my father would come back if she waited. You see, whatever they say about me, I tried my best to be a good son, and I respected and loved her, even though of course I could have been a better one. Make sure you write that down.'

'But he'd died of typhus!'

'I know. He did, I saw him. Not when he died, but when they buried him in the lime pit.'

'Why did she think he'd return?'

'I told you, a human and an animal are two different things. An animal gives up, a human doesn't.'

'But it was an illusion.'

'Of course, but strange things happen, there are mix-ups, people do come back from the dead, that's what she said. How could I tell her I saw him being shovelled into a mass grave? My own mother.'

'What happened to your grandparents in Mád?'

'Up the chimney, of course, what else?'

'And Berta's family?'

'The same.'

So this was the big silence that had deadened my childhood. I understood a little better. How could any of it be spoken, and to a child? My parents held it all inside them, like their own blood.

'So what did you do next?'

'Back to the old trade. Why give it up now? I should deprive those girls of a living when they saved my life? When they sheltered me?'

'How did that work under communism?'

'Good question. Communism crept up on us when we weren't looking. I didn't notice. Then there it was. But the need for the services I provided doesn't go away under the socialist paradise, whatever the women's libbers say. I kept to my trade, it was just that instead of having my office at a table in the Hotel Astoria, I was assigned a position, a post. I was still in the café, that was the same, except now I was a waiter. The same people came, what was left of them. The same intellectual discussions, the same pastries, all the same old talk, just as it had been before, which reminds me, I'd totally forgotten, I went to Maison Bertaux and I got the cake, you want a slice?'

'No thank you. Why are you smiling?'

'Why not smile? I'm alive, aren't I? They tried to kill me, they failed. Isn't that a good revenge on those demons, those evil spirits?'

You go down into the darkness, you emerge into the light, this is the nature of a subway system, and when you arise, you are in another place. You don't see the transitions. The map turns the city into a grid, a diagram, you don't have any sense of the distance between stops, it's all relative. I travelled to King's Cross, through that dreary interchange, the wait on the platform, the two stops on the yellow Circle line, the walk down Portland Place, turning into our street, up the lift, and putting my key in the lock, until I got inside and my mother was in the kitchen. I said to her, 'Why do we never talk about the war?'

She was straining green beans in a metal colander.

'The war? Why do you raise this now? It was a long time ago.'

'I just want to know why we never discuss it.'

'Well, I told you. The bombing was terrible and the rationing—'

'Not the war here, in London. I mean in Europe.'

'We were not in Europe, we were in England, thank God.'

'But you had relatives there.'

'Yes, I did.'

'What happened to them?'

She shrugged. In the kitchen of the window of the next mansion block, a smartly dressed woman was standing at the sink, filling a kettle.

'She's new,' my mother said. 'What a turnover they have in that place. Must be something wrong with it. Maybe damp, do you think?'

'They're my grandparents.'

'Who? This lady?'

'You know what I'm talking about.'

'What is this interest all of a sudden? You watch a film?'

'I just want to know.'

'What can I say? They all died.'

'And did you have brothers and sisters?'

'My lunch is getting cold, it's already quarter to two and I'm starving. You want something to eat? I'm having this poached egg. Should I make you one?'

'No, I'm not hungry. Why do we never talk?'

'About what?'

'Anything.'

'What do you want to discuss? Name a subject, I'll try, though I didn't have your education, you know that.'

'What happened, for example, to Uncle Sándor during the war?'

'Well, naturally, he had a terrible time, no one denies that.'

'Such as?'

'But it didn't change him for the better. He could have made amends and set out to live a better life, but he chose not to. His decision.'

'I feel like I'm talking to a brick wall.' Nothing had changed and I couldn't make it change. I thought that the revelations of the morning would alter everything but it was all just the same.

'What is it you want to know, Vivien? Why do you bother

with all this old history? What's got into you? You're bored, your head is full of speculations. Maybe it's time to find a nice new boyfriend.'

'Maybe I have one,' I said, out of malice and anger.

'That common boy I saw you with?'

'Which boy?'

'A week or so ago, I saw you on the street with a boy with a jacket made of a leather skin, with all kinds of straps hanging from it.'

'I didn't see you.'

'No? Well I was there, it was not long after lunch. If this is the boyfriend, you want to be careful he doesn't drag you down to his level. This is always a danger when you mix with unsavoury types. I don't understand how you touch him after Alexander.'

'You're such a snob, Mother,' I said, turning away so she would not see my embarrassment.

She picked up the plate and hurled the poached egg and green beans into the bin.

'That's it. I have no appetite now.'

'There's an iron curtain,' I said. 'I'm banging my head against an iron curtain.'

'Good, I hope you don't bang so hard your brains fall out.'

She was at the sink washing the plate.

'Do you want a cup of coffee?' I said.

'Why, do you want to join me?'

'Yes, let's have a cup of coffee together, we hardly ever do that.'

'Lovely. There are some biscuits in the tin, see what you can find. I like the arrowroot at this time, the long fingers.'

I put the biscuits on a plate and we took our coffee into the sitting room. My mother picked up a television magazine and began circling the programmes she and my father planned to watch that evening, her finger hesitating between a quiz show and a play.

'Didn't you want to make friends with other refugees when you arrived?' I asked her.

'Well, we might have done, but your father was a little sensitive.'

'What about?'

'Oh, you know, he doesn't like gossip.'

'And what would people be gossiping about?'

'Vivien, I feel I am in that programme *Perry Mason* and you are the lawyer and I am the accused. What do you call it, cross-examination. I wish you would stop.'

Calmly she deflected all my questions. I couldn't get anything out of her at all, and it wasn't that she knew nothing, because it was she who, around a year later, after Sándor had died, told me that when he was doing labour service he had been beaten so badly on the testicles that it sterilised him.

Throughout that summer, my parents' fear and paranoia had been growing, until their anxiety burst out on to the surface and what had been a dream existence, a pleasant half-life, suddenly seemed to them like a waking nightmare. These external events – the political forces that were emerging in 1977 and would carry on for the next two years until they subsided and a kind of order was restored – made me want to help and protect them because they could not help themselves. They did not even have to leave the house to feel terrified: their precious television had become the bearer of dreadful warnings of what could happen when you put a foot outside the safety of Benson Court.

'You *see*,' my father said, pointing a finger of his fine, craftsman's hand at the screen, a hand precise in all its movements, the nails clipped every other day to a length he measured with a tiny ruler: '*now* it starts.'

They clutched each other as they sat on the scratched brown leather sofa, their backs upright, away from the enlivening beige cushions, ramrod straight, as if iron had suddenly entered their souls.

'The government won't allow it,' said my mother, who had put down her knitting, a useless sock for a refugee who would never arrive. 'This is England, not Hungary.' But her throat closed on the words as if they choked her.

'The Arrow Cross, back again. Who stopped them last time? Tell me, who?'

'They're not called the Arrow Cross, it's something different, wait, I'll get a pen and write it down. We need to know, it's important. Vivien, where is a pen? You have many pens in your bedroom. Get one right away. And a paper.'

I went to my desk and gave her a lined notebook and a biro.

'You write it, darling,' she said. 'Make sure we got the spelling right.'

National Front, I wrote.

'Look at them,' my father said, his face writhing. 'They're criminals, you can see it all over them. Hooligans, thugs. See this one here. What a low-life individual. The Englishman is a gentleman but this is not the best sort, not by a long chalk.'

'Horrible,' said my mother. Fear ran down the walls.

'Why do they march through the places where the coloureds live?' said my father.

'To control the streets, of course,' my mother said, who suddenly seemed to me to know far more than she let on. 'So people are scared to walk around and do their business. Then when they are scared, they can beat them. I saw it in Budapest, exactly the same. Look, the police are protecting them, they're giving them the right to march. The police are not so innocent, you can see it.'

'Not all,' said my father, whose face looked very grey and sickly.

'They go into shops and beat up innocent shopkeepers just because they're black,' I said.

'Who? The police?' said my father, outraged.

'No, the National Front.'

'Where do you get these ideas from? I thought you spent all morning in a library, with the books. Do you read this in the books?'

'No, it's not from books, it's from real life.'

'What real life do you know about?' my father said, with a look of anxiety in his face.

My parents' reclusiveness had been reinforced by a horrifying encounter with this unknown property, real life, in mid-February. My father arrived home from work with blood on his face. My mother screamed out loud when she saw him, a piercing yelp like a cat. 'Ervin!' she cried. 'What happened to you?'

He ignored her and went straight to the kitchen, poured himself a glass of water and sat down. The blood was clotting in his hair and my mother wet a tea towel under the tap and gently began to wash it away but the gash reopened, the blood dripped down into his eyes.

He kept very quiet until she had put a bandage on him, and allowed her to take his hand and lead him into the living room, to his armchair, and sit him down with a cup of strong coffee. After a while, he began to talk. He had seen something. What? we asked. He just shook his head, it was terrible, no need for the details, but we wanted the details, we demanded them. He described, in a whisper, how a young girl was walking along the street and a gang of brutes came along *and for no reason* grabbed her hair and began to bang her head against a wall. What kind of brutes? we asked. You know, the ones with the boots, the shaved heads, that type. And what kind of girl? The kind who came with Sándor that time, you know, a coloured girl, but perhaps a little more respectable, she had nice sensible shoes and big glasses on her nose.

So how was he involved? Nothing, he had no choice. He just stood there watching in horror this incident, which took place on the corner of Farringdon Road, in broad daylight, just past five o'clock when the shop had shut, and he was waiting for the traffic lights to change – and when he saw what he saw, he might even have taken the drastic step of crossing on the red light, but the traffic was too heavy. So you see, he said, this wasn't even going on in a corner, an alley, but right on the main road, and then they turned round and saw him, and they realised they had a witness.

Now they began screaming horrible words at him, hateful filth, he wasn't prepared to say what. He didn't confront them, of course not, what did we take him for – a hero? Had he a gun or an arrest warrant? The traffic lights changed, he broke into a run (and I had never seen my father run) but as he reached the middle of the road he tripped over his shoelace which he had failed to tighten properly before he left the workshop. He went down on his hands and knees and his head cracked the pavement. The lights were changing once more, the traffic was starting to move, he couldn't believe it, the drivers were putting their foot down on the accelerator, they were revving their engines and moving forward because they had the *right* to go forwards, and my father was lying there on the ground, in their way.

A lady ran into the road and helped him get up. She stood with her umbrella erect in her hand, holding back the traffic – like a demon, she was, he said, waving that green silk stick above her head. She got him to the other side and then he was all right. She wanted him to go to the hospital but he said it wasn't necessary, because by now he was so frightened (even of the woman with the umbrella) that all he could think of was to get home as fast as he could, to be safe inside Benson Court, where everyone was kind and generous and kept themselves to themselves.

The long period of calm in my parents' lives, which had lasted from the end of the war to the present day, years that were placid and uneventful, which was how they liked it, was coming to an end. They felt they faced a frightening, uncertain future and they had no idea at all where they might go next, if it became necessary to flee once more, and anyway, they were too old now to start new lives.

But me, it wasn't too late for me, if things got bad, they said, I could always go to America, surely? But I replied that I had no intention of going anywhere.

The magnetic pull of Benson Court and my parents' inert lives had weakened to a faint, plaintive tug and now reality lay all around me, clear and finely etched, visible. King's Cross, Brixton, Wood Green, Harlesden, Islington, Southall, New Cross, Lewisham, and far beyond to *terra incognita*, the Thames estuary and its islands – the Isle of Dogs, the Isle of Grain, Sheppey. This London was a great eye looking upwards, blinking by night and day. Railway lines crossed it, gouging scars into its face. Bridges. Steeples. The serpentine river. Derelict factories. Blocks of flats. The smell of human flesh and orange peel, chip papers, asphalt bus shelters, old age, queues for everything.

And everywhere this:

It was on bus stops, bus seats, bus windows. On railway bridges, shop windows, litter bins. Tattooed on to fingers and foreheads. The elegance of its form simplified everything, you could write it easily, even if you were no good at writing. It was as blunt and uncomplicated as a fist. But what did it actually mean?

There was a lot of discussion at the time about this. To some it was an old nostalgia for times lost, when Britain had an empire and ruled half the world; the white man had lost his place and the Queen on her throne, celebrating her silver jubilee in a jewelled coach, crown and sceptre, riding behind plumed horses trotting through the streets of London, this emblem of monarchy, mysterious and divinely ordained, was reduced to a dumpy, ageing woman in reading glasses and a canary-yellow coat with matching shoes and buttoned gloves. Others said no, this was the real Nazi McCoy: that the British Fascists who had been forced underground after the war went on breeding and thrived on grievances, like white maggots in the dark. In Yorkshire they will build the gas chambers, believe me.

Or there was a third take on the situation: that they were just teenage thugs who enjoyed beating up niggers and queers to get a taste of White Power in their parched mouths.

Myself, I had no opinion. I didn't have the means to arrive at any conclusions, other than hearsay.

Now, no one in my family had ever joined a movement or a party. The Kovacs went on living, they had this capacity to adapt to circumstance, either by leaving the country like my father, or working out ways and means of beating the system as far as they could, as my uncle had worked up the pimping side of his business when he was forced out of real estate by the race laws. The bigger picture didn't interest them. They were not ideologically driven in any particular direction, communist or Zionist, it was just a matter of keeping your head above water until the flood subsided, as they believed it eventually would. Even in the labour service, my uncle was never involved in plans to escape or mutiny. The 'look out for number one' quality was too ingrained in him, and he wasn't given to romantic or quixotic gestures.

All over London a badge with this design on it began to appear on people's clothes, pinned to lapels, dresses, jumpers, shirts:

At first I had no idea what it meant and had to ask someone standing at a bus stop. He took a leaflet out of his shoulder bag and that explained everything.

It seemed to me that it was the least I could do, to avenge my uncle's horrible suffering, to join this organisation, this league, and fight the Fascists here in London.

What an eye-opener that was. As if my eyes really had been shut and my parents' paranoia had some substance.

I was sent to stand outside pubs and hand out my own leaflets. They received a varied response. Human nature is not necessarily a pretty sight, close up. You see walking towards you a perfectly respectable man with his dog with a running nose and a poorly leg – a dog which he pats and says, *Poor lad, you've been in the wars haven't you?* So although you are afraid of dogs, and particularly don't like the smell of this one, which is sick, you bend down to touch its rough fur and force a smile and try to hand its owner the leaflet. Which he examines, then tells you that dusky immigrants, monkeys barely down from the trees, are going to swamp the white race, Enoch Powell was dead right, and did you know they pushed their stinking turds through old ladies' letterboxes, he'd set his dog on them when Buster got better, he was training him to smell a nig-nog, ha ha.

I would come home and find my mother handing me sheets of paper covered in messages in her strange, erect Mittel European handwriting: *Mick telephoned, he says, urgent you must come to the Red Lion with the leaflets and give them to Claire. And Dave has the money to give you to give to Steve which they need to pay for the printing. And on Saturday you have to assemble on a corner, the one he says you know, at Old Street.* 'And who are these people, these Micks and Daves and what kind of family do they come from? A good family? Do you know? Vivien, I'm talking to you!'

Sándor was concerned only to protect Eunice. 'She must come and live here, with me,' he said. 'Wood Green where her flat is, it's not a good neighbourhood for her. Those people are all over the place. But she won't come, she won't live with me, she says it's not respectable. What can I do?'

'Is this what it was like in Hungary with the Arrow Cross?' I said.

'*This?* Ha, ha. Nothing will ever come of these people, they're scum. They like to make a big noise, that's it, and you deal with them the same way you deal with any scum, anywhere.'

'What's that?'

'Well, you know, on their own terms.'

'How?'

'You fight fire with fire, what can I say?'

I told him I had joined an organisation. 'Very nice,' he said. 'And what do you do in this organisation?'

'I hand out leaflets outside pubs.'

'Oh! A *leaflet*, very good. I feel safe now, and so will Eunice when I tell her.'

But I didn't care. You only had to remember four things about the Front (though nearly thirty years later I can't recollect what three of them were: only what they said about themselves – *The*

National Front is a racialist front. I still don't know the difference between racist and racialist, though I'm certain it was once explained to me). The content of my leaflets spoke for itself, I had nothing to add. Out on the street with the leaflets, I could talk to anyone as long as I kept to what was on the piece of paper and didn't get sidetracked into other discussions. This single-minded insistence on one topic was not easy for me, I wandered away from the point, I was told, and was too easily led into other people's agendas. But I stuck with it. I went out every weekday evening leafleting. I picked up discarded leaflets from the pavement, I rescued screwed-up leaflets from litter bins, smoothed them out and came home and ironed them so they could be distributed again tomorrow. I went everywhere with those sheets of paper, anywhere they sent me. I'd even go across the river, south, to Lewisham, Brixton, Tooting, Morden, places that were just names to me on the tube map. The world radiated outwards from Benson Court, and the mansion block on Marylebone High Street became just a pin-prick, a dot, an intersection.

The dirt of London was under my nails and the dust of its pavements under the soles of my shoes. These were my streets, this was my territory. The slight incline of a hill beneath the concrete slabs of civilisation, a hill with an old stream, a meadow buried under traffic got inside my own body's navigation system. I had a right, I felt, at last to say that I belonged here.

To belong to a place, now that is really something. No Kovacs ever felt that before!

There came a morning when I was holding the hairdryer in my hand as I straightened my bush of black hair, looking in the mirror at myself, and thinking, What would it be like if I didn't have that jungle round my face? And all these bloody old clothes. Claude laughed at them. He thought they were completely weird and I realised that what had begun as a liberation from my parents had turned into just an affectation.

It was a complicated manoeuvre, what I was trying to do. Whenever I try to describe this early part of my life to people I feel that they don't have a clue, or maybe I don't know how to explain myself properly. I was a kind of embryo that can't make its mind up if it's going to be a chicken, a carrot or an Australian bushman. It keeps acquiring feathers, then turning orange, then growing skin. I look back on that fragile, uncertain young self with some humour and some compassion. I can sympathise with the young Vivien, even though the lengths she went to to try and form herself into a person now seem so absurd. But that's it, being young – you're free to be ridiculous, to wear hideous clothes because they're all the rage, and to strike attitudes and postures. You see yourself in those old photographs and you wince, when what you should do is touch the glassy paper with your finger and try to revive inside you the naïve audacity you have at twenty.

Claude said, 'Why don't you let me cut your hair? I can do it. I'm handy that way.'

For the black bush, he said, got on his nerves, he couldn't see my face. Our relationship was erotic, and nothing else. We were definitively sex objects for each other. He read the leaflets I gave him, and he looked at them with little interest. Politics gave him a headache. 'We have a few of those around our way,' he said, finally, under pressure. 'They all have heads that look like they was boiled. A lot of them have dogs, and I told you, I fucking hate bow-bows.'

Ours was not a relationship of shared interests or exchanges of views, we didn't even talk about music. Claude was a pill-popper, a speed freak and, apart from his coloured fish, he had no hobbies. The marshy dampness of the Isle of Sheppey ran through his veins, and the sharp-eyed instincts of his tinker forebears. He was always looking out for an advantage.

If anything interested him, it was his own body. He was saving up to get himself an elaborate tattoo, had already drawn experimental sketches in a notebook he would not show me. 'It's gonna be big,' he said, 'and all over my shoulder, that's the bit I'm sure about. You can't get rid of a tattoo so it's got to be bang on target. You've got to be dead sure, but by the time I've got the money together I will be.'

He had a strong sexual curiosity, would paint his face, using the little mirror of my tarnished gold powder compact, and his male hardness dissolved into a disturbing androgyny. When he was at work in his guard's uniform, I'd dress up in his jeans and leather jacket and when he came home he would have to beg me to take them off so we could go for a drink to the pub. Not because he didn't want to be seen with me dressed like that but because he had nothing else to wear. Get your own bloody jeans, he said. They suit you better than those ratty dresses.

So he wanted to cut my hair, he was sure he could do it. I sat down on the edge of his bed with a towel round my neck, while he knelt behind me with a pair of scissors, held that dense, wiry mane in his strong fingers and hacked it off. There was no mirror in the room, just hair everywhere, hair drifting across the floor, floating like dead pieces of myself. Hair got inside the crevices of my body, in my mouth, my ears, my nose, under my fingernails and inside my socks, settling between my toes. Hair floated on the surface of the fish tank. The shorter the hair on my head got, the more I felt full of suppressed emotion, tearful, like the prisoner who is released from jail after a twenty-year sentence, free at last from the neurotic, slightly mad girl carefully nurtured in the dusty corridors of Benson Court.

The mirror of my gold compact could not do justice to the violent transformation that had come over me, the inch of black halo, the dark shadow on the upper lip, the kohl-fringed eyes, the slash of red across the mouth.

'Fantastic,' Claude said. 'You look the business now. You should get some monkey boots. Go and show the fishes.'

We went to bed, struggling and thrashing on its narrow platform. I fell asleep for a while. Maybe snakes and butterflies and other things which change from one form to another have to have a rest after the strenuous endeavour to alter themselves, both inside and out. I slept heavily, one of those descents straight into dreamless blackness.

When I woke up, Claude was looking through my handbag and I watched him for a while, though narrow slits of eyelids. He pushed my lipstick up and down in its tube, stared at his face in the gold compact mirror, and then examined all the bits and pieces in my wallet. I thought he was going to take the eight pound notes that my uncle had paid me, but he merely counted them, licking the tips of his fingers, then put them back, with care. No corpse-robbing today, I thought, then pretended to wake, stretching my arms out towards him, and he put the bag down and came back to lie next to me, stroking my hair this way and that, like iron filings.

My uncle got it into his head that he wanted to hold a birthday party for me, in his garden. I was going to be twenty-five. His plan was to bring in workmen to clear the ground, raze the weeds and saplings, push back the bushes and erect a marquee. He even thought of hiring a dance band for the occasion or, failing that, borrowing the large sound system that they used at the dance classes. The birthday party plan was part of his show-off side, the man who had once owned a house in Millionaires' Row, who had flown first class to New York in 1961 and had seen Eartha Kitt perform live at Carnegie Hall. The love of indulgence, of cream cakes and fleshy whores, had been there before he became a slave in the Ukraine, but when he was no longer a slave, it returned with ferocity. He had a hunger, a greed, for life, for material possessions. Food, luxuries, flesh. Then fourteen years back in prison. His existence was a series of heavens and hells.

So he dreamed my birthday party. He was no longer a millionaire, and even when he had been, most of it existed only on paper; but he was not poor, and he had nothing to spend his money on. Whatever else you could say about my uncle, he was never a miser. It wasn't money he loved, but what you could buy with it. Wealth for its own sake didn't interest him.

I did not believe he was serious about the party until workmen arrived with sawing equipment, scythes, a flamethrower, gallon plastic jugs of weedkiller, and shears. The dandelions, daisies, buttercups, saplings, the tightening ivy, the lines of mint sending their underground runners through the fence, the fence itself with its rotting boards, were obliterated. Bald earth with a few tufts of bleeding, wounded grass, the lilac bush and an ash tree were all that was left. The following day after this scorched earth policy had reached its conclusion, they came back, dug a hole, and planted a flowering cherry tree which they promised would burst into blossom the following spring.

I don't know if Eunice tried to dissuade him from his increasingly elaborate ideas. He was hurt by her jealousy. I was all he had; I was the one who would redeem him, not just through the relating of his story, the book he really imagined would be printed and published and for sale in bookshops, but through an enduring memory in another mind, a sense that he was as much a father to me as his brother. Or even more so. For he must have understood that I was closer to him on the scale of human extravagance and lust for living than to the pale bespectacled jeweller in the dusty suit who counted out his days through the shadow land of the TV screen.

And he was right. I am like him. I do bear all his faults.

So the plans for the party took shape. A marquee was booked; Eunice arranged the catering.

'Do you mind,' my uncle asked, 'if I invite some of my associates? I want them to see what a beautiful secretary I have, and what a book she is going to make of me. Of my life.'

'Sure,' I said, amused at his hubris. The party seemed to me to be a farce, I didn't know if anyone would come. But Sándor was inviting everyone, Jim from the dance class and the instructor with the double-sided crocodile handbag. 'We're going to have an exhibition tango,' he said.

'What are you going to wear?' Eunice said. 'You look more of a beatnik than ever.'

'Well, of course,' said my uncle, 'we'll take you to the shop to buy you a dress. Special for the occasion.'

'It's fine,' I said, 'I have a dress, the one you bought me.'

'No, no, you have to have a new dress. Oh, and by the way, will you invite your parents?'

'Why not?'

Even though they had never been friends, not even in childhood, I believed they should be brought together again. And then I found out that this was exactly what my grandmother would have wanted and that it was up to me, the next generation on, to carry out her last wishes.

It was her death, in November 1956, which brought him here to London, not the failed uprising against the Soviet tanks. A tumour had grown unnoticed in her chest; no hand had touched or caressed it since her husband had been taken off for labour service in 1939. She lay in the hospital ill and frail, and said, 'Son, go and find your brother, go and be with him, my two children belong together. Go,' she said, '*go*.'

She cherished the letters my father sent her from the end of the war onwards, in which he carefully stuck to generalities and avoided any mention of his life in London, to avoid the censor's pencil. This was the first time Sándor mentioned, obliquely, that he had a niece, waiting to see if I would take the bait, but I didn't, not then. I was digesting the information that my grandmother had known all about me from my birth until I was three years old, when she died. She had a picture of me in a silver frame which stood on the little bureau in her apartment and came with her to the cancer hospital. I was there, with her when she died, Sándor said, both of us were: him and the little girl. He still had the photograph but not the frame, of course, he had to abandon that when he got out but the picture was inside his breast pocket, next to his heart, as he left Budapest.

He would show it to me a week later, after the party – a piece of paper with deckled edges and me on it, a round-headed black-haired baby, held in my mother's arms in our living room at Benson Court. I had forgotten how luminous my mother's eyes once were and how softly shining her hair. A disembodied hand with manicured nails is on her shoulder: my father. I have no idea who took this picture.

On 1 December, two weeks after my grandmother died and her oldest son stood in the cemetery knowing that he was bound now to no one, that there was no one left alive who was once a Klein who came from Mád who was not 'up the chimney', he walked in the snow with a party of other refugees across the border into Austria, the army firing at them as they disappeared into the trees. It was easy for him, he said, 'just a little stroll in the forest compared to what we did during the war, and this time with a good coat and boots'.

A blizzard came down and covered their tracks. The lights of a village were visible ahead; the wind dropped, everything went silent. Someone said he thought he saw an eagle, and everyone laughed. How could there be an eagle, which was a bird in books and fairy stories? A child was wiping his nose with his sleeve, and his mother began to tell him off for ruining a good jacket with snot. My uncle was thinking of all the girls he had ever slept with, and their names, the order they came in. The one with the wig because her hair fell out, the one with the crippled foot, the one with the deformed hand, and he suddenly realised that he was drawn to females who were disfigured in some slight way, not quite perfect or whole. He wondered why.

But he was not of introspective disposition and he dropped the thought.

They crossed the border. My uncle saw the West for the first time. Was given a new suit. He spent a couple of weeks in a refugee camp; then Vienna and the journey in a railway carriage to what he had never seen before, a coast. The sea. Grey, furrowed. Unstable. The ferry, making landing at Dover, and the steam train north to London. A beautiful clear, bright day, frosty and cold, he said. Overwhelmed by everything outside the window, the steam billowing across the lemon sun, and inside the carriage the maroon plush seat he sat on, damp from his excitement.

Houses!

'They all had gardens, you could see them,' he said, 'because they backed down to the railway line, some with fruit trees, others with rose bushes and others that were wild and overgrown, like no one cared for them. Windows long and the houses tall. I never saw nothing like this in Hungary, just apartment buildings round a courtyard and everyone knows everyone else's business. Later I heard the saying they have here, "an Englishman's home is his castle." We have a castle in Buda, where the King used to live, I suppose. But in England, every man could be a king, even me. That's what I understood, before I even got to the city.

'I looked at the houses, I devoured them with my eyes. I wanted to know who owned them and who were the people who lived inside them, and how much rent do they pay, and who do they pay it to? What are the laws governing these transactions? How much money could a person like myself make from them? These were all the thoughts that were going through my mind as the train took me closer and closer to my new life. A lot of cats there were, too, in the gardens I saw from the train. And even squirrels running up and down the trees, and birds' nests, very clear, in the bare branches. I marvelled at everything.'

The time to be here was just after the war. If Uncle Sándor had not been demobbed in 1944 and sent back to Budapest, if he had been liberated by the British or the Americans and sent to a Displaced Persons camp, he might have got to England a decade earlier than he did. Back then, he told me, you could go to the auction room in Queen Victoria Street and buy a house for £10, even £5. That was how it was in those days. You bought dirt cheap, you sold dear. It was a bonanza and no capital gains tax. If Sándor had been in London then he would have become a property millionaire and be retired by the time they put him in prison. But arriving in 1956, he asked a few questions, got some answers and formed an opinion about how a man such as himself – a refugee with nothing – could make a good living, could even prosper and become rich.

It was a chance meeting on the street which took him into his new line of business. My uncle always like to be at the heart of things, where the *people* were, that's where you saw an opportunity, not sitting by yourself in a bedsit, staring at four walls. He found out that the place to be was Piccadilly Circus where the statue of the boy with the arrow was that everyone thought so much of, or Oxford Circus where four important streets met, and each one with big shops and a lot of people; people with money in their pockets, wanting to make purchases, there was an opening, everyone knew that.

On Regent Street, around five o'clock on a winter Saturday just before Christmas, Sándor came across a young lad selling wind-up clockwork bears from a suitcase.

The poor boy could only be twenty-two, twenty-three and already he had gone bald and wore a terrible wig. In his cheap suit and blue suede crêpe-soled shoes he was winding up the bears, which ran around the pavement under the legs of the crowd who gathered to watch. My uncle was not interested in childish things but he had nothing else to do. He watched the boy selling the bears, making a good success, he sold them easily. But the lad, for his part, saw Sándor watching him and Sándor understood at once that he thought he was a policeman, because he started to throw all the bears into the suitcase in a panic.

He was not a good shot. Bears were standing on their heads on the pavement. Some of the heads and arms broke off because it was obvious that they were just cheap shit, and probably stolen anyway. The sight of the bears with their broken arms and legs, decapitated, frightened the children, and some of them started crying.

'I want my money back,' a woman demanded and she tried to snatch the purchased bear from her son's hand but once a child has a toy he will never let it go and now there was a lot of screaming and crying, and in the meantime, the lad with the wig was running around trying to pick up all the bears.

In his very basic English, Sándor explained to him that he was not a policemen and to prove it got down on his hands and knees and started to help him put the bears back in the suitcase. Together, the two of them tried to fix the heads and arms back on and wind them up with their keys to see if they still worked, and now they had a lot of bears running round and, quite naturally, they found that the best language to understand each other was not English, and not of course Hungarian which the boy didn't know at all, but their *mama loshen*, their mother tongue, the one they learned when they were children themselves, one in the village in the Zémplen, the other in Bethnal Green; the language that is spoken, or was, not any more, in every country in Europe, crossing every border, and this way an Englishman and a Hungarian could talk to each other. In Yiddish.

His name was Mickey Elf. They went to a pub for a drink and my uncle explained his situation so that Mickey knew from the beginning that though Sándor was the immigrant, the refugee, while Mickey was born here, that it was he who would be the employer. And so they started out together, Mickey taking care of one thing, and my uncle the other. Mickey had all the connections.

On Mickey's advice, my uncle set up a letting agency, which anyone could do, you could run it from a bedsit, but owning the houses and taking the rents was where the money was. You could buy houses very cheap, Mickey explained, but the problem was the controlled tenants, the ones the law protected: you couldn't get rid of them or raise their rent. You had to find ways and means to get round this problem, but my uncle said that there were always ways and means, of course there were. It just required brainpower, which he had.

What I knew, what anyone who followed the trial knew – or what they read about him in the newspapers, gazing on *the face of evil* – was the squalor, the walls running with condensation, the children dying of bronchitis, the shivering, bitter cold those first arrivals from the Caribbean endured as Uncle Sándor's tenants.

'Let me tell you who nobody wanted to rent to,' he told me. 'The coloured people, the West Indians who came off the boats from their islands, the ones they brought here to drive the buses, and all that. Why? Why did they not want to rent to them? Their money was the same colour as anyone else's money, no different. The ten shilling note was the same brown in an Englishman's hand as it was in a Jamaican's.

'Prejudice. This is all there is to it. They arrived at Victoria station, same place I come to, by the way, and all their luggage is just put in one big pile by the platform and the pickpockets and petty thieves, the nice Englishman, would just go and buy a platform ticket, and help themselves. They came with high hopes in their hearts, and what did they find? Signs. No Coloureds. No dogs. These signs I knew from my own past experience, though my skin is pale.

'No one forced the coloureds into my houses. I didn't have to send out any bullyboys to tout for custom. Everyone knew my name, the name of Sándor Kovacs was as familiar to them in those days as Duke Ellington or Sonny Liston. In court a West Indian gentleman tried to speak up for me: "He was a saviour, and people respected him," that's what he said, and he was not even one of my tenants, but what they call a social worker. So I charged them a higher rent than a controlled tenant would have paid? Am I a charity?

'A flat, a room which was unfurnished, you couldn't get the tenant out, they could stay put for life and you can't even raise the rent without going to a tribunal. That was the law. A furnished flat, this was a different proposition, tenants of furnished flats you could charge as much rent as the market can stand and you could give them a month's notice, and if they didn't get out, you could send the police to *get* them out.

'Now what West Indian has furniture of his own? He doesn't come here with a bed and a table. I provided everything – the bed, the table, the hotplate so he can cook his rice and peas. Maybe the mattress stinks of piss. So what? Where I come from, there wasn't even so much as a mattress. Let me tell you, the rooms I rented would have been a palace to me, during the war. They called me a parasite. Listen, the parasites were the aristocrats, the owners who sat on their bottoms for a hundred years, waiting for the leases to come up. Me, I worked all hours in the early days, collecting the rents and emptying the gas meters, the pennies I emptied into buckets and schlepped them home on the bus, before I had a car. That's how it was.

'Later, I got the rent collectors. I always employed their own people, other West Indians, just like them, I gave them a job when every door was slammed in their face. I told them, six pound is the rent. You keep five shilling. You see they are on commission, they have an incentive. In court I hear that they threaten the tenants if they don't pay up on time. Whose fault is this? I never threatened no one. It's their own people they should complain to, not me.

'Of course when the West Indians moved in, the white tenants, the ones who paid a pound a week and still they complained, these rents are so low it was hardly worth collecting them, they screamed blue murder. How dare I give them these dark-faced people for neighbours? They play music all night long, drink rum, have parties. Animals.

'You don't like it? I said. So move.

'Now they accused me of forcing them out of their homes, of putting pimps and prostitutes into respectable houses. This is another matter. You know me, by now. You know that I always dealt in this line of work.'

But what about his brother? I interrupted. How did the reunion go?

My uncle looked very angry. 'No,' he said, shortly, 'that didn't work out.' And he reached forward to turn off the tape recorder so I should know that our session had come to an end and it was time for me to start typing.

A new set of workmen arrived the day before my party and roofed over the garden with a crimson marquee which cast a rosy flickering glow above everything as the canvas rippled in the light wind. They stood on ladders and decorated the tent with swags of flowers and gold cardboard 25s and at one end they put up a floral arch and three gold-painted wooden steps which led up to a platform with a golden throne, above which a crown hung suspended from a length of cord attached to a pulley. White-clothed trestle tables were piled with ice buckets, rented glasses, plates and cutlery. Small tables and chairs were dotted around, each chair tied with a gold bow and a gold 25 with a silver tassel. The uneven ground had been rolled and strips of plastic turf laid down.

'Look at this,' said my uncle. 'Have you ever seen such a sight? Magnificent! And I don't even think it is going to rain. A beautiful evening, they say.'

'You did very well, Sándor,' said Eunice. 'It's like a fairy palace out here. Much better than the jubilee.'

'That was for the Queen but this girl is a queen, also. Wait until it gets dark, they got lanterns, paper, but with real candles inside them. And the food! Sumptuous. This is a word, sumptuous?'

'Yes, it's a word,' I said.

'See? My English is getting better all the time. What a lucky break for me that I met you that time in the park.'

'Yes, what a coincidence.' Sándor and I each knew by now, I think, what the other knew. Two cats held our tongues, they dug their claws in but tonight would be the night of revelation, the reunification of the two brothers and the remaining secrets out in the open. 'Who arranged all this?' I asked, looking around in awe, reminded of the Hotel Negresco and all its opulent swagger.

'Harrods, of course! The finest shop in the world where, like I told you, you can buy anything you want, a cat a dog, a tent. They took care of everything, very, very fine people. And I got a surprise. A big surprise for you, Meeranda.'

'Oh, yes, *Miranda*,' Eunice said, turning to me. 'Who all of this is in aid of. Because she has a birthday.'

'It's not every day a person is twenty-five,' said my uncle. 'The day I was twenty-five, that was another matter.'

'And you're not even a relation, are you, Miranda?' Eunice said, drilling me with her black eyes.

'But tonight we will meet her family. You say they're going to come all right?'

'Yes, they're coming.'

'Wonderful. What a surprise they will have,' said my uncle.

'Indeed. Who is going to be sitting on the throne, by the way?'

'You, of course. You are the queen.'

I looked at it, aghast. Cold dread came over me. 'I'm not sitting there!'

'Don't be silly, who else should sit?'

'I don't know, but I'm not going to.'

'Why not?'

'It's embarrassing!'

'You afraid you get a red face from people looking at you? Don't worry, you're amongst friends here!'

'I don't mind sitting in a throne,' Eunice said. 'I don't see twenty-five again, but if a man wants to treat me like a queen, I don't throw it back in his face.'

I began to panic. Was it possible not to turn up for my own party at this late stage and stop others from attending?

'And we got a new dress for you,' Sándor said. 'Wait till you see it, it's a beauty. Eunice ordered it special.'

'Yes, from Italy.'

'Where is it?' I asked, looking around.

'I had it sent,' said my uncle.

'Where to?'

'Your house, of course.'

'But you don't know my address.'

'My dear, I have associates, they know everything about a person.' And he picked up my hand and kissed it, his eyes wet. So then I was certain.

Everyone was coming to the party to meet the mysterious man with the large library who had been my employer for the past two months. My parents had agreed to attend, Gilbert, the cartoonist, promised to put in an appearance, the ballerina and the plutocrat, they would definitely be there, for they loved parties of any kind, particularly ones where he would meet new, unattached young ladies, and she would get a chance to reminisce about her days *en pointe*. Several of my comrades from the Anti Nazi League had accepted the invitation, and of course my uncle's sidekick, Mickey Elf, and his wife Sandra. Only Claude could not come, because he was on late shift; he would arrive when the last empty bottle was being thrown into the bin, but he had a present for me, 'because I've got wages,' he said, 'and I can afford it. It's a surprise.'

So many surprises.

I went home in the early afternoon and found my mother standing in the hall holding a box. 'Something has come for you, what is it?' she said. 'I can't wait for you to open it.'

'I think it's a dress.'

'Who bought you a dress?'

'An admirer.'

'Oh, you and your secrets.'

'Don't talk to me about secrets,' I said, as I opened the box. 'You're the one for secrets, not me.'

My parents had spent several days worrying about the party: how they would get there, what they would wear and whether it was appropriate to bring some kind of gift to the host, perhaps a box of After Eight mints or Black Magic chocolates, which they had seen in shops and considered to be highly sophisticated and upper class. My mother found a cream linen dress, only a couple of seasons out of date, in the Oxfam shop. She tied a ribbon on to her brown, rubber-tipped stick, 'because it's such an ugly old thing, I feel ashamed to carry it sometimes.' I watched her twisting the loops of the white satin into a bow, the girl who all her life had had to bear this stigma of her disability. She looked up. 'There,' she said, 'that's much nicer, don't you think?'

I had not understood until now how much my mother must have hated the symbol of her lifelong handicap. I thought because she wore the brown felt waistcoats she didn't care how she looked, dressed only for practicality. I was embarrassed that I had never before realised that the ugly stick was always with her and that it must have made her feel ugly too.

She saw my face.

'What? No good? Should I take it off?'

'No, leave it. It cheers it up a bit.'

"I don't want to make a show of you in front of your friends and this important man who is employing you. Your father is enough on that count.'

'You'll never make a show of me,' I said. 'Don't think that. When you were my age, did you hate having to always carry a stick?'

'Of course, what young girl wouldn't?'

'Did it make you shy with boys?'

'Yes it did.'

'So how did you meet Daddy?'

She paused, and then smiled. She had a lovely mouth, which I am told I inherited from her. Her washed face had a healthy shine which had dulled with the years, cracked deeply, but those occasional smiles illuminated her.

'Let me tell you a secret – now don't repeat this to your father, I'm only telling you because it's a special day. It wasn't Ervin I met first in his family, it was his terrible brother. He walked past me when I was in a café with some girlfriends and he tipped his hat, just like that. Not at the others, at *me*. My stick was leaning against the table so it wasn't a mistake. He knew. I was so surprised and blushing, but he came over and asked me to join him the next day for an ice-cream. Well, you know, no one had ever paid any attention to me before in that way, so I turned up. Why not? It was an adventure for me. All by myself, I went, I was eighteen.'

'Where was this?'

'Oh, a café along the river where you could sit out and eat ices and look at Buda on the other side and the boats sailing along. Now after only a few minutes even an innocent could see that he was a bad man, a womaniser, not for me at all, but then who should turn up but Ervin and he introduced us, and then Ervin – well.'

'So you knew Sándor *before* Daddy?'

'Yes, only a day. But I have to admit, if I never met him, then I never met your father, and where would you be now, eh?'

'Nowhere.'

'Exactly.'

'And then of course Ervin had the sense to bring us out of Hungary in the nick of time. Sándor has no such sense.'

'What was he like?

'Ugly, but very attractive at the same time. Look, he was a pimp, he knew how to talk to women.'

'Why do you think he tipped his hat to you and asked you for ice-cream?'

'I don't know. He is a complicated person.'

'What did you see in Daddy?'

'He had beautiful eyes. Even under his glasses. The eyes of a man who looks.'

At breakfast the next morning they gave me my birthday present, a seed pearl necklace, 'because we know what a terrible time you have,' said my father, 'and you need a special thing. Don't think we don't know or don't care what you been through. One thing after another.'

'Exactly,' said my mother.

This pearl necklace was a symbol of my parents' love for me, odd, badly expressed love, but love all the same. And love is stronger than death, as the psalm says, and fiercer than the grave. Is that not so?

I didn't go to Sándor's until late afternoon. He told me he was busy with a lot of different matters. More surprises, no doubt. My mother washed her hair and I helped her style it. We experimented for a few minutes with some make-up but we agreed she looked better without and she washed it off.

'I'm a plain person,' she said. 'That's the way I am.'

When my father came home from work he went out with a pair of scissors in his hands down into the communal garden for the first time since 1944, the final night underground in the air raid shelter. He cut a yellow rose – a bud in the process of uncurling itself – carried it back upstairs in the lift, its thorny stem gingerly wrapped in a piece of toilet paper, then sat at the table and neatly snipped the thorns, and put it in a glass of water, to wear later in his buttonhole.

'Now *that's* an effort,' said my mother.

The garden was waiting. I had to hand it to my uncle, he had made a wonderful job of event management. The weather stayed fine for us, it was a balmy summer evening, not too much humidity, a bare-arms night, with perhaps a little shawl, and there was every chance that this party was going to be a roaring success. I was reminded of a remark that Claude had made a few days before – that the railways would work perfectly if it wasn't for the passengers.

The three of us stood under the rosy canvas roof nervously waiting for the first guests to arrive, my uncle holding hands with Eunice. I glimpsed him, for a moment, in his heyday, the Bishops Avenue house and all its expensive trinkets, the diamond wristband of his watch, the suede shoes. He whispered something to her and she laughed.

Minutes passed, and all three of us experienced the panic of party-givers that no guests will turn up, though I knew my parents were already on their way, setting out for the tube station.

But then two figures appeared, a gnome-like individual in a glaringly obvious toupee with a red-faced blonde woman a few inches taller than him, dressed in electric blue velvet.

'Ah, Mickey!' said my uncle, embracing him. 'Nice and early.'

'Somewhat, somewhat.'

'He's not long had breakfast,' said Sandra. 'Cold fried fish and ketchup. He calls this a breakfast? I have to stand all day frying fish for him?'

'Protein,' Mickey said. 'Gives you energy. And fish is brain food.'

'We all know who has the brains round here, don't we, Sammy?'

'But your Mickey has a good heart, Sandra, and that counts for a lot.'

'You must be the birthday girl,' Mickey said. 'Do I get a kiss?'

I held up my cheek. His breath smelt of whisky and plaice and tomato sauce.

'What have you been up to, Mickey?' said my uncle.

'Shooting around, here and there.'

'He slept in the lock-up last night,' Sandra said.

'Business, petal, I didn't want to bother you.'

'What do you keep in your lock-up?' I said.

'All sorts,' he said, briefly. 'Anything to drink round here?'

'Of course,' said my uncle, 'and you don't even have to help yourself, we got waiters will bring it right to you.'

'What a posh dress,' Sandra said to me as the men went off to get the bar service started.

'It was a present from Sándor, but Eunice chose it.'

'The *shvartze* lady's got taste, I'll give her that. Look at this gown I'm wearing. Only three quid and a few bob extra for the alterations. My Mickey's got his best wig on. It was made special for him. Beautiful shade of chestnut, and very natural looking, don't you think?'

'But you can still tell it's a wig,' I said.

'Well obviously. If you're going to spend all that money, you want something to show for it.'

The garden now held that air of quiet excitement, of a space that is about to fill up, though some never do and collapse into forlorn despair. Jim from the tango class arrived, and then a couple I didn't know, and then more tango dancers. Everyone exclaimed about the marquee and the decorations and soon a couple from the Anti-Nazi League entered. The anti-Nazi comrades looked about uncertainly at first, appalled by the decadence of the marquee and the buffet and of course the terrible throne and the gold and silver 25s. I don't think they even recognised my uncle; it was a long time ago, they had just been children, like me, and furthermore, who would expect to come across the killer of black babies in freezing bedsits, with a woman like Eunice on his arm?

Then seeing the tango crowd looking round in admiration at the décor, they gravitated towards them and soon they formed an animated group discussing the political situation.

'They would come in the shop,' said Jim. 'They'd terrify the children buying their sweeties and the old lady with her magazine. You should see the way they dressed, with the trousers rolled up halfway to their knees and the big boots with the laces and the head with the hair shaved off.'

'You have to understand,' said Dave, 'that Tyndall and his mob are using these kids from the estates to bring back Nazi ideology, exploiting the working class. They're not just racists, they're Fascists and instead of the Jews this time, it's people like you who are in the front line. And we've got to *counter* attack, every chance we get.'

'Why can't the police just come and arrest them?'

'Because the police *are on the same side*. They support them, they have members *in* the police.'

'But the government doesn't allow—'

'Oh, the *government*, those class traitors. You think they care about working people, look at all the unemployment . . .'

'And they say we take their jobs. I've got a shop—'

'Exactly. But blacks in this country have always had the shitty end of the stick. Look what happened when you first came here, the terrible housing.'

'Oh, yes, that was a bad time but . . .'

The garden was filling. The guests were mingling, eating and drinking. I was scanning the door, waiting for my parents to arrive. Gilbert came, and the ballerina and the plutocrat, bearing their presents.

'This is a laugh,' Gilbert said, looking round. 'What's going to happen with the throne?'

'I'm supposed to sit on it, then I imagine people will sing Happy Birthday.'

'You're not going to, are you?'

'No!'

'How are you going to get out of it? He looks very determined. It's Sándor Kovacs, isn't it? I remember doing a cartoon of him during his trial. Eating babies. It was after Goya, of course.'

'Yes, it is him.'

'So *that's* who you've been working for. Fascinating.'

'Actually, he is fascinating, in a way.'

'I always wondered if your family was related to him.'

'We are. He's my father's brother.'

'And who's the pixie in the wig with the buxom blonde?'

The bow in my mother's brown stick thrust forward into the garden to test the unstable ground. Only once before had I seen them in such a situation, at my wedding, and the enormity of that occasion had so overwhelmed them that they had barely begun to enjoy themselves before it was over, and what reminiscences they might have had, any chance to relive vicariously the pleasure they could have felt, had been obliterated almost at once, at the very outset of the honeymoon. So I saw that this time they were determined to make as much of the party as they could, to accept glasses of wine, and twirl the stems around their fingers, even if they took no more than a sip, and to eat what was handed to them without sniffing and making suspicious enquiries about the content and preparation of what was on their plates.

My father saw me and smiled. It was a smile of relief, that they were not in a strange house, entirely amongst strangers.

'*Look*,' said my mother.

'Beautiful,' said my father, with tears in his eyes. 'Our daughter in this setting – like fairyland. We made a daughter, didn't we, Berta? And look how she turns out, even after all the tragedy.'

My mother lifted her beribboned stick.

'See, over there.'

'What?'

'Didn't you polish your glasses before you came out? Look where I'm pointing.'

The stick was raised towards my uncle, who was standing with his arm round Eunice's waist talking to a couple of meat-faced men in tight blue-black suits whose hands looked as though they could barely hold the wine glasses without inadvertently crushing them.

At this moment a crocodile of schoolchildren pushed past us, led by a woman who was evidently their teacher, because one of them was saying, 'Miss, miss, I want to go to the toilet.' My parents shrank back against the wall.

'They're here!' cried Sándor. 'At last. The proceedings can commence. Now, young lady who is twenty-five today, it all starts.'

'Come on,' said Eunice, and took my wrist in a bricklayer's grip. 'You come with me.'

I was dragged towards the throne and pushed up the steps. '*Sit*,' Eunice said. The pulley descended and the crown was lowered on to my head. A number of the guests applauded. 'Bravo!' cried the plutocrat, and the ballerina ran forward to the foot of the throne and curtsied, holding the skirt of her party dress. More applause. The crocodile of children arranged themselves into a semicircle in front of me, and my uncle stepped forward and raised his hands. He was using all his power to keep the trembling lower lip under control.

'My lords, ladies and gentlemen,' he cried. 'Can you hear me? Yes? I shout as loud as I can. OK, I don't think we have a lord here this evening, but if there is such a person, then you are very welcome. This is a great day for me. Some of you here know me, some do not, some are thinking, wait, I recognise that man. Yes, I *am* Sándor Kovacs, the one you read about in the newspapers, the same.'

It had been many years since my uncle's name had appeared in any newspaper. He was a forgotten man. It took a few moments for my comrades in the Anti Nazi League to recall that this was the monster who bled dry the poor immigrants, but activists are always handy with slogans, which they carry around with them like hand grenades, ready to lob at a sudden foe.

'*Racist scum!*' Dave shouted, raising a clenched fist.

'There's no need for that kind of talk,' Jim said, mildly, but Eunice had more than slogans at her disposal.

She snatched the plate of food from his hand and threw it into a potted palm. 'You eat a man's food and call him names to his face?'

'That was good salmon,' Mickey said. 'What a waste.'

'You can pick it out and eat it yourself,' said Eunice. 'And you,' she said to Dave, 'shut your mouth and listen to what he's got to say, maybe you'll learn something.'

My uncle would not be stopped. He had seen demagogues make speeches at various times in his life, before and after the war. He knew you just drove on and rode out the heckling, and he had understood that there would be heckling. The only guests whose reaction he was interested in were his brother and sister-in-law, whom he could not quite see in the crowd towards the back of the garden, blinded by the spotlight that fell upon the stage. They were his audience, and the young men and young women in their ridiculous clothes and their babyish leaflets were like lint a well-dressed man brushes from his suit. His only worry was the choir of schoolchildren, whose teacher, with a ghastly face, was trying to quietly escort out of the garden without him noticing, but found her way barred by Mickey Elf, who was pointing out to her that she'd been paid cash in hand for the job and he didn't take kindly to anyone who broke a contract, even if they had a pair of glasses on their nose and a leather music case in their hand.

'Since I came out of prison,' my uncle went on, 'two wonderful things have happened to me. The first is that I found, for the first time in my life, the love of a woman, a *good* woman who has had her own share of suffering. I fell in love with her because of her beauty, her elegance, her exquisite taste (except where it comes to me, of course, that is baffling, and not just to you, ha ha). But I also fell for her because of her spirit, her strength and dignity and her loyalty.'

He pointed at Eunice. 'This is her. Does everyone see?'

She was dressed exquisitely, as always, in a black cocktail dress and high-heeled shoes with small bows at the back of each heel. But her face, raised to the stage, dabbed with a spot of rouge on each cheek, was irradiated with an internal brilliance as if a ruby light was switched on inside her. We experience such happiness only once or twice in a lifetime, when we believe (usually falsely) that all our troubles are finally behind us and the future will be what we always hoped. I have never forgotten her face that night. What it meant to her to receive the public recognition of those qualities she'd worked so hard to make real and permanent: the manicure late at night when she was so tired her eyes were drooping and she would have to erase the polish she painted on her nails when she had smudged them and start all over again; the elocution lessons; the fashion magazines she bought instead of records, and studied each night so that when a customer asked her for the latest news about hemlines, she could answer without hesitation.

If my uncle did a good thing in his life, it was that speech: what he told the world about Eunice. And then he went further.

'So this is the first thing. In front of all these people I declare my love for my beautiful girlfriend, Eunice. Except now she is no longer a girlfriend, she is a fiancée, because this morning I proposed marriage, and she accepts, and we do not yet have a ring, but we are coming to that in a minute.'

Jim's stricken face. His hand to his head, holding it, as if he feared it would fall off. Eunice, seeing for the very first time what she should have known, what was *obvious*, even to me, when I first met him at the tango class, when he held me as we danced but his eyes were always on her. How could he compete with the man who bought her flashy presents and took her to expensive restaurants?

But my uncle had not finished with the revelations. 'What is the second thing we celebrate here today?' he asked, smiling. 'Look at another person, the person sitting on the throne, like a princess.'

I wanted to die.

'I have a niece and today she is twenty-five year old and a beautiful human being. What is she like? Intelligent, curious, sceptical, a high morality and many other qualities. She does not like to see an injustice – she try to put it right. That's the kind of girl she is. And I see here somewhere, hiding in the dark, like always, my brother, Ervin. Look what you made, look at this beautiful daughter, Vivien! A *tribute* to you, a *tribute*. And now we will have a song. Children! Sing. Now.'

The children raised their faces, opened their mouths and warbled together, *And I think to myself what a wonderful world*. When they got to the end they went straight into Happy Birthday. It was a flawless performance. Applause, and then they broke away, towards the birthday cake which was being wheeled out on a trolley. I was trying to get down from the throne. Once again Eunice took my wrist, as a teacher drags an unruly kid by the ear. 'You're going to cut the cake,' she said. 'And do it nice.'

'Congratulations,' I said, breathless. 'On the engagement.'

My uncle handed me a serrated knife. 'You make the first cut,' he said.

I was looking around, trying to see my parents. I had not thought that the reconciliation would happen like this. I had hoped to make a quiet introduction, preceded by explanations and entreaties. I was going to invoke the words of my grandmother, her heartfelt desire to see her two sons together again, I would remind them of all the ghosts who could not rest while there was bad blood between brothers. I had imagined them pausing, then falling into each other's arms and crying with joy like those TV programmes which reunite long-lost relatives. Despite everything, I was trying to overcome my Kovacs blood – I yearned for a happy ending, when history should have taught me that the best you can hope for is tragicomedy.

I cut the cake then hurried away to find my mother and father but Sándor was there before me.

'Ervin,' he said. 'You came. My little brother.' He took my father in his arms and embraced him.

I suddenly remembered I had implied that my father had cancer.

'You!' cried my father.

'Yes. It's me. I'm so happy to see you. You look . . .' He searched my father's face for signs of sickness. 'No, you look fantastic, you'll live for ever, you'll see us all out. You know how long a creaking gate lasts.'

Understandably, my father took this the wrong way but Sándor pushed on.

'What, is it four year since you come to see me in prison and you bring me the picture of Vivien graduating from university? I want you to meet my fiancée, Eunice, and I want to ask you, as a brother, to make her engagement ring, before your sight fails.'

'Pleased to meet you,' Eunice said, holding out her hand.

I had seen my father silent, but not speechless. His eyes swam around behind the lenses of his glasses like circling sharks.

'You are the man with the library?' said my mother.

'What library?'

'She told us she went every day to catalogue a library.'

'No, there is no library. Berta, I'm just telling her my life story so she can make it into a book.'

'A book!' cried my mother, aghast.

'Yes, I don't have a daughter like you. I got nothing to go forward into the future, I want to set the record straight.'

'You could have done that at the trial.'

'No, back to the beginning, the very beginning.'

'What beginning?' said my father, finding his tongue at last.

'You know she asks me things I don't even know I remember, like the village. You remember the village, Ervin? You remember the day our father had the fight with our grandfather? Do you remember the beautiful shul? The stone lions? Oh, what a time it has been for me, going back to those days when we were children.'

Fear crossed my father's face. 'What right have you to tell her such things? Who gave you permission?'

'Why? There is no secret. I enjoyed remembering and I enjoyed telling.'

'What's the harm in telling me about the village?' I said. 'It was interesting.'

My father turned to me. 'We bore you, we brought you up, we protected you from all the monsters, all the filth that's in the world – *his* filth.'

'What filth?'

'Did he tell you what he does for a living?'

'Of course.'

'So you,' my father said to Eunice, 'are you one of his girls? No, no, you're a bit too long in the tooth for that. Maybe you retired.'

I saw Eunice's face turn to ash, as if she had been consumed by fire and nothing remained but the cold, dead coals.

'You little *klipe*,' said my uncle, his own face suddenly suffused with blackish blood.

'You with your names,' my father said.

The two men faced off. They circled each other like wrestlers. I saw my uncle summoning all his energy – the scars on his back, the ruined lungs, everything made an effort to form themselves back into a body that could do combat with a mortal enemy. And my father rising fast, like mercury shooting up in a thermometer and spouting out the top in a silver fountain, unable to be contained by the glass tube.

I don't think my father had ever touched another person who was not his wife and daughter since he kissed his mamma goodbye at the railway station at Budapest. Even shaking hands was a torment to him, he hated it. Sándor got thugs to do his dirty work for him, but he was a soft man, a ladies' man. So these two lifelong enemies now reached for the main means they each had to inflict punishing damage on the other.

'I'm going to kill you. I'll bury you in the ground like a treasure no one ever finds because there's no map,' was my uncle's first assault.

'Yes, yes, and while you're digging may you shit green worms,' my father hit back.

'I hope your troubles are so bad they bleed from their own wounds.'

'May you burn down your business and forget to insure it first.'

'May you have a thunderbolt in your sides.'

'You should have a lament in your belly.'

'And pepper in your nose . . .'

'*Please*,' I said, terrified by this cataract of curses. 'Stop. I just wanted you to be friends, brothers. My grandmother wanted the two of you to be reunited.'

'What do you know about your grandmother?' my father said, grabbing me by the wrist which was already bruised by Eunice's grip. 'What's he told you?'

'He said she was a—'

'If anyone tells you about your grandmother it's *me*.'

'But you *didn't* tell me.'

'So you could have asked.'

'And what would you have said?'

'Nothing! What's she got to do with you?'

'You see, Ervin – this is what drives her into the arms of her uncle. Because she is a clever girl, with curiosity, she wants to know everything.'

My mother was bent over her brown stick, undoing the white satin ribbon. 'Please,' she said to Eunice, who was standing silently, still grey in the face. 'Take it.'

Eunice took the ribbon and twisted it in her hands.

'What do you give her that for?' said my father.

'It's a pretty thing and this is clearly an elegant lady who likes pretty things. What's a pretty thing got to do with me?'

'Berta, are you mad? What you talking about?'

But my mother turned her face away and looked down the garden where the guests, oblivious, were continuing to enjoy themselves. The throne was being removed from the raised platform and Fabian had climbed up the three steps with a young woman. He held up his hand as he did in class. Some music began to play, that dark, night-time sound of the tango.

'Look,' said my uncle, 'the exhibition tango starts.' My mother's face was stone, like the Sphinx at Giza.

'What is this party for,' my father said. 'To rub your sex life in my face?'

'Get out,' said my uncle. He turned to me. 'Your father has no human feeling. He never did. You can't bring us together. Nice that you try.'

'Yes, we're going. Come on, Vivien. And you, a curse upon you, Sándor, may your wedding be an evil hour.'

My mother took my father's arm and pointed her stick towards the door. She reached up and picked the yellow rose from his lapel and threw it on the ground. My uncle bent down and picked it up and put it in his pocket.

'Next time we meet will be in the *yane velt*, that place, the *other* world. Goodbye,' he said to my father. 'And you, Berta . . . what a ball and chain I gave you, that you have to drag behind you all your life when you already have your own burden to bear. I apologise. If I only knew.'

I looked around the garden at all the people laughing, drinking wine, eating salmon, tapping their toes, the two figures on the little stage bent in each other's arms. The scarlet glow fell deeper and deeper on everyone's faces and the red rippling sky moved above us. Paper lanterns were being carried out, and candles lit inside them. The older dead, back in Hungary, were watching, they paid careful attention to this important scene with me at its centre, the damage I'd done.

My parents left, the guests remained and so did I. I apologised to Eunice for what my father had said to her. 'It's unforgivable,' I said.

But she had her own scores to settle.

'Why do you lie to Sándor? Why didn't you come out with who you was straight away? Were you spying on him?'

I did not know how to tell her what it was like to be unemployed, lonely, feeling your life was a failure before it began. I thought that she would sneer at these little woes, pointing out my life of privilege, with the degree from York University and the incomplete thesis, unfinished because of my own lack of backbone. So I just told her about the library, the book, the photograph.

'And do you think he's evil, now?' she said. 'What's your opinion?'

'No, I don't think he's evil.'

'*Good*. Because you don't know what evil is.'

The party was still in full swing. People were eating, drinking, dancing, in the lanterns the candles were burnishing their way through coloured paper. Fairy lights came on in the corners of the marquee. The tango set were taking it in turns to sit on the throne and soon the anti-Fascists ran out of slogans and started to join them. The rain did not come until midnight, the first drops unheard, then beginning to beat down on the canvas roof. We danced on, oblivious. The rain came down harder and harder and now the canvas sagged under the weight of pools of water but still no one left. My uncle ascended the steps and sat on the throne and took Eunice on his knee and began to kiss her. Someone started to throw food about. Meringues flew through the air like cloudy angels.

Finally the guests began to leave, drunk, shouting, happy. Apart from the meeting between the two brothers, it had been a huge success. Claude arrived, sweating and wet on his bicycle, his hair flat and plastered to his face. 'How did it go?' he said. 'Did you enjoy yourself, birthday girl?' It was time to tell him who I was, my real name, Vivien Kovacs and my relationship with 'the special Mr K'.

'I knew who you was,' he said. 'I guessed you was some kind of relation and then I saw your library card with your real name on it in your wallet. There was a different letter but it sounds the same, so it must be the same.'

'Is that why you're sleeping with me?'

'No. I only sleep with girls who get me going. I wouldn't screw some rich old slag if she didn't look the business. Anyway, I got you a present. Here. I hope you like it, it's better than the one I've got, better quality.'

A leather jacket.

'Put it on, I want to see you in it. I don't know if I got the right size.' The leather creaked as I put my arms tentatively into the sleeves. 'Go on, zip it up. Yeah, fantastic.' The short laugh. He touched my breasts under it. 'Now let's get it off again.'

The long night should not have ended the way it did: me, slippery with sweat, my body bruised, my hands clinging to his forearms, digging in my nails, his mouth all over me. I should have remembered the bloody dead, I should have sat and thought about what I'd done, this catastrophe I had caused, a final rupture between the brothers and the insult to Eunice. I did not deserve this piercing pleasure. And yet I took it.

I still have that jacket. It's folded in a drawer somewhere in my house. It doesn't fit me any more, I forget how thin I was. I don't know what to do with it, how can I throw it out? I put it on occasionally, with the red lizard shoes Alexander bought me, and think about how it can be that it is these clothes that have survived when everyone who had anything to do with them is gone or their whereabouts unknown.

When my father walked out of Sándor's garden with my mother, blackened in the face with rage as if he had been scorched by the fires of hell, the crimson glow of the marquee reflected in the panes of his spectacles, I knew that I would never spend another night in my childhood bedroom. I went back to Benson Court to pick up my things.

My mother came to the door when she heard my key in the lock. It was early afternoon, the time I would have returned after a session with Sándor, interviewing.

'What happens to you now?' she said.

'I can't live here any more.'

'I see.'

'The painting is coming along well,' I said, looking at the stool and the three kitchen chairs which had broken tumultuously out of their brownness and resembled grasshoppers standing upright on their jointed legs.

'Yes, you were quite right about green being a lively colour.'

'I'm sorry.'

'About what?'

'Being so thoughtless. I should have known it wouldn't work.'

'You had your reasons, I suppose.'

'He told me my grandmother wanted the two brothers to be reunited, I just thought . . .'

'Don't be ridiculous. Your father never stopped seeing Sándor, he tried to help him, he met him off the train when he arrived here, did you know that? He had a job all arranged for him.'

'What kind of a job?'

'In a factory. It made venetian blinds, I think. He didn't want it, he preferred to continue in his old ways, to be a criminal.'

'He's not the kind to work with his hands.'

'Exactly, too good for him. He always preferred to go the flashy road, whatever the cost.'

'But a *factory*.'

'What? You think he should walk into a job behind the counter at the Bank of England? Or your father should fix him up running an introduction agency for married ladies? It was a good factory with good wages, near Hackney marshes, I believe. It was applying the paint.'

'I thought his lungs were damaged. Wouldn't the chemicals be bad for him?'

'Maybe Ervin didn't think of that, but Sándor could have put it a bit nicer, instead of the things he said.'

'What things?'

'Why do you pry into other people's conversations? When did we ever bring you up to do this? All I'm telling you is that your father was never a bad brother, never. He went to visit the prison. Not often, but he went.'

'Why didn't you tell me?'

'It was only you we tried to protect from him. We wanted you to have a start, to be a respectable person. This is all we wished for you. We got you a certificate from the church so you were a proper person from the word go.'

'But *how* could he harm me?'

'It's not a matter of harm, it's about a bad influence and people thinking we are not a nice family.'

'Well, he's settling down now. What do you think of Eunice?'

'Oh, her. She's a lady, anyone can see that.'

'Apart from Daddy.'

'Yes, apart from him.'

'How could he have said that to her? It was *appalling*. I felt sick, I wanted to hit him, it was such a vile thing to . . .'

But my mother shrugged. She said, 'Your father is not like other people. He says what comes into his head. He isn't like you either, he doesn't have any experience of company. We never went out into society like the rest. You see how we live, it's only what is to be expected.'

'Do you regret marrying him?'

'*Regret*? What are you talking about? Of course not, what a crazy idea. I love your father.'

'What do you mean, you love him? What do you actually mean by that?'

'It means I know him, Vivien. I know him, with all his weaknesses. This is love.'

'And what about his strengths? Where are they?' For to me my father was now a grotesque caricature of a human being, a mean-spirited misanthrope. I hated him.

'You try going out to work for forty years, doing the same job every day, working until your eyes ache and water, your bones are stiff, your hands are full of spasms and you have to put them in a bowl of hot water in the filthy sink in the back before you leave for the night. Tired you do not know the meaning of.'

She turned away and walked abruptly into her bedroom and

shut the door. I stood there looking at the green stool, the window looking out on to the mansion block next door, the closed blind of the opposite window, the taps, the cooker, the pots and pans.

My uncle gave me a flat, rent free ('You think I charge family?' he said), the best flat in the whole place, apart from his own. He must have kicked someone out to make way for me: paid them off, or sent round one of Mickey's 'contacts'. I know whoever they were, they left in a hurry, with the bed unmade, sheets stained and full of crumbs, as if they had been disturbed at night.

It was in that room that I started to read again. A leaflet says little, a whole book is full of thoughts, ideas and makes you fall prey to complicated feelings; there is no anaesthesia in the pages of a novel. Often you find discomfort, as if you were sleeping like the princess on the mattresses on top of the pea. The books that I read were about faraway lands, places where there were temples, rice paddies, brass gongs, murderers hiding in the mountains, distant coups.

But the history of the Kovacs family, our history in Hungary, continued to crowd in on me, and the many dead and their past lives set themselves up in the darker corners of the room. In a few weeks I had gone from being a girl without a history to a girl whose past was what was meant by teachers when they spoke of it, book history. The various choices made by my uncle and my father: one to survive against all the odds, the other to exist in a half-life, required me to ask myself what I would have done in their place. I did not have, innately, my uncle's ruthless instincts, his calculating trader's brain which was prepared to deal in any commodity, including human beings. But nor could I have stood the decades of self-immolation that my father had imposed upon himself; his abject surrender to all authority exasperated me. *I wanted to live. I just wanted to live.*

And if life took you to the uncertain, strange margins, to the places where people struggled to express their whole being, through dress or sex or whatever form such individuality took, then that's where I would go.

So I spent my mornings with the tape recorder and typewriter, afternoons lying on the bed reading, early evenings outside the pubs with the leaflets, and nights with Claude, if he was on day shift. I didn't delude myself about what was going on, we didn't have a relationship, we had sex, that was all, much-needed, hot and hasty sex. Yet he had bought me the leather jacket and it had cost him a lot, he had drawn on the savings for his tattoo. He knew I could afford my own jacket, if I'd wanted one, but having seen me wearing his, he couldn't get the idea out of his head. There was something about me in leather. 'You're a different girl in that skin,' he said. 'You look like you own the ground you stand on. Which you don't in your mouldy old dresses.'

'What's the matter with my dresses?'

'They smell.'

'Of what?'

'Old ladies. And old ladies' pee.'

What did he want from me? It was always half in my mind that he thought I was the route to the Special Mr K's money. I'd got his window fixed, what else could I do for him? Maybe the old geezer would give me a huge cheque, *thousands*, or he'd just pop off one night and leave me the lot. Or perhaps his ambitions were more modest, that it was just the idea of walking through London with a 'posh, rich bird' on his arm that appealed to the boy from Sheerness.

Or simpler still. Claude was the victim of his own hormones. Men like him must expend a great deal of energy each night finding a girl to go home with them, and if they are intelligent they understand that it's important to come to an arrangement to make it regularly available. I didn't think of myself as his girlfriend, but I was his girl. His regular girl. There might have been others, I'm not sure. I did not mind, and he would have known that I didn't. We had a situation, it was suitable for both of us. It met a need, it was its own point.

The feeding of the tropical fish, the hours he spent lying on the bed watching them swim fluorescently about in their tank, absorbed his spare time when he was not working or screwing. Their aimless short existence and extreme colours and patterns were what he liked about them. They ate and circled around behind the glass to no purpose. Watching the fish allowed his imagination to run free while he worked on the design of his tattoo. He was *dreaming* that tattoo, whether awake or asleep, watching the fish or riding to work on his bike at dawn through north London's empty streets.

Before he left Sheerness he had bought a sketch pad which he kept in his locked suitcase. I was not allowed to see it, nor did I wish to, for I loathed tattoos, hated the idea of his body disfigured with coloured inks, pictures needled into his flesh. What was wrong with a tattoo? he said. I thought they were common but I couldn't tell him that, so I asked whether it would hurt. He thought it might and admitted that he was curious and anxious about the pain and whether he could live with it. It mattered to him that he would be prepared and not let himself down by yelping out loud, or even breaking down and crying (especially in front of the tattooist, who he assumed would be a tough character). He began to conduct cautious experiments to test his pain threshold, stubbing a cigarette out on the back of his hand to see how long he could go without screaming. I had to go out of the room and stand in the corridor when he did this. When I came back the coal had singed his flesh and left a circle of blackened, charred skin, and he held it out and laughed at it, a laugh that sounded like a dog with its paw caught in a trap.

He moaned in his sleep that night, reached out for my breast and laid the back of the burnt hand on it, as if it had healing powers.

Only because he set fire to the suitcase did I finally see what was inside. He was going through an arsonist phase, finding dead birds and cremating them on pyres of leaves. He would talk of setting fire to London's landmarks. I told him about the Great Fire of London, the city razed to ashes. I sometimes think he would have enjoyed a sudden incendiary episode, like the firestorm after Dresden, and wandering along across the scorched and blackened surface of an empty city. He was a little weird, I suppose, but I had grown up amongst weird, it was nothing new to me. I was only a few weeks away myself from biting down on drinking glasses.

He took the suitcase out into the garden to make an altar on which he placed a small pile of sacrifices: his guard's hat, which he would have to pay to replace, a pair of underpants, one of Mrs Prescott's satin blouses.

The clothes did not burst into flames as he had hoped but set up a low smoulder and a chemical stink, mainly from the hat. Eventually the blouse transformed itself to ashes but the hat stubbornly held its shape, browned and singed; sparks glittered briefly at the peak. Claude got bored, closed his eyes and fell asleep. I continued to watch the burnt offerings. After a few minutes the suitcase caught fire.

I shook him awake. 'Did you mean to burn your suitcase?' I asked him, laughing.

'Holy fuck,' he said, and picked it up to shake off the little bonfire, but the handle was metal covered with leather and had heated up. He screamed and dropped it. We were nowhere near any water to put out the fire.

We had to wait nearly an hour before the suitcase was cool enough to carry indoors. The lock was twisted in the heat and he had to use his penknife to prise it open. He was desperate to know whether its contents were safe. But what have you got in there? I asked him. What's so important? It's my *stuff*, he said.

Inside, the case was filled with small baffling treasures: a paperback of James Fenimore Cooper's *The Last of the Mohicans*, well worn on the spine, which he said he had read many times, containing, he implied, all of life's significant lessons. But I had never read it, and all I knew was that it concerned Red Indians. A girl's bracelet made of those coloured plastic beads that plug together. A postcard showing Edinburgh Castle. Blackbird feathers, held together by a rubber band. Letters postmarked Sheerness. And a bag of sweets.

But it was not the letters, the postcard, the book, the bracelet or the sweets that he anxiously removed from the suitcase. The sketch pad, spiral bound, was taken out and each page checked to make sure that it had not been damaged. Here were the designs for his tattoo, from the first, crude efforts at seaman's anchors, or ruby hearts with a name inscribed inside them (HELEN – his mother, he said, though he wasn't that sentimental about the old bat, but you had to put something) all the way to the increasingly ambitious and sophisticated schemes, quite well executed, involving schools of fish swimming around an upper arm, some of which I recognised from the tank. Until finally he turned the page, and there it was, his final design. The finished version.

'What do you think?' he said.

I couldn't take my eyes off it, however much I wanted to turn them away, to his face. I was trying to see if there was some error, that if you looked at it from another angle the form would reassemble itself and become something more innocuous but even though my eyes swam on the page, it stayed the way it was, anchored to the sheet of paper by its four points.

'It's a swastika.'

'Yeah, I know.'

'Don't you understand what it is?'

'Yes, it's a shape.'

'Not just a shape. Do you know what a symbol is?'

'Of course I know, don't fucking talk down to me.'

'It's a symbol of Fascism.'

'They can be a symbol of anything you like, but I agree they're sort of heavy. They've got a lot of power in them, that's why they've been around for thousands of years before the Nazzies got hold of them. The Indians the ones in India, not the Americans, they had them first. I think they're amazing, I love them.'

'Don't be so naïve. In this day and age they have only one meaning, and you know it.'

'Who cares?'

'I do.'

'Why? Why should you care?'

We argued for a long time. He jumped out of the window into the garden and stood under the newly planted flowering cherry and smoked. I saw him through the open pane, sitting on the hard ground, his hands round his thin knees, with that frail toughness that attracted me, that mouth I had to kiss. He was a shape in the garden, full of blood and hormones.

I wasn't going to tell him the truth about my uncle, about who he was and where he had come from, about the slave labourer years. It was none of Claude's business. Nor was I going to talk to him about being Jewish, because I didn't feel Jewish inside. The village in the Zémplen, the great-grandfather with the curls in front of his ears, the synagogue my uncle and father both remembered (despite my father's denials) were like folk stories of another century.

My parents thought this island, this Britain, was an oasis of tolerance and fair play, but across the Channel a howling wilderness of big ideas could inflate into an ideology, and once a man had an ideology, he was always on the lookout for enemies. When you are the enemy of a person with an ideology, you're in serious trouble. But I knew different, from the evenings handing out the leaflets. I knew that quite ordinary people, who had no thoughts at all, just feelings, could be equally dangerous.

Of course, I knew Claude was no Nazi, but what upset and frightened me was the discovery that I had no power to change his mind, that he was resistant to logic, indeed to understanding. He was his own planet, and on it he made his own rules. In Claude-land, a swastika could mean whatever you liked, it was up to you to assign your own meanings, he said, though not in those words, but that's what he meant. His tattoo had symbolic significance for him alone. He was solipsistic and nihilistic, I told him, and he laughed longer than I had ever heard him laugh before, to hear that such big hard words applied to *him*. He made me write them down in his sketch pad and then practised copying them, in a variety of artistic scripts.

But I would not sleep with him and he was surprised and angry that some drawings in a book should deny him what he needed every night.

After the triumph of the birthday party, my uncle and his future bride began to plan their own wedding. She had ordered for him a silk suit from Italy, and for herself a dress, the details of which were a close secret but which was thought to have come from one of the great French houses. All my uncle had to do was write the cheque, and he was overjoyed about that. The marquee and the caterers had been re-booked for late September. There was a date. The wedding was a reality.

And even before that, Eunice would be moving in with uncle; they would be living together, as she said, 'as man and wife'. They already slept together three nights a week, and it was during those nights my uncle had thought deeply that this was what it must be like to be a married man, to go to bed with the face of a woman next to you on the pillow, to kiss her while she slept. How could a man who did not have it in his blood to say yes to a boss surrender to another human being, even if she had lovely breasts and smelt of flowers and spices? Still, her body warmed him while he slept.

And then there was the business of the skinheads in Wood

Green who were terrorising everyone with their marches and their ugly shaved heads and their horrible laced-up boots with the trousers rolled up to the calves to show off the brown leather and the eyelets. If he married her she would leave behind for ever all that, he would make some different arrangements, such as knocking though to the next flat to make it bigger – he could afford to lose £6 a week rent.

'And what does she think?' I had asked him when he first told me of his plan to marry her.

'Well, you see, Eunice does not have a favourable view of marriage. She tried it once, it was a disaster. She's an independent woman so if you are going to pin her down you have to have something to offer her that she don't have already. And money is not enough, because she can earn her own living.'

But he had eventually prevailed, had overcome his own anxieties about the loss of his freedom. It was a huge step for him, this would be the rest of his life – a married man – but he was going to do it for he could not leave her unprotected in Wood Green and he did not even dare consider suggesting the idea that they should live together as a common-law couple. Without the wedding, even if it was in a registry office, without an engagement ring and a dress and a cake and a speech, Eunice would not budge. And the ring was the declaration that he was absolutely serious and not pulling the wool over her eyes.

I don't see no ring, she had said, when he proposed, over lunch at an Italian restaurant on the day of my birthday party, an ostentatious lunch with silver service and a trolley with the desserts and the option of having a waiter standing next to you flambéing a piece of veal over a live flame in front of your eyes. He knew what impressed women. Nothing about my uncle was ever mean.

And in order to rescue Eunice from the skinheads in Wood Green, he needed to buy an engagement ring, since there was now no chance that my father would make it.

Sándor had a keen eye for jewellery but he wanted a woman's opinion so he asked me to accompany him to Harrods to make the selection. The purchase was not actually going to be made there, he no longer had the kind of money that could afford a ten or twenty thousand pound ring; the rents from the two houses in Camden kept him comfortably with some room for extravagances like my party, but there was a limit to his liquid assets.

His plan was to pick out a few suitable rings and then give a description of them to Mickey, who would look around for a week or two and come up with something similar, or even exactly the same thing, not a fake, absolutely out of the question, but it didn't need to be. For Mickey's London, which radiated out from his Dalston lock-up miles and miles in all directions to the suburbs north and south (but no further than the orbital motorways, beyond which were things he didn't understand and didn't want to understand, like cows, sheep, birds) had all kinds of individuals inside it who could get you pretty much anything you wanted, such as a piece of moon rock or, later, chunks of the Berlin Wall.

It was true: my uncle had wanted my father to make the ring. He saw himself generously paying his brother for his time and his labour, praising his exquisite workmanship, but Ervin had nixed that one. 'I tell you again,' Sándor said, as we were on the bus to Knightsbridge. 'I see him next in the other place. Then we'll talk.'

'What is that other place?' I asked him.

'It's where they do the final balance sheet. The counting up of days.'

'How do you think you'll come out? Are you afraid?'

'Not at all. The Expert isn't concerned with the things they worry about here in this life. He sees things in a different way. I'm not worried. He wants to know not how a man lived but *did* he live? Did he waste the gift the Expert gave him, or did he make the best use of it he can?'

'So you believe in God?'

'Who said anything about God?'

'Isn't that what we're talking about?'

'No.'

But this riddle of my uncle's beliefs remains unsolved, for the bus swung round into Sloane Street and we got off and walked down to Harrods, him stopping at the windows of the shops all along Brompton Road and exclaiming at the luxury goods.

The rings lay on velvet and satin beds; they held their heads up to the light and sank their gold and platinum shanks deep into the blue and white luxury of their opulent pillows.

I could name all the stones, I grew up in this business. There were diamonds, sapphires, emeralds, rubies, and then the lesser gems – garnets, opals, amethysts, topaz – but it was only the sapphires my uncle was interested in. 'Blue is an aristocratic colour, don't you think?' he said. 'It says quality to me, but maybe I'm wrong. What is the stones that the Queen has in her crown?'

The salesman was delighted to be asked this question and began a scholarly speech on the matter, because there was more than one crown. We looked carefully at the rings and my uncle enquired about the prices, a nominal question so as to establish our credentials as bona fide purchasers, not time-wasters. We discussed whether she would prefer a solitaire or a cluster, a square-cut stone or a lozenge shape. And what would be the setting, of what material?

For my uncle cried out, 'You see my curse and my blessing? To fall in love with a woman of elegance and style, and everything has to be exactly right or she turns up her nose. I want it to be perfect, you understand, Vivien? I want her to open the box and she *gasps* because this is what she has been waiting for her whole life, ever since she was a little girl in school in Tiger Bay and she reads stories about princesses.'

'Look,' he whispered. 'This one.'

An ice-blue square-cut solitaire on a platinum band.

'What do you think?'

'It's perfect.'

'Elegant?'

'Yes, it is.'

'We'll think about it,' he said to the salesman. 'Thank you, you have been a big help.'

'How are you going to find something like that?' I asked him, as we walked through the aisles.

'Well, Mickey will have to do his best. He'll manage, he never let me down so far. You want to go for coffee?'

'Are you going to take a picture of it or something?'

'Why? No need. I remember it exactly. The picture is inside my head already. I got it.'

We ascended in the lift to the tea rooms. The little tables sat like débutantes, waiting to be asked to dance.

'This is a very nice one,' my uncle said. 'It's important in a café to know which table will get you the best service, and I know this because I used to be a waiter. How you treat a waiter is very significant too, if you want to be offered the best pastry.'

The cakes, stiff cream fabrications looking exhausted already under the over-brilliant light of the chandeliers, were offered to us on a silver tray.

'You got anything special today?' my uncle asked the waitress, and he gave her a smile; it was mainly in his eyes rather than his lips, and they seemed to address her with a whole speech composed of warmth and sympathy and humour, a smile that knows everything about swollen feet and swallowed-back responses to insults.

'I'll go and see if we do, sir,' she said, and she winked. She returned with a second, smaller tray bearing fresher gâteaux. 'I recommend the raspberry and chocolate roulade.'

'Then this we will have,' said my uncle. 'I always accept a

recommendation from staff. Because you know, don't you? You are experts, and lovely experts, every one. Thank you, my dear. May your day be a happy one. You see?' he said, turning back to me. 'It doesn't take more than few words to get the best service.'

'Have you set a date for the wedding?' I asked him. I don't say I was under my uncle's spell, but I was drawn to a person who made their own rules and was scared of no one. Such individuals, who do not care what society thinks or what it says about them, are full of energy and they make the world go round. My husband was this way.

'Soon. But Eunice wants time for preparations, that's what women are like, you have to accept it. Oh, this pastry! This is a good one. You didn't see this on the tray, did you? The *main* tray. Vivien, in life there is always the main tray which is for the ordinary people who don't know that waiting in the back there is something special. Always. I learned this a long time ago. Wait for the special tray.'

'But life isn't cakes.'

'No, it isn't, of course not, but the principle is the same. You have to know that there is something else, something better, that is hidden from you, that they don't want you to find out about, that you have to ask for, and sometimes you just have to go and take it. Your father never knew this, that's his great failing; don't let it be yours.'

'My mother told me quite recently that she met you before my father.'

'That's right. I'm happy she remembered. A poor girl with her stick, a pretty girl who had no idea she was pretty, the stick beat her itself if ever she told herself she was. And intelligent, too. I knew she was just right for Ervin.'

'You introduced them on purpose?'

'Of course. It was all arranged. Ervin didn't know he was going to meet a girl, I just told him to join me for coffee on the banks of the Danube, but this was my plan, to bring them together. He needed a girl and he was too cantankerous to meet one himself.'

I felt that everything had happened already, that we living ones were just shadows of the real events, weak outlines cast down the decades.

'But why?' I cried. 'Why was *she* to be a human sacrifice? Didn't she deserve better?'

'No, no, you don't understand. She elevated him to her level, not the other way round. She turned him into a human being.'

'I don't think that's true. She told me he used to sing her American songs, from the films.'

'Did he? I never knew that.'

'She said he was different, then.'

'Well, maybe she knows him better than me – I only knew him as a brother. And as a middle-aged man who insults his future sister-in-law. Deliberately, as you saw. But I never heard him sing no songs and I never knew him going to see no films either. But always you ask the questions not me. What do you do with yourself, how do you spend your time?'

'I fight Fascism,' I said, with some pride, hoping for his approval. I hoped he would think that I was doing some small thing to make amends for the years he had spent as a slave.

'And how do you do this?'

'I told you already, I hand out leaflets.'

'A leaflet. *Very* nice. What does the leaflet say?'

I explained our important political message to the people of London about this Nazi menace hidden behind a lying face of British patriotism.

'Well, I'm sure they will listen. Who could disagree with a leaflet? What about the boy Claude, does he go with you?'

I had tried to conceal my relationship with him. I felt my uncle would not understand what I was doing with a common boy, a rough boy, as he called him, with the leather jacket and the job below ground. But he must have caught sight of the two of us together, coming home from the pub, or of me sneaking out of his room in the early morning before I got my own flat in the house. And the swastikas. I was ashamed.

'Are you worried about Eunice?' I said, changing the subject.

'Yes, of course I am. That's why I'm in a hurry to marry her, so she will get out of that flat and come here where she will be safer. It's not a good neighbourhood.'

'Sándor, tell me, why do you always go out with black girls?'

'Why?' He looked at me and smiled that same kind smile he had given the waitress, a smile full of charm and somehow the lower lip, that Hitchcock profile, softened into a sensitivity I'd only occasionally seen in him before. For he could be the cold businessman, the beast who roared for his profits, who carelessly bought on credit the tawdry goods he craved because once he was a slave whose balls had been beaten until they broke, but then his features once or twice would melt, re-form, assume another shape.

'I never saw a coloured girl until after the war. I barely knew such a person existed except maybe in those American films your father says he went to see, which I doubt. But when I left it too late to leave Hungary, when communism stole up on us when we were not looking, we were cut off from the rest of Europe. The dance bands, Tommy Dorsey, the singers, Frank Sinatra, people like that, they never came to the East. We had brotherly love, we had comrades, and among our comrades were the Americans. American communists. Once, there came to the café where I was made to work as a waiter, a torch singer from America, a *communist* torch singer.'

He threw back his head and laughed. 'What an idea, but you know, that's what she was. Her name was Elvira. She had a sequined dress and high-heeled shoes when the women of Budapest wore a man's jacket and leather boots to keep out the bitter winter cold. Elvira from Kansas City. The most beautiful woman I ever saw in my life, before or since. I don't know what happened to her, I tried to find her records, but I don't think she ever made any. She was a true communist, a Party member. I made sure she had the best pastries, the ones we kept on the special tray for the Party officials and the visitors from Moscow. Ever since then I lost my taste for white women. Her grandmother was a slave, and I told her that just four years ago I too was a slave. I drank Tokaj from her shoes. I'll never forget that, in my little flat with a bottle of wine from the vineyards of the Zémplen, drinking it from the heel which smelt of her sweat and all her odours and still it was the sweetest drink in all the world.'

When the last train leaves for its destination, when the passengers have disembarked at the final terminus, and the train's lights flash, then darken, the trains roll on to their night-time rest.

What do they get up to, down there in the dark?

'I want to do it with my bird on a train,' Claude said.

'*What*? In broad daylight?'

'After we stop running. I'll take you to the depot.'

'Are you allowed to do that?'

'No, but it doesn't mean to say that you can't, neither.'

We had no common interests, no social life together; mostly we just lay around in bed looking at his tiny fish with their dot eyes. Sometimes a fish would develop a white fungus and die slowly, occasionally they jumped out on to the hotplate, with self-evidently suicidal intentions: it was a very constrained world in there.

The death of a fish upset him for days. The little bodies would be wrapped in a tissue and buried in a shallow indentation he made with a teaspoon in the garden, but then a week or so later he would dig them up and examine their skeletons before they too disintegrated. He felt sad that they had to lie in the cold English soil when they came from faraway seas and warm climates.

The night after I accompanied my uncle to scope out engagement rings at Harrods, where I had seen what there was to be had on the *special* tray, I got dressed in my jeans and leather jacket and waited close to midnight on the platform at Camden station, northbound.

The last passengers were on their way home, the pale revellers and weary night workers slumped against the walls; the final train is a lonely business, the day closing behind you. A strong wind blew along the tunnel, signalling the train approaching. The indicator board lit up and faded, trains came and went until the last train of all. The doors opened and Claude swung out, searched the faces of the crowd and beckoned me on board. I stepped on lightly in my monkey boots, the doors closed behind us and we were on our way.

'Come here,' he said, 'let me cuddle you, you look cold. You been waiting long?'

'I'm all right.' We were in the little space between the rattling carriages, the shifting floor where the carriages are coupled together and you feel that you might be torn asunder, one half of your body moving away from the other.

'Can I blow your whistle?' I said.

'Yeah, here it is, go on, have a go.'

I put it in my mouth, it was still warm from his lips, and I blew, long and hard and piercing.

We rushed north. Claude ran through the carriages, his cap down shadowing his eyes, his jacket loose around his shoulders and grey with ash. He wasn't handsome: his nose was too sharp, his hair too fine, everything about him came to a point, except that mouth, those lips that looked like they had been grafted on to his face not for talking but sucking, kissing. But the young girls homeward bound after a night out stared at him with bold laughing eyes.

He said I was his girl and I laughed. I said we were just fuck-mates. So it was true, he was too common for me, he taunted. I'm here, aren't I, I said. Look at me, you've got your common hands on my breasts. You just want a bit of rough, he said. And what do *you* want, I asked. What's your agenda?

'I'm after your money, girl, what do you think?'

'Take it,' I said. 'Eight pounds a day is my fortune, I'll give you all of it.'

'I fancy being a kept man, the plaything of a rich old lady. An old lady like you.' The sudden, abrupt laugh. 'It's funny, ain't it?' He couldn't keep his hands off my hair. 'Let me stroke you, old lady. You're like the Queen of Sheba. She was in the Bible and the King gave her gold and presents. I'd give you gold if I had the money.'

I wished I could have shown him my bedroom at Benson Court, the ballet picture, the china dog, the horse bookends, the horrible hand-me-down clothes in the wardrobe, but he would never see inside Benson Court. That was his attraction. We were just bodies, in free fall.

At Golders Green we came out from the deep tunnels up on to the overground tracks. Above ground the train seemed more frail and vulnerable, as if an underground creature had burrowed up to the surface and was exposed to all its natural predators.

The train stopped at Hendon, Colindale, Burnt Oak, then reached the end of the line at Edgware. Sleeping passengers were woken; they struggled through the ticket turnstiles and made their way home. 'But don't you get off,' he said to me, 'we're not there yet.'

A long time we waited, the carriages standing silently and emptily at the darkened station before we moved again, shunting slowly south, then gathering speed, black outlines of trees, houses on the embankments above us, and above that, a sultry summer moon.

'There are trains that are supposed to be haunted, did you know that?' he said. 'Passengers die on the trains all the time, and some trains have killed people, they're murder trains, but you don't know which ones, they change their numbers.'

'How do they kill people?'

'Suicides throw themselves down in front of them and the blood flows along the tracks.'

We pulled into the Golders Green depot. I heard the driver's footsteps echoing along the walkway as he left for the night. We were alone in the silence. Outside foxes moved stealthily through the bushes, Claude said; he saw them sometimes.

'So it's just you and me, girl,' he said, taking off his cap and jacket. 'I wish we was moving but I couldn't risk it.'

There was nowhere to lie down but the floor, a surface covered in empty crisp packets, torn newspapers, plastic bags, cigarette ends, chocolate wrappers, a baby's dummy, a wallet with its contents removed, a hat, a shoe, a shirt, torn-up tickets. He opened the windows and let in the night air.

'Unzip your jeans,' he said. He unzipped his own, reached forward and pulled down my panties to my hips then placed his hands in the straps that came down from the roof of the carriage. It was so dark in there, I could hardly see him, he was a shape, and an echoing voice. 'Kiss me for a bit, then put it inside you.' I pulled myself up until my knees gripped his narrow hips. We hung there suspended, him from the roof and me from him. When it was over he wiped my thighs with his jacket.

I didn't say anything. It was his fantasy, not mine. I felt we had gone too far: like the tube train leaving its designated path on the map, we had lit off out for unknown quarters. He rolled a cigarette in the dark. I sat down.

'Do you mind if I sit on your lap for a minute?' he said.

'OK.'

His body was as light as a bird or a phantom.

'You're so thin,' I said, holding him carefully so that he would not break. You don't eat enough to live,' I said, stroking his face.

'I'm living, aren't I?' he said, turning his head away.

'You're wasting away, you were much stronger in the spring. Those tablets you're taking are slimming pills, did you know that? That's what the doctors prescribe them for, it's why you have no appetite.'

'I live on air,' he said. The voice came from the little coal glowing in the blackness: 'that's what my grandma once told me. She's one of the tinker folk and they're related to the pixies.' He laughed. 'I'd like to be from the other world. I sometimes think I don't belong in this one.'

I knew that it was almost over, but that did not mean that I would ever stop longing for him, or that the tenderness he sometimes showed would not continue to move me, or touch a heart that was already healing itself with invisible calluses

'Shall we each tell each other a secret?' he said. 'That's what the night's for, isn't it, stories?'

'I don't mind.'

'Who's going to go first?'

'It was your idea.'

'All right then. Here's one.' He began to talk in a low, quick voice, as if he was hunting down his thoughts to kill them. 'It happened when I was little kid just starting at the big school, right? And we had to have a pair of long grey socks that come up to your knees. That's how you knew you was in the big school, them socks. When I come home the first day, my dad sent me out to the yard to clean the dog's dishes.'

'What kind of dogs?' I knew his fear of them. He had told me before how the smell made him feel sick.

'Two big mongrels with pointed teeth and matted fur. And they had black lips and their eyes was always crying. I don't know what my dad wanted them for because he never took them walks or nothing, he just left them chained up but he come from Ireland, somewhere in the country, and he said a man's not a man without a dog.

'So I'm bending over to pick up the dishes and this dog, Alf, my dad called him, after a bloke down the street, he picks up his leg and pisses on me. I could feel it trickling down on to my socks, warm and wet and stinking of that ammonia smell, all yellow. And I ran inside bawling my head off and me mum was just standing there laughing. She gives me a kiss and takes the socks off and washes them and dries them overnight in front of the fire. But when I went to school next day the whiff was still coming off me and all the kids was calling me names so come milk break, I ran away.'

'Where did you run away to?'

He laid his face against my cheek and I kissed it, as you kiss a child.

'Down to where the ships come in, some sheds I knew about. I slept with the tramps and they gave me cider. I was only eleven, but I liked the taste and the way it felt when it got into your veins. They were all right, I didn't mind them, though they stank of course, but then I stank too. I was like a cat that's gone wild, do you know what I mean? Have you ever felt like that? Like you don't belong to nothing or nobody? I thought I could stay there for ever and never go back to school but they came for me in the end, with a policeman and a woman from the social and I had to go home. My mum threw the socks away and bought me another pair but I always thought that people could smell that dog's wee, that it would follow me around as long as I lived.'

'You smell fantastic,' I said. 'Didn't you know that?'

'Yeah, girls have said it before now. But you never really believe them, do you? I wash a lot, to make sure.'

The doors opened and further down the train the cleaners began their work, with rubbish bags, mops, cloths. He stood up.

'We've got to go now,' he said. 'They might report me. I liked sitting on your lap, we'll do that again some time.'

It was still only 1.30, the long night was ahead of us.

'Where are we going now?'

He said we could start walking home when it got light, but we would have some tea first in the mess room. 'And now you can tell me a story. Make it a good one, eh, girl?'

I remember the tiled clinic, the green waiting room, the frightened girls, my mother's hand wiping the sweat from my neck, the bus, the smell of the plastic seats, the awful pain. But who can really remember pain? It's impossible, you don't remember it, you only fear it returning. These thoughts are like stitches – you sew together a memory with them and the flesh heals over into a scar. The scar is the memory.

My mother brought me tea in bed. 'You must be careful how you wash,' she said, 'you must not get an infection. The place down there has been opened to the air.'

The tea tasted like iron filings. 'I can't drink this.'

'A glass of water?'

'That would be better.' But when it came it was oily and rank.

What does the body know? It understands very well that it has been invaded, whether by a fused cell or a tube that aspirates away the clump of living matter. It will *never* let you forget. There were holes in my body. Gaps, deficiencies. I tried to pay them no attention.

*

'Oh, shut the fuck up, will you? You can't kill a baby.'

'I didn't kill a *baby*.'

'Yes you did. It's dead, ain't it? If it's not dead, where is it? Where's the baby, Viv, show us your baby.'

'Stop it.'

'Stop what? You killed a little one and you want me to feel sorry for you, is that it?'

'But I told you the story, don't you understand I *had* to. What choice was there?'

'There's *always* a story, people are full of excuses. You hear them all the time, oh, he said he'd marry me, I thought you couldn't fall the first time, the silly slags.'

He threw a bag of sugar across the mess room; it rained down from high on the plastic chairs, the maroon vinyl floor, the Formica table.'Look what you made me do.' His face was sickly under the fluorescent light, half starved, demented.

I remembered the hand on his back as his father pushed him up the hill to church.

'Some priest has been filling your head with rubbish,' I said.

'Hell's a real place. Just because the priest talks about it, don't mean it's not true.'

I didn't know him at all. I didn't understand the first thing about him, he was an opaque mass of matter in a leather jacket and a T-shirt. Behind his eyes some complicated person lay in hiding. I had not touched him at all.

'I'm going,' I said. 'I'm walking home. You're crazy.'

'Great. See ya round.' He began to roll a cigarette but his fingers were trembling. When I turned back at the gate, he was standing at the window watching me, as if he belonged, suddenly, to another time, another dimension, framed in the rectangle with the light behind him, one square of light in the utter blackness of the depot, like one of those ghosts he believed wandered the empty trains at night, the ghosts of suicides.

The sky gradually lightened as the dark broke over London. City of towers and steeples, railway lines, wormed with tunnels, and the closer I got to home, the faster I went until I broke into a run, running through Chalk Farm until the whole bright day dawned, the sun rising in along the estuary.

Past factories and workshops and lock-ups, I ran. The energy of London transmitted itself to me, all the energy and vitality of a city awakening rose up inside me and my thoughts ran quicker still.

If I'd kept that baby, she would have most of the things she needed to become a real person by now. A head, legs, arms, hands, hair, and she would be developing feet and fingerprints. Her brain would be starting to receive messages and form memories of her time in the womb, which she would later forget, because everyone forgets. Resourcefully, she would be growing, intent on who she was going to become, her DNA deciding on Alexander's long bones and blond hair or my short limbs and dark moustache. The DNA would be working out what it was going to send on into the future – the code string could reach back east to the village in the Zémplen, with the rabbis and plums, or to the county towns of western England, their churches and oak trees. My body would be a busy machine turning out this brand-new person.

This time next year I would have been wheeling her in a pram through Regent's Park, past the rose garden. I would have showed her the lake with the water birds and explained the inner life of a goose, as her daddy understood it. And such an intense wave of regret came over me, such a searing sense that I had done the wrong thing and that Claude in his simple crude way was right, I was pierced to the core by his harsh words.

At last I got home and went into my little flat, dropped down on the bed, unwashed, fully dressed and fell asleep. I dreamed of my baby. Her name was Gertrude. What a stupid name! She had blue eyes and wore a velvet dress. She took my hand. 'Mummy,' she said. 'Yes, darling?' 'What's *your* name?' I tried to tell her but my tongue was wood. I tried to shape it with my lips and the harder I tried, the more success I had. Yes, I could definitely hear myself.

'Vivien,' said my uncle. 'Vivien! It's ten o'clock. Are you still sleeping?'

'You and that boy had an argument,' he said. 'I can see it written all over your face.'

Yes, I admitted it. His face lit up. He said he would get rid of him; a few pounds and he could leave the next day. But I said Claude had a right to live there and of course he rolled his eyes – 'You and your rights.'

'Tell me,' he said. 'What did you see in that character? He was beneath you, a girl with a degree like yours.'

How could I explain to my uncle the erotic drag that pulled me towards him?

'Oh, I understand now how it was. Don't be embarrassed. Don't make of that part of your life a prisoner and an exile, like my brother did. OK, you deserve a little toy after all you been through. But the toy is broken now, you throw it away, you move on to something else.'

'Is that all that women are for you?'

'In the past, yes. But I've changed. It's true, even a villain like me can change his stripes.'

'Spots.'

'What spots?'

'A leopard cannot change its spots, that's the saying.'

'I don't know, I never saw a leopard so about whether he can change his spots or not, I have no opinion. But me, I have changed. I am going to be a very different man, you'll see.'

We were in his flat, under the mural, drinking coffee, him in his cane peacock throne and me opposite him in my T-shirt and jeans with my legs pulled up and my hands around my knees as if I was protecting my abdomen from external assault.

We were not taping his life story; he saw I was exhausted and he wanted me to preserve my strength for a favour he had to ask me – would I go in the morning to Wood Green to help Eunice pack? She was moving in with him, to his flat, at long last. The boxes had been delivered and the removals van was coming tomorrow, she had taken the day off work but reluctantly admitted it was going to need two pairs of hands.

'Why me of all people?' I asked. 'She doesn't like me.'

'That's only because she doesn't know you, and to tell the truth, you are not such an easy person to know, like your father in that respect – though not in any other, don't get me wrong. You don't have his personality at all, thank God.'

'*Why* am I hard to get to know? I don't understand.'

He smiled. 'So, what shall I call you? Miranda? Vivien? What? You know, you are a girl who likes to put on a different face every five minutes, like a new dress, when she doesn't need to at all because she is lovely in herself, with her own face. And all because she is not confident, she doesn't trust her own instincts in case they lead her up a wrong path to disaster. I know that's what you feel. I watch you when we are tape recording. Inside you are uncertain and must ask questions. This why and the why and the why. That is what you hide behind, your whys. You think if you ask why, it gives you a little time. You were like this as a child? Because I remember you, you know, standing by the door with a face full of eyes and I was trying to give you chocolate, but your father snatched it from my hand like it was poison.'

'Yes, I remember it too, it's the clearest memory I have of my childhood.' I was busy storing away these remarks about my personality to examine later, when I had some quietness. I found them very surprising and even alarming because I thought of myself as someone constantly scrabbling to hold on to reason and logic in the face of my irrational parents and their old grudges, insecurities, neuroses and cranky opinions.

'*Really?* What do you remember of me?' He sat forward in the cane throne, eagerly.

'I remember your blue suit and your suede shoes and your diamond watch, and the girl you were with in her leopardskin coat and her hat. I was watching you from the window when you both left, you were out on the pavement and she had chocolate round her mouth.'

He smiled. 'Yes, that girl. I don't know what happened to her, they come and go. I don't know what happened to the suit either, or the watch. But what a nice child you were. I never had a child, or not that I hear about, anyway.'

'Do you wish you did have one?' I said, for I did not know then about my uncle's sterility. His face froze a little. Grey shadows appeared in the creases of his face.

'For many years I thought about a son. It's normal for a man to want a son, but then you see a little daughter and your wish turns into something different. You realise that the way you treat a woman is the way your little girl will be treated by men in her own life. It can strike you like a plank of wood around the head, this thought. You know, I was never unkind to women, just careless. You shouldn't be like that with people. I don't want you to be careless, which is why I didn't like you being with that boy. He was a plaything for you. But enough, it's none of my business,

I just express an opinion, and that's it. Now it is time for the news.'

He switched on the set. They were interviewing John Tyndall, the leader of the National Front who was talking about the 'white race'. I looked down at my hands to see what colour they were. A dirty olive brown. He was flanked by supporters, the men all wore white shirts and dark ties, and their heads seemed to have been boiled so that all the blood came to the surface.

'Look at that frozen piece of shit,' my uncle said. 'You see I'm not worried for myself, it's Eunice. Now *she* worries me sick, what's going to happen to her. These people with the lace-up boots all over the place, who can control them?'

'Well, I'm going on a demonstration next week,' I said, with pride.

He laughed, the lower flabby lip trembling in his face and his brown eyes full of cynical mirth. 'I seen demonstrations. People march in a crowd with signs in their hands, I saw it in Budapest in '56. Does it ever come to anything?'

But despite the bravado he was afraid. I saw his face turn chalky in the cathode ray light of the screen and his hands clutched the sides of the cane peacock throne.

'Eunice!' he cried, as the lines of marching racists crossed the screen. 'What is going to happen?' he said, turning to me. 'What are you going to do?'

I tried to explain to him about the days when it took me a long time to get rid of my leaflets, and the other times when people took them so eagerly they seemed to be snatching them from your hands, and thanking you, blessing you, for just being there, and showing that if there was going to be trouble, there would be some people who would stand up to be counted.

'Oh, you foolish girl,' my uncle cried, in despair. 'With all the brains in your head, your Shakespeare, look at you, dressed like a boy, and all your lovely hair gone.'

'I'm going to grow it again,' I said. 'I don't want to be a punk any more.'

'Good. That makes me happy. And will we go on with the recordings? I haven't told you anything yet that is important, the real story is coming, of what I did and what they did to me. You don't know, you only know the beginning. You give me a kiss?'

'Of course I will.' I kissed his forehead gently and he reached out and grabbed my hand and put his lips to it. I felt those wet lips on my skin, the pressure of his fingers on my wrist, the nails whitening. My uncle, my flesh and blood which had suffered and made others to suffer. Revulsion and empathy, these were my feelings. He picked a white speck of lint or plaster from my hair. 'You are dusty,' he said, and his hand tentatively touched my cheek. 'Grow it again, won't you, your lovely hair. Let it be what it wishes, when I saw you when you were little you had corkscrews coming our of your head. So did my mother, exactly the same. And she used to try to fight the curls, like you do, but it was never a completely winning battle. I like a girl with a curl best of all.'

We went on watching the news but he had lost interest. I wrote down Eunice's address and he thanked me. I wish I had finally got to the meat of the story, about how he had bought the west London houses and started to rent them out. I had a lot of questions I wanted to ask him about what he did and how he could defend himself, but it turned out this was the very last conversation we had, sitting in his flat in front of his mural, with the palm trees swaying on the wall and the sun shining in the painted sand.

He had a plate in his hands with a piece of cheesecake with strawberries under a red glaze which he had gone to Swiss Cottage to buy but he had barely eaten, for though he talked of cakes a great deal and did everything in his power to obtain them, I think it was the *idea* of cake that compelled him, because his digestion couldn't stand the richness of so much sugar and fat. Thirty years later I still see him sitting in front of the mural with the plate of cheesecake, looking at me with a face of timid love and longing, then the brown eyes filming over, and his handkerchief rubbing at the panes of his mock tortoiseshell reading glasses.

I always thought that Eunice would live in a fussy flat with plenty of decoration and it was true, she had bought a few nice things – some pictures and ornaments, velvet curtains and African violets in plastic pots, but it was like a tidy hotel room, as if she came back here only to eat a meal, watch TV and sleep, and her real life, the public display, was in the shop or on my uncle's arm. Her home was a place in which a child's best doll was carefully put away in its original box and wrapped in pink tissue paper. She lived behind the front door of a Victorian terrace with a cracked dusty, stained-glass panel. It was just the door that interested her, the separation barrier between herself and the world.

She pointed across the street to the flats. 'A different class of person lives over there,' she said. 'And not a nice class.' A lot of bad boys, she said, petty criminals, cat burglars, receivers of stolen goods and kids who were just wild and impertinent and had no respect for their elders. One day one of them had run off with her handbag as she was walking to the tube station, and everything was in it – her purse, her keys, her lipstick, her national insurance card. She searched the neighbourhood and found it in a rubbish tip with everything gone and she had had to go to all the expense of changing the locks.

'And then worse came along after that,' she said: 'the white boys with the boots and the shaved heads.'

So I told her about my activities in the Anti-Nazi League, hopeful of a favourable reaction that would make her like me, but with no great confidence that she would think more highly of them than my uncle. 'Well,' she said, 'it's good you take a stand, we have got to stick together, us and you Hebrews. But these ones with the boots don't take no notice of a leaflet.'

'So what do you think should be done about it?' I asked. For at least I was there, out on the streets, instead of hiding indoors.

She shrugged. 'Well, you know, this is the one time that someone like Mickey Elf has his uses.'

I thought he was a strange character and my uncle's close relationship with him was baffling, but she reminded me that they went back a long way, to the time when Sándor first came to London and my father had not been at all nice and welcoming to him, offering him a job working with his hands, in a factory when he was obviously a man with a businessman's brain. Mickey had got him started. Mickey had the connections, Mickey told him what he could do, what anyone could do, if they were willing, or in the case of my uncle, had few other choices.

But how, I asked, could Mickey of all people be recruited into the fight against Fascism? Well, she replied, he had helped Jim with the ones who were bothering him in his shop, they hadn't come back no more.

The dwarf-like figure in the bad wig had beaten up skinheads? I asked amazed. No, no, she said, not Mickey himself, of course not, his *contacts*. He knew a lot of people. She didn't say it was the right way. It wasn't, but it was one way, and sometimes one way is the only way.

She had all the boxes labelled so as to know in advance what would go in each one. Everything was done according to a system she had learned during many years in the retail sector but it was only mundane items like sheets, tea towels, cushions, knives and forks, some cans of food and packets of dried soups that she allowed me to pack. Her clothes she kept for herself, folding them with nimble fingers and placing them in suitcases as if she was handling a delicate child.

The monotony of my task was soothing for it allowed me to make peace with all the warring thoughts that raged inside my head since the row with Claude. He had picked up some idea from his Irish father, the old hypocrite, because Claude was an only child so they had to be defying the Church one way or another. How was I to know that my story of Alexander's death at the restaurant table and the abortion when I came back from London would send him so demented? He looked half crazed there in the mess room.

I knew how very different it would have been with Alexander. We would have sat quietly at the kitchen table together and discussed it in a rational manner, and he would have said, quite gently, I think, 'Well, Vivien it is entirely your own decision, your own choice. Of course I have an opinion, but it's your body, not mine.' And these platitudes would have been the wheels on which we span forwards, these common mental agreements, the mutual language of educated people. But I was long beyond all that.

When the packing was all finished, and I was exhausted, only then did Eunice make me a cup of tea. 'I haven't got a cake to offer you, like Sándor,' she said. 'I like to keep my figure.' But then she made me an offer, a suggestion so surprising that I had to reassess completely, from the start, the woman who sat in beige soft trousers, embroidered velvet house slippers and a mocha silk blouse, drinking tea from a china cup with rosebuds on it.

'Would you like to share a spliff?' She took out a silver foil with a little bit of hash in it and started to roll a joint. 'I like a smoke at the end of the day, it's relaxing, better than a glass of wine. Sándor don't like it. He tried it once, I gave him a few puffs but it just made him sick, he doesn't have the constitution for it.'

My uncle had made many disparaging remarks about drug addicts – hopheads, he called them. He liked to be in control as much as possible, and letting himself go, apart from with cakes and with women, was a dangerous idea, for letting yourself go was surrendering to the power of someone else and he was only prepared to do this in the case of Eunice. But this was her sole vice and so he would forgive her for it, because she drank only a few sips of wine and closely controlled what she ate.

It was Eunice's last joint. She had decided she would not introduce drugs into her new home, for the police were always looking for a chance to arrest her fiancé who was still on parole, not because of anything he had done, just out of spite, she said. Eunice was no more fond of a policeman than my uncle.

We shared the hash in silence. As much as I tried to relax and focus my attention on the rosebuds on the exterior surface of the teacup I was still holding in my right hand, and as the rosebuds grew in size and in the intensity of their colour until they started to resemble cartoon roses with giant thorns and to appear faintly foolish, I could not keep out of my head, like a running commentary, thoughts of my unborn child. Whether I had really done the wrong thing, and if the child was going to stubbornly refuse to leave, to stay around, in spirit, as a ghost. Next Alexander's small blue eyes looked down at me from heaven, his lips contorted into a smile. The dead gathered around thickly, my little baby, my grandmother with the lump in her chest, my grandfather in the lime pit. They spoke in foreign tongues; even Alexander began to speak Latin to me, and the baby babbled, accusingly.

'This is strong shit,' Eunice said. 'What do they mix with this, opium?'

'I don't feel good,' I said.

'No, you don't look good. Go and lie down.'

She took me to her bedroom and put a blanket over me. 'Sleep it off,' she said. 'I'll wake you in a couple of hours.'

I fell into an exhausted doze full of highly coloured dreams and was woken up with the command to come into the kitchen and eat a poached egg on toast. Its yellow eye looked up at me from the plate but when I'd eaten it I felt much better, alert and energetic. It was time to go. Eunice wanted to walk me to the tube station but I said I would be OK.

'Thank you for coming,' she said. 'I know it was Sándor's idea. He wanted us to get to know each other. Well, I see you are a hard worker and your heart is in the right place, even if you have faith in a leaflet. If I wasn't moving out tomorrow I'd say you was welcome in my house any time.'

'After tomorrow we'll be neighbours,' I said.

'Yes, we will.'

'And I want to apologise, again, for what my father said to you.' But I realised I had uttered the wrong thing for that insult was now in the category of events that were unmentionable and which she suspected were only raised in order to provoke embarrassment. She nodded curtly, and opened the door.

I said I would be around the next day at the house in Camden to help her unpack, but she said it wouldn't be necessary, 'because Sándor will be there, I don't need any more help than that'.

Still, I tried to reach forward to kiss her on the cheek, and she stood, stiffly, accepting the touch of my lips, but not offering her own.

As I turned the corner at the end of Eunice's road, opposite a noisy dirty traffic junction near the tube station, a gang of boys came along, four abreast, in the other direction. To an outsider who was unfamiliar with the clothing of that period, the late 1970s, we were dressed in the same way, but not quite, for I had adopted Claude's off-duty punk style, which had certain significant coded differences to the clothes of the skinheads. For example, they wore laced leather boots, we wore canvas boots; they wore their jeans rolled up to the calf, we wore tight, drainpipe jeans; they wore braces to hold up theirs, we didn't; our hair stood up in spikes which were, that summer, growing higher and higher into Mohawks, dyed pink and blue, and they shaved their heads to a close stubble; our jewellery was safety pins and they had none at all. So there were all these differences that you could see at once and they knew, and I knew, that we were enemies.

I had never seen skinheads so close up before. I could smell the leather of their boots and see the pink skin of their scalps.

They grabbed my bag, yanked it from my hand and began to throw its contents out on to the ground. Perhaps there was something else cut into the hash, apart from the suspected opium, because instead of curling into a ball and dying, quietly, there on the street corner, or running back to Eunice's, I began to shout at them, calling them dirty low-lives and Fascists. I snatched the bag from their hands and began hitting one of them about the head with it. The metal clasp caught the side of his face and gashed his cheek. I'm bleeding, he cried, and began to dab at the blood with a handkerchief. The others started laughing at him, calling him a crybaby for being upset about a little cut from a girl's handbag. They knelt down and began to tighten the laces on their boots. I gathered my things that were strewn around the pavement and put them back in my bag.

As I bent over, I felt a boot go into the small of my back and I fell face down on to the concrete. The road grazed the skin from my hands, and beads of blood began to spread along them.

The skinheads stood and laughed, then they picked up my handbag and stuffed the wallet in my mouth, because I was a filthy Jewess bitch who loved money, they said. But it didn't matter what they called me because as soon as I freed my jaw I went on screaming at them, all the names under the sun, until they got bored and walked off and then I ran after them and they turned back and beat me again. But in my rage I barely felt the blows and I went on running my mouth at them in revenge for what their forebears had done to my uncle. The more I talked the more they kicked, but my legs were iron and felt nothing. My mouth spewed fiery wrath like God bringing down plagues on the enemies of his people.

When he heard me come in my uncle knocked on my door, but I didn't answer. I really didn't want to see anyone, I was dog-tired, aching, dumb. I came home shamefully, shaking along the railings like a beaten animal. He called out, 'Vivien?' You there?' I said, 'Yes, I'm here.' My voice a cracked tin plate. 'You OK?' 'Yes, I'm fine.' 'What's the matter, did someone hurt you?' 'No.' 'You sure?' 'Yes, I'm sure.' 'OK, OK, I see you in the morning.'

The front door opened and closed all evening. I heard Claude come in, the creak of his leather jacket, a cough, a slight pause as he passed the door of my flat. I heard him open the door of his room and close it. An hour or two later, it opened again, I heard him go upstairs and knock on Sándor's door. There was a conversation but I couldn't make out what either of them said, then Claude came back. The bed sagged as he lay down in it. I thought about him lying there, looking at his fish, their simple little lives.

Finally, after a few hours of fitful sleep I noticed that my jeans were torn at the knee, my leather jacket was ripped. I got undressed and my legs and arms, covered in short coarse dark hairs, were growing huge bruises, and a fingernail had gone bad. I got into the bath but the hot water made me very sleepy. I dozed for a long time, the water cooling, until someone banged on the door and asked me if I'd drowned in there and, regretfully, I pulled myself out, wrapped the small thin towel round me and dried myself. My naked body looked so frail and damaged that I thought it could be folded down into a matchbox. I wept.

Night fell, at last. I lay down on my bed and began to read a sonnet but after few words, I fell asleep. The warm damp of the towel held me. I was slumbering, deep in dreams. I am a big dreamer, always have been, they come easily to me. I love to dream.

Sándor in the dark. His eyes wide open. He thinks about what he has seen, the sight will not leave him. It glitters with a metal brilliance.

How do you protect the ones you love? He doesn't know, he never had the opportunity before. His little brother ran from him, his father was distracted in his books, his mother was far away, and when you think about it, safer than he was, even when she was in danger. Now suddenly, everyone is vulnerable – his niece, his sweetheart: what is a man like him to do?

My uncle's brain is one of calculation. It's true he had goons to beat up his tenants if they could not pay up, or would not pay up, but he always employs those goons from their own people; for himself, he has a distaste for violence, he will not be there when they are doing the beating. It's their own business how they get the money, he turns away his head: don't involve me. I don't see what you do. That is what he told Mickey, who had the connections.

But now something is winding down in him; that intense drive which had accompanied him all his life to keep his head above water, the life-saving act he had done on himself for forty years – he's no longer sure it matters. He remembers the December afternoon he first saw Mickey on the street, the lights of the shop windows blazing, full of beautiful things that you could not buy in communist Hungary, and the clockwork bears running around the pavement as if they had business of their own to do. I'd like to see them bears again, he says to me, in his thoughts. I had no bear like that when I was a child growing up in the Zémplen. The toys we had were made of wood and never moved, you moved them yourself, with your hand, soldiers and so forth. Horses, with straw tails. A wind-up clockwork bear, *that* would have been a miracle.

He misses the village, the quiet streets, the drays, the plums in the orchards and the grapes ripening on the vines, the smell of his mother's hands on washing day, the lye soap: all these memories that had lain dormant inside him for so many years that had been brought up, struggling to the surface like gasping fish, by that machine with its whirring tapes, the typewriter, the paper.

But what can you do? You see it before your eyes, still metallically gleaming. It won't leave you alone, this torment. Even a sound mind plays tricks, he learned that in prison, because like everything he knows, lessons have always come to him the hard way.

When I was finally bathed and dried and in bed and sleeping, and the sodium streetlights were burnished through the undrawn curtains, the branches of the flowering cherry in the garden black and mysterious, the traffic lights turning red amber green to no one, and I was dreaming of fairgrounds, wooden bucking horses with gold manes, I heard my name. Like a hot needle, it came.

Vivien help me where are you Vivien.

Had he fallen?

I turned on the time delay switch and stumbled through the hall. His door was open. Help me, he cried.

In the room the light bulb was smashed out: the time delay switch outside illuminated the scene then put it back down into darkness. I saw a heap by the bed, a hump shape of a body or a bodies. The fish tank was smashed and the fish lay in puddles of water, gasping, dying. My uncle was beside them on the floor and Claude was on top of him but it was Claude who was calling my name. *Get the knife*, he moaned, and blood gurgled in his windpipe.

I saw a knife on the floor a few inches away from my uncle's hand. I bent to pick it up and the blade was black and smeared. The last time I held it was to cut my birthday cake.

'What's this?' I said.

'He fucking tried to kill me, I was asleep and he came in and stabbed me in the neck, look at what he's done, help me.'

'Don't call the police,' said my uncle, 'please, Vivien. No police.'

'No,' I said. 'I won't. What happened here?'

'Viv, I'm bleeding to death here, for God's sake get me an ambulance.'

My uncle looked up at me: the lower lip was shaking uncontrollably and the jacket of his pyjamas was pulled up round his shoulders. I could see the famous scars on his back, white lines crossing and crossing again, buried under the mottled grey skin.

'What did you do?' I cried in horror, for Claude was passing out, he was making a bloody gurgle in his throat.

'I struck back,' my uncle said. 'I saw what he really is. How can he live? I saw, Vivien, I *saw*.'

'I don't know what you saw. I'm going to ring for an ambulance.'

'No police!'

I went into the hall where the payphone was and I rang the emergency services.

'I need an ambulance,' I said. I heard laughter in the background, I think someone had just told a joke before I came on the line.

'What's the nature of the injury?'

'A person has cut himself.'

'Where?'

'In the back and the neck, I think.'

'Has he been stabbed?'

'Yes.'

'So you want me to send the police?'

'Exactly.'

I still held the knife. I went to the front door and opened it and sat on the step. After a while the sirens started from far away and got closer and eventually they all came, running up the steps of the house and through the door, all those uniformed men and women, who saw me with the knife in my hand and the fear came back, the dark terror I remembered from my childhood, of the world outside my little room.

My uncle was in a cell and as soon as I saw him, I knew he was finished. I could tell that he would not survive and he didn't. The spasm of rage which took hold of him, that took him down the stairs with the knife in his hand to kill the beast – the beast that was under his own roof and put its hand on the skin of his own flesh of blood – this senseless, irrational clot of anger, overcame not just Claude's body, but his own: three strokes in twenty-four hours.

Elsewhere in the hospital, Claude was being patched up. His family arrived from Sheerness, the mother, the father, and a young girl his own age who was carrying a little baby which she held up to him and Claude kissed him on the cheek. The girl sat and held Claude's hand and asked him if he was coming back home now, and they'd manage, wouldn't they?

Don't run away, she said to him, don't run away again. He's our lad, we'll find a way to get wages, I know you were dead scared but it's all going to be all right. Look at him, our lad, he wants you back, he needs his father.

I only saw him for a few minutes. The girl stood outside, smoking a cigarette, glaring at me. She was very pretty.

'I don't know what I did,' Claude said. 'I only went up to hand in my notice. I took a load of pills after you went and I was fed up with the lot of you. I wanted to piss off down to south London or somewhere, get a job in a different depot. But we didn't have an unpleasant word.'

'I don't know what happened either,' I said. 'I only told him we'd had a row. That's not enough to try to kill you.'

'Claude don't want to see you no more,' the girl said, returning to the room. 'He's coming back home with me, aren't you, babe?'

'I dunno,' he said, 'I've got to think.' But the girl held up the little child.

'Look at him,' she said. 'Look what you've been missing. See his little toothie?'

He stared up at me helplessly from the pillow, and I knew I could no more save him than I could my uncle. He would never have his tattoo, it would remain unseen in the pages of the sketchpad, and one day she would find it, and quietly, when he was out at work, it would be thrown out with the rubbish. He would remember it for many years to come, until at last it had faded from his memory. What was disturbed in him would give way, I supposed to drinking, or depression. Which was not hard on the Isle of Sheppey.

When I went back the next day they were all gone. I never saw him again, or I only see him in my dreams, running along the train in his guard's cap and jacket, opening and closing the doors, shooting up and down, through London, beneath the river in that long soot-blackened metal tube. Or on the river that night, on the slow dredger as the bodies were pulled from the water, and his hands were on my breasts.

'I'll warm you,' he had said.

My father was Sándor's only next of kin, unless you count myself, so he had to take responsibility. My parents came to the house and looked round his flat, at the mural, the peacock throne, the wicker furniture. 'So this is how he lived,' said my mother. My father said nothing.

After a while, Mickey Elf turned up with a dishevelled wig and red-rimmed eyes. 'Look,' he said, 'I'm no relation, it's none of my business, but if you ask me—'

'So who asked you?' said my father.

But Mickey wasn't afraid of my father, he pressed on, insistent, holding his hand up to straighten his hair. 'I know what he would have wanted. I know exactly what he was after. Trust me, I know.'

'Well,' said my father, 'we can't begrudge a man his last wishes.' But only because he didn't have a better suggestion

He had gone very quiet when I told him the news. He turned his head away. A few minutes later I saw him polishing his glasses on the frayed end of his tie. 'So, he's dead,' he said. 'It was always going to end up like this, a murderer in the family.'

It was a large funeral. Mickey and his associates took care of everything down to the last detail. They had him buried in the Jewish cemetery in Bushey. I had only been to one funeral, Alexander's, the Anglican service in the same chapel where we had got married, the handsome mahogany coffin with brass handles, carried by six churchmen and laid on the altar while we sang hymns and his father delivered the eulogy, full of grace, and quotations from the life and sayings of Jesus. In Bushey, we all gathered in a small building designed for the purpose, neither a chapel nor anything else I could understand, and my father was offered a prayer book to say the particular prayer that was said by the chief mourner for the dead but he didn't know how to read it.

The pine coffin with rope handles came down to the grave. There were many underworld types there, and of course the press, they came, and wrote short paragraphs the next day, reprinting the old picture of him, that *face of evil.*

Eunice was alone, dressed in black with a black hat and a small black veil, looking, for the first time, frail.

'That good man,' she said. 'That lovely man, and all he suffered, in the grave.'

Who is being buried there? asked mourners at other graves. A slum landlord, and a pimp, said a reporter, snickering.

Eunice lashed out at his legs with her umbrella. 'No one knew the man like I did,' she said from beneath her veil.

'I knew him longer than anyone, apart from your dad, over there,' Mickey Elf said to me. 'I knew him when he was just off the train from the old country, and I knew him through the high times and the low, through thick and thin.'

'I washed the wounds on his back,' said Eunice. 'I saw what was done to the poor fellow, the terrible things he suffered, I heard what he cried out in his sleep. I saw this man, a big strong man, in tears, crying like a little baby in his pram.'

'*I* knew him when he was king, King Kovacs, when he had the house in Bishops Avenue and all the toffs came to his parties. He had a swimming pool and a ballroom, all the quality came to that place, the film stars and nobles, he had the lot.'

'You don't know a man until he's seen trouble,' Eunice said, pointing her brown finger at him.

People took turns with the shovel and threw a handful of earth on to the coffin. Mickey took something from his pocket and threw it in. People murmured, 'What's that he's chucking at him?' I saw the brown ear of a bear fly past me. Some of the gangsters had clubbed together and bought the biggest wreath they could find but Mickey made them leave it at the gate. 'No flowers at a Jewish funeral,' he told them. 'That's not the way we do things.' Later, they came back and laid it down on the hump of earth where it stayed, withering and rotting in the early autumn sun and rain, until several months later when we returned to erect the stone and found the metal frame. Years later I went back to Bushey, and the grave still stood, marked, as is the custom, with pebbles, and a withered bunch of irises.

There was nowhere to go afterwards, so we all went our separate ways. I returned to Benson Court with my parents. We went up in the lift, and I entered once more that flat with its smells and its dingy wallpaper and its old-fashioned pre-war kitchen fittings but in my absence my mother had been hard at work with the tin of green paint. She had covered everything she could find that the paint would adhere to. Green stabbed you in the eye wherever you looked.

I opened the door to my bedroom. There, the paint pot had not dared to penetrate. 'You see I left everything as it was,' she said. 'I wanted that if you came back, you would see that nothing had changed.'

'And that's the problem,' I said.

'What?'

'That nothing changes.'

'What should change, for heaven's sake?'

'Everything. Life should change, all the time.'

'Why do you think this?'

'Look at you both, you and Daddy, you live here in this museum, this immolation.'

'What is this word, immolation? I don't know it. Your father and I came here as refugees, we made ourselves a decent life. What more do you want from us?'

'How can you not want to live?'

'To live? To live like him, that poor wretch, in his grave?'

'*I* want to live,' I cried, weeping tears of frustration.

'And you will, of course you shall live. What do you think? That this is for ever, this period, this time of all the deaths? It's just a moment, don't you understand? It will pass and you will live, believe me, you will live.' She leaned against the wall for a moment, then put down her stick beside her and used my shoulder as her crutch, to steady her as she kissed my face and stroked my shorn head with her hand.

Later that evening, I asked her to tell me all she could remember about Uncle Sándor in the days in which she knew him, before they left Budapest. She nodded.

'He was a charming, dangerous man,' she said, drinking a cup of coffee, 'a man who makes girls laugh, who listens to them with sympathy, who penetrates all their secrets in order to take advantage of them. A man who did not understand anything about deep feelings, not until after the war; then, I think, he understood a little. Maybe in later life he learned more. Perhaps these thoughts came over him lately and he didn't know how to handle them. I was very surprised when I saw that nice woman at the party. Not his normal type at all. He always preferred tarts.'

My father never said another word about his brother. He stayed quiet on the subject until the day he died, but my mother told me about the prison visits he had paid him over the years, to show him pictures of me leaving for York University, my graduation, my engagement to Alexander. He boasted about all my achievements, wanting him to know that he, the small, quiet, industrious, obedient one had made *this*, and look at him, the flashy older brother, sitting at a table in a prison visiting room. Still, my mother implied, my father always came home dissatisfied, as if Sándor had somehow managed to get the better of him, in ways my father couldn't put his finger on.

I went back to the house in Camden Town and I decided to take my uncle's flat and live there for another two months until the house grew too squalid to stay in any more.

After a few days, I found the keys to Claude's room. Someone had come in and taken most of his stuff. The remains of the shattered fish tank lay strewn across the floor but the little bodies were missing. Only the clothes still hung in the wardrobe. His guard's uniform and cap, his jeans, his T-shirts, his leather jacket.

The smell of the leather jacket was part of him, and of his young body. I turned it to look at it, the zips, the collar, the pockets. It swung round on the hanger. And then I saw what he had done. How he had found a way to defy me. He had gone to Camden Market, into one of the shops that does this kind of thing, and got them to put a pattern on the back of his leather jacket, a pattern of his own design, because I recognised it, the four arms rendered in metal studs, his own decorative swastika.

The Talmud says nine hundred and thirty kinds of death were created in the world. The most difficult is diphtheria, the easiest is a kiss. The kiss is what is called the *mise binishike*, which is how you kill the six people over whom the Angel of Death has no sway – such a person dies by the mouth of God. The nine hundred and thirty-first was created for my uncle. He died of his own eye.

My uncle's story, in his own words

Should a man be hunted? Is a man to be beneath a dog? You beat a dog, maybe he turns back and bites *you*, this is my warning.

Yes, I am Sándor Kovacs, it's me. The one you read about. That terrible person.

What were my crimes? Show me the sheet.

To act instinctively but with cunning? Yes. Guilty.

To count my personal survival above the survival of others? Of course.

And for this I was to be hated, hunted, misinterpreted, turned into a symbol?

Back in those days, 1964, just before I went to prison, they told a lot of stories about me in the papers, and even on the streets. Some of them made me laugh so hard I used to have to sit down to rest my chest, because since the TB my lungs have never been up to scratch and it didn't help that in those days I liked to be seen with a cigar.

First they said I started out as a prize-fighter in Chicago. Or maybe I was stevedore in Poland, or a circus strongman in Peking. Then they went really crazy and I hear that I'm the lovechild of Joe Louis and Sophie Tucker. It's a game now, to come up with the most ridiculous combinations – Benito Mussolini and Fay Wray, Joe Stalin and Wallis Simpson, Princess Margaret and Lobby Ludd.

Later they all tried to wriggle out of it, didn't want to be taken for fools and said they were jokes I started myself, and got spread around by my associates. But how would they know anything about me? They say I never gave an interview for the papers. And you know why? No one ever asked me for one. That's why.

The other people who wouldn't talk were the ones they called my victims. Some victims! Only one person spoke to the press and he never even met me, that politician, that member of the high and mighty parliament, the Welshman, Clive Parry-Jones, the lone crusader, very nice they were about him, that frozen piece of shit with the boom-boom voice and the Jesus talk.

What I read in the papers about my properties was full of lies. He says – this Parry-Jones – that I kept West Indian families thirteen to a room, no kitchen or bathroom. He talked about rats. About cockroaches, crawling over children's faces as they slept. He said a rat went for a three-year-old's throat and tore it out; he said I paid the family off, arranged a funeral with a fine child-sized mahogany coffin and a band of Trinidadians in white tails and white top hats playing steel instruments, marching in front of the hearse through Kensal to the cemetery.

Nothing like this ever happened.

I got here, December 1956, from Hungary. I was worse off than them, the Negroes, I was a refugee and the iron door had slammed shut after me, nowhere to go but forward, no past for me, only future. I remember everything about that day, *everything*, how my brother came to meet me at the station, the insult he made to me. I walked the streets not hearing my language spoken, for six hours I wandered, up and down. I came to the river, the bridges, no one stopped, no one said a word to me, not a kind word or a harsh one. I was lonely in my soul, I was tired of walking, I wanted to give up. I had a mackintosh, a scarf and a leather satchel, that's all. I saw men in bowler hats and women in fur coats, a shop that sold pipes and tobacco and cigars, theatres, and everything was cold and alien and strange and I was hungry.

Finally, I heard my own language; they took me to a place, a hostel for refugees. They gave me coffee, soup, meat, vegetables and a bed. This was it, I was here. London, my home. I have not got another one.

An immigrant is very different from a native-born person. Nothing is owed to you, you have no expectations. You have to take what you can, as soon as you see it. You can't hang around. Not at my age, certainly. I was already forty year old when I got to London but my eyes had a very keen focus, and I could recognise a business opportunity. Life in the Eastern Bloc hadn't squeezed those instincts out of me. There was no communist re-education camp capable of indoctrinating me, Sándor Kovacs, with a love of the proletariat and my fellow man.

I came here with nothing and within weeks I started my business. People compared me to the Kray twins, those thugs, those cretins. They were just louts, men who liked to inflict pain, and that is not me. I don't agree with suffering. It's against my principles. The Krays had everything, they had a family, they had what they called a manor, their neighbourhood, where they grew up. I never had any of that.

I remember when the warrant went out for my arrest, walking down the Strand to buy some cigars, a beautiful sunny spring day it was, like now, as it happens. Warm sun on your face, the trees green and starting to grow lush. I remember days like this from long ago, when you hated the sun for shining, you hated the fact that to others it brought pleasure, but you had to admit it brought pleasure to you too, and you hated it even more for that.

Where is Kovacs hiding? This is what it says on the *Evening Standard* placard. I'm laughing. Hiding? Where should I hide? A journalist is a born liar. He's a man with an imagination, how else do you explain the rubbish they printed about me? They say I'm living in a stately home in Buckinghamshire, guarded by slobbering Alsatian dogs kept on short rations. No, no, says another one. I'm in a penthouse flat in Chelsea, with a steel front door. Did you hear about Kovacs, says a third? He's holed up on a luxury barge moored in the middle of the Thames, upriver, somewhere around Chiswick or is it Teddington Lock? Anyway, they have to send special police boats to get him.

And one night on television, a man I never heard of, Kenneth Tynan, he is something in the theatre I think, anyway, he has degrees from Oxford University, he says I don't live nowhere, I don't exist, I'm a figment of the national imagination, like the Loch Ness monster.

This was the worst of all. I feel my soul shrivel when I hear this. And I hate him. But to this day I don't understand why a man should say such a thing, and this is one of the issues I intend to raise. I have to get to the bottom of it.

When I came out of prison, a year ago, no one remembered me. I heard on the bus one time, someone discussing me. Didn't Kovacs die in prison? No, no, he escaped, you know like the Great Train Robbers, like Ronnie Biggs and he's living in fine style, somewhere in South America.

I wish it was true.

Because what it is, is that everyone just forgot about me. It was like I was a craze, such as the hula hoop or the yo-yo. What they call a *Zeitgeist*, which is a German word, I used to know that language. So maybe that Tynan was right after all, to some extent.

When you read about me now, which is very rarely, I'm just a slum landlord. The slums (*so-called slums* – they were beautiful houses in their day) I owned were pulled down and over them the government built brand new housing. Tower blocks of concrete. Very nice. They looked like slums to me even while the builders were making them. They were prisons, anyone who has been in a prison could see that.

This was King Kovacs' condition. People talked about what I represented, but no one understood what it was to be me, Kovacs. How could they? In England they have here what is called the rule of law, not the law of the jungle, which is what I know. A government that believes in social progress, in rebuilding a man's soul to make sure he is pure and healthy, not with a sickness inside him. We had this back in Hungary, too, after the war, when the communists came in, but they did it with tanks, and here they do it from the pulpit.

They say, oh, Kovacs isn't interested in any of that. He is coarse and brutal. He is the impediment. You have to get rid of Kovacs if you want to build that Jerusalem they talk about, this fair, this just society.

There's a Japanese paper game called origami I once saw, someone showed it to me in prison. You fold a sheet into any kind of shape you like if you're dextrous enough: a bird, a bear, a dragon. That's what they tried to do to me. But I am *not* paper, I am flesh and blood, and come what may I refuse to be folded.

Now when it comes to the manner of man I am in my private life, I acknowlege I was not a better son

I had not meant to spend all day sitting in my father's armchair in the empty flat listening to the tapes, not eating, barely drinking. I hadn't expected to hear once more after so many years that guttural accent, the pendulous lower lip trying to close on the words, his hearty laugh, his cynicism. I heard my own voice from thirty years ago, and was it my imagination, or did the accent sound a little different? Did I really talk like that in those days, was I actually what Claude called me, a posh girl?

The tapes contained the evidence of the enduring gift my uncle had left me: a past. He gave me my grandparents, the village in the Zémplen, the plum trees, the vines, the horse shit in the streets, the cafés of Budapest, my mother sitting with her stick in a café on the banks of the Danube, her brown hair around her face, her raisin eyes, her cleft chin. Whether they are true or false (and I have no cause to doubt them), this past is the only one I've got, there is no other available.

When I had finished, I packed everything up, put the tapes and the tape recorder in a cardboard box and left the flat, shutting the door behind me. I waited for the clanking gate of the lift to open, placed the box on the little leather stool while I descended. In the hall I removed the card with my parents' name on it from above the brass plate of their postbox in the hall, and wondered how many last times there would be for me, and this building, this mansion block in red brick, that I could spend my whole life avoiding, trying to find a different route, another direction.

It was a sunny late afternoon, just after 5.30; long shadows, sirens in the distance, anxiety and excitement in the faces of passers-by. *They caught a terrorist, did you hear?* The city was still hot, nervous, febrile, people didn't want to travel but they didn't have a choice – whether it's the tube or the bus, they'd get you either way. I walked round to Seymour Street, to the shop, carrying the box. The last customers were working their way through the sale racks with frenzied attention.

The spotlights on the ceiling illuminated her hair and cast sparks on her false eyelashes. I don't know how she held that mask in place, day after day, the face of the professional sales lady for whom the customer is always right, even when she is obviously wrong and the dress she's trying on is too tight, and you tactfully suggest that yes, that's very good, but perhaps here is something better.

I admired her for her forbearance, for keeping a civil tongue in her head, for tolerating the timewasters, the ones who just came to look, but she told me once, 'If a young person tries on a cocktail dress they can't afford and anyway they never get an invitation to cocktail parties, I let them try. Because you see, you never know what life has in store for you, and one day this poor working girl could walk in with a diamond ring on her finger and she remembers the kind sales ladies who let her try on dresses when she couldn't afford them and because of this she is not intimidated by the idea of cocktail parties. This is why selling is a profession, but tell that to the children they employ on Oxford Street, who turn away their heads at the sight of the customer.'

I watched her folding, smoothing, wrapping in tissue paper the day's final purchase; her hands with the silver nails were still agile, but she massaged her elbows when no one was looking. I remember my mother making the same gesture.

'So you came back,' she said, when the last customer had left.

'Yes, I have something for you.'

'What's this, what have you got in that box?'

'Do you remember the tapes we made?'

'You have them? Sándor's voice?'

'Yes.'

'Sándor alive on them tapes! Oh, I'd give a lot to hear his voice again, that dear man.'

'They're all here, and the tape recorder too, and what he was writing, the day I met him in the park. His own words.'

Thank you,' she said. 'This means a lot to me.' She looked at her watch. 'Near enough to six,' she said, and locked the door. 'Wait, let me finish up, and then we'll talk. You're tired, girl, look at you. Sit down.' She pointed to a yellow velvet chair with gilt-painted arms.

'But *you* must be exhausted, *you* should sit.'

'I sit when I get home. That's when I sit.'

'Do you want me to show you how to operate the tape recorder?' I said. 'It can be tricky at first.'

She stood by the counter checking her receipts. 'I know how to do that, don't you worry. I understand little machines. I do all the credit cards with the new gadget, it didn't take me a minute to learn how to do it.'

'I listened to the tapes myself this afternoon,' I said. 'It all stopped, so abruptly, I never heard him explain how he came to be a landlord or what he—'

'What they did to that man is a crime. That judge, *he* is one who should have been in prison.'

'But he—'

'Oh, but. Don't believe what you read in the newspapers. I never pay any attention to that rubbish. A person who has the marks of a whip on his back, who has been a slave, like the slaves in Egypt, where his people once made their exodus from, is a king, in my opinion.'

'The tenants, he—'

'I'm going to the back to make a pot of tea, and when I come back, I'll tell you about those tenants.'

'Can I help you?'

'No. Sit there. Don't fidget, I'll be back soon.'

I looked around the shop. She had turned off the spotlights and locked the door, put the closed sign up. It was a very small room in which to spend most of a lifetime – the eau-de-Nil walls which had been fashionable when it first opened, fifty years ago, the little velvet chairs, the glass-fronted display cases, the marble table bearing only a vase of early bronze chrysanthemums (a flower that even when it is growing looks as though it's longing to be cut), the curtained changing rooms with hooks for coats and a shelf for handbags, old perfumes hanging in the air, a mingling of the scents of many women's skin. Shalimar. Poison. L'Air du Temps. Magie Noire. Blue Grass. No 5.

All the time that Eunice had been serving in the shop with that charming continuity, so many things had happened to me, so many twists and turns and interruptions.

I had wanted to live, and I had lived. I had wanted to escape from Benson Court, and I escaped. I was in the Fountain Room at Fortnum and Mason eating an ice-cream sundae, I was at the table, all by myself. Opposite, drinking a cup of Earl Grey tea, my future husband looked up from his newspaper, saw me with a drip of ice-cream on my chin, spooning a red glacé cherry into my mouth and he burst out laughing. I turned my attention from my Knickerbocker Glory. What had he seen to cause him to laugh? It was my look of earnest concentration as I attacked the sundae and the white moustache of cream that flecked the dark hairs of my top lip. A black, serious creature with a child's sweet, he said. A thin girl on her own in a café devouring ice-cream unselfconsciously. 'And when you finished you took out a little pouch of tobacco and rolled a cigarette with those hands which look too big for the wrists to support them, rattling your matches in the box. I thought, now *here's* a story.'

You know, my life turned out more banal than I ever expected, for as I found out, to live *is* banal.

I got a couple of book reviews published and then a job on a little magazine, moved in with Vic to his flat in Clapham, started to dress like a woman approaching thirty, I had my first child, then another. Daughters! What a steep learning curve that was. We bought a big house by the Common, then Vic, who was in software design before anyone knew what those words meant, got a job in America. We were in St Louis for five years. I wrote a couple of children's books which were quite successful; they're still in print, I look them up every few months on Amazon to check their sales ranking. Vic got a big pay-off when the company was taken over by Microsoft and we moved to Deya, that rock-ribbed village on the island of Mallorca, to fulfil his dream to open a restaurant. He loved cooking.

It was a happy life, interrupted by a couple of affairs, one his, one mine, but you get through it. Then one lunchtime he had a heart attack taking a rack of lamb from the oven: the grease from the metal pan fell on his shoes. By the time the ambulance arrived from the city, he was dead. That's all.

I sold the restaurant and came back to London eight months ago. It is true that I have let myself go, the girls talk about it all the time – my daughters, those fair, fat English girls with none of my anxieties and uncertainties who have spent their whole lives crossing borders without impediment. I watch them get dressed, I see the choices they make when they look in the mirror. They have passed out of that teenage phase when they must dress exactly as their friends dress in jeans that expose a naked slab of belly; they are with gathering certainty starting to define themselves, each going in a slightly different direction, Lillian and Rose, destined for their own little greatness.

The clothes you wear are a metamorphosis. They change you from the outside in. We are all trapped with these thick calves or pendulous breasts, our sunken chests, our dropping jowls. A million imperfections mar us. There are deep flaws we are not at liberty to do anything about except under the surgeon's knife. So the most you can do is put on a new dress, a different tie. We are forever turning into someone else, and should never forget that someone else is always looking.

Eunice came back with a tray, a china pot of tea, cups, saucers, a bowl of sugar and a jug of milk. 'I hope you don't expect biscuits,' she said. 'I only eat sweet things when I go out to a nice restaurant. Sándor used to take me to some lovely places, with the sweets on a trolley that they wheel right up to your table so you can choose what you want. Now, tell me. What became of you?'

'I told you already.'

'Oh, I know that café in Spain where all the rich people used to go. I read about all that in the paper. I mean, why did you run away so fast?'

'What do you mean?'

'Why didn't you stay on in the house and collect Sándor's rents for him? Why let everything go to waste and rack and ruin like it did, until there was nothing left, and those houses were slums, like they were when he bought them, and he spent all that time and money making them nice?'

'What did it have to do with me?'

'You inherited everything, didn't you? You were his niece.'

'No, I didn't.'

'Who did?'

'My father.'

'Oh, him! So why did he not take over the business?'

I smiled to think of my father with a leather satchel over his shoulder, knocking on the doors of all those strangers, haranguing them if they were late with their rents.

'It's not the kind of person he was. He never had a head for finance and he certainly had no social skills.'

'Yes,' she said, 'I remember that, all right.' She gave me a piercing look with her old eyes. 'But he didn't want the money?'

'No. He wouldn't touch it.'

'What a wicked thing to do. Why wouldn't he take his own brother's legacy?'

'He thought it was tainted. He didn't believe in breaking the law, for any reason.'

'And what do you think?'

'About what?'

'About breaking the law.'

'I don't care much about the law but I still think about the tenants.'

'Oh, yes, those people. Well, you know some of them lived in a terrible way back home in Jamaica. They never knew about an inside toilet, or a sink or anything like that and when they came here they kept respectable people up in the middle of the night with their noise, their parties. And some of them didn't want to work, they just lay around and smoked their spliff all day, making trouble. I don't say there's anything wrong with a little weed once in a while, but then other things come into it. And decent individuals who were born here had to keep their children away from them, they corrupted those good children.'

'Is that what happened to your son?' I said.

'What's that?'

'Your son. Was he corrupted by them?'

'My son is dead,' she said briefly, and swallowed her tea as if she was trying to drown him inside her.

'I'm sorry.'

'Why? Why should you be sorry?'

'It's horrible when a mother loses a child.'

She shrugged. 'Death is death.'

'When did your son die?'

'Not so long ago.'

'Who was his father?' I asked her, feeling that I was entering a place in her life that was so hidden from view behind the suits and the hair spray and the false eyelashes that it seemed like the dark night that cannot be penetrated.

'You want to know *that*?' she said. 'Of all the questions!' She laughed. I don't think I ever heard her make this sound before, a gurgling giggle in her throat.

I waited for a few moments to see if she would tell me, but evidently I had finally struck her dumb, because all she did was swallow her tea and look out the window at the passers-by, the crowd streaming south to the tube station, so helpless and vulnerable they looked, in their summer skirts and dresses, those thin fabrics, the sandals that barely held their feet, the lightness with which they passed along, almost floating, evaporating as they went in the steam of the humid early evening.

And Eunice went on drinking her tea in silence, a line drawn between her eyes, her head drooping as the cup emptied, and that gesture I saw in the morning through the glass, of her lifting her chin with her hand, pushing it upwards.

'Jerome,' she suddenly said, 'it's a long time since I thought of *him*.'

I waited for more.

'Well, you know, it was the war, I was a young girl, in Cardiff, and there were a lot of Americans, of course. GIs. So I met Jerome one night at the dance hall, I remember I was wearing a sky blue dress with a short net skirt which I made myself out of bits of material I found here and there, because you couldn't get a lot during wartime. And Jerome showed me how to do the latest dance from America, the Lindy Hop they called it, he came right over and picked me because I was wearing such a lovely dress compared to all the girls in the room who looked so drab. He went overseas but thank God he wasn't killed and he came back. So we got married and I went to live with him in Mississippi. But it wasn't at all what I expected. It was not what I was accustomed to.'

'In what way?' Eunice in America. I thought she had never once left these shores.

'I didn't know about houses with no toilet inside, and pigs and dogs everywhere, and the white people who looked at you like you were not a human but a relation of the pigs and the dogs. No one raised a hand to me, before I came to America. To beat a person with a *broom*, a *chain* you use to tie up the dog? I had to run away with my baby, and it was very hard here, all on my own, trying to make a respectable life with a son who has no father and gives in to all the temptations. I don't know why it happened, he was a lovely chubby baby and he turned into a lean young man with eyes in his head that see everything and don't understand nothing. That's how I met Sándor, when I used to come and visit my boy and I stood in the queue with Mickey Elf. Poor man, he had nobody to visit him but that one. So we struck up an acquaintance and in the end it was him I came to see, not my son because he didn't want to know me any more.

'Many years of work behind the counter it took to get this job in this lovely shop. And I remember when I was closing up that night, the day Sándor got out of prison, and he was waiting for me on the pavement outside, he'd been sitting in a café opposite, just waiting. And then he stepped up with a bouquet of roses and he bowed. *He bowed down before me*. To treat a person like me as if she was a queen when she had been hit and beaten and looked at in the street as if she was not human! Do you understand? *This* is dignity, *this* is respect.'

'I understand.'

'Do you? I never know with you.'

'I'm not your enemy, Eunice. I was just a young immature girl who was lost and lonely and couldn't find her way in life.'

'Well, you seemed to me to know exactly what you wanted, with all your scheming.'

I stood up and lifted the tray with the empty cups. 'I'll help you,' I said.

She nodded quickly. Behind the curtain there was a little room with a kettle, a sink, bills, inventories. A little bunch of pansies with short stems stood in a small vase which was placed on a lace doily.

'What's this?' I said, picking up a framed picture.

She looked frightened. 'Don't tell anyone about that,' she said. 'I could go to prison.'

'It's cut out of a book, isn't it?'

'It was in the library. I took it home and I saw this picture. I got a pair of scissors and I thought no one would notice, but it's a serious crime, isn't it, to deface a library book?'

I looked at the photograph. It showed a line of men, in hats, double-breasted jackets, trousers with turn-ups, carrying suitcases, valises, briefcases, leather satchels. One or two of them wore tinted glasses in what must have been strong sunlight because of the shadows it was casting on the road. My uncle had stepped forward towards the camera and was smiling, that lower lip was unmistakable, even in the face of a young man. I recognised what everyone had seen in him, the cocky sexiness, the eyes with all their humour and avarice, that look of complicity, that intimate knowledge of the little one inside who cries out for life and is greedy for the whole world.

For that tiny naked figure, with its terrible hungers, cries in me, too.

We shook hands for the last time. She let me out and stood at the door of the shop, watching me walk up the street. The newspaper placards proclaimed the capture of the would-be terrorist. I was thinking about the bombs last year, just as I got back to London, the pieces of tattered cloth on the rails.

I was walking across the park, holding between my fingers the strings of the bag containing a new dress. It was a beautiful late afternoon, geese taking off in the sultry air over the lake. I hear the buzzing saw of a branch being felled, and the tree stood like a one-armed man against the clouding horizon. A new dress. Is this all it takes to make a new beginning, this shred of dyed cloth, shaped into the form of a woman's body? The crowd hurried past, their faces lit with anxiety and excitement. Our vulnerability suddenly touched me, all our terrible, moving weaknesses contained in a jacket, a skirt, a pair of shoes.

Acknowledgements

I have drawn on an account of Labour Service Company 110/34 by Zoltan (csima) Singer in Randolph L Berman (ed.), *The Wartime System of Labor Service in Hungary: Varieties of Experience*, New York, Columbia University Press, 1995.

The character of Sándor Kovacs was inspired by that of the Notting Hill landlord, Peter Rachman, who was born in Lvov, Poland in 1919, survived the war in a Siberian labour camp, came to Britain as a refugee in 1946 and died in London in 1962. At the time of his death he was still searching for any surviving relatives. For information on housing in London in the post-war period, I have drawn on his biography, *Rachman*, by Shirley Green. London: Michael Joseph, 1979.

I would like to express my heartfelt gratitude to George Szirtes for his help in describing Jewish life in Hungary and for his family insights into the horrors of the slave labour units. Any errors are mine and mine alone.

My warmest thanks, too, to Antony Beevor and Artemis Cooper for the generous hospitality at their house in Kent during the writing of this book and where, in the unlikely setting of a bedroom overlooking the garden, Ervin and Berta Kovacs put in their first appearance. I would also like to thank Gillian Slovo and Andrea Levy for kindly agreeing to read an earlier version and for their helpful comments.

My thanks, as ever, to my agent Derek Johns who has pulled me out of so many scrapes, to Susan de Soissons and Elise Dillsworth at Virago, and above all, to my editor Lennie Goodings, who never, ever gives up.